I0635349

When Falls the Night

Jo Wilkinson

TSL Publications

First published in Great Britain in 2020
By TSL Publications, Rickmansworth

Copyright © 2020 Jo Wilkinson

Cover image: Jo Wilkinson

ISBN / 978-1-912416-71-4

The right of Jo Wilkinson to be identified as the author of this work
has been asserted by the author in accordance with the UK
Copyright, Designs and Patents Act 1988.

All characters and events in this publication, other than those clearly in
the public domain, are fictitious and any resemblance to actual
persons, living or dead, is purely coincidental.

All rights reserved. No part of this publication may be reproduced,
distributed, or transmitted in any form or by any means, including
photocopying, recording, or other electronic or mechanical methods,
without the prior written permission of the publisher, except in the
case of brief quotations embodied in critical reviews and certain other
noncommercial uses permitted by copyright law.

1

Spring rain drummed on the forest leaves. It was oddly silent. The camp lay ahead, swallowed in the camouflage of its protective gully.

"I ..." her voice was stifled by a strong hand as he thrust her against the trunk. Eyes wide, body pressed against the concealing bark, she watched, silent, as he shrank beneath the ferns. *Had they come?*

He beckoned. Rustling unfurling stems, they crawled, hands trembling, her enlarging belly catching on the undergrowth. Sinking into the shadows they gained their feet.

"Can you run?" he hissed.

"The others ..."

"Too late! Can you run?" She nodded. Grasping her hand, he raced through whispering branches. She began to stumble. He paused, noting her laboured breath.

"The children ..." she gasped.

"I can only save ours." He ran a protective hand over her belly. "The woods are full of troops, hundreds of them. We need to move, after they're finished, they'll come looking."

As if in confirmation, guns rent the stillness, echoing through the silent groves. He wiped a soiled sleeve across his eyes.

"We have to go ..."

She nodded. Pursued by cries and gunfire, they melted into the ancient refuge of man. Tall sentinels guarded the way, as increasing rain erased traces of their path.

ɤɤɤ

"Did they have dogs?"

"Didn't see any ... I hope not. The stream should throw them off the scent if they did. Sleep now. I'll keep watch."

Bathed in tears, she surrendered to exhaustion. Greg scrutinised their surroundings. The forest had been their refuge for the past two years. The forest where he'd met her, where they'd survived, hidden from prying eyes. Now ... now it was all over, his companions, closer than brothers, their families, dead ... He brushed the tears away, but they kept coming, here in the darkness with none to see but the trees. Why couldn't they let them be? What harm had they done, simple folk, farmers, travellers, living off the land.

There was nowhere to go. Only in the wildernesses could they hide, but for how long? There was no real escape, only the game of cat and mouse he'd been playing since he'd left it all behind. It had just been internment camps then, people disappearing silently, one day there, the next gone, never to return. Now there was no need of subterfuge. They killed openly; the remaining voices of protest silenced in those last Easter raids. He'd not been near civilisation since. He'd grown hard, his frame lean, but strong, nourished on roots and herbs, fish, and meat from the traps. His grandfather had been obsessed with the "outdoor life". He'd groaned at the time, but those things had saved him. Gramp's rifle lay across his back, loaded, the few remaining bullets in his backpack. There'd be no more. He pulled out the wrapper – four, plus the three in the rifle. What good would that be if they were discovered? How would he get meat for winter if he used them?

"God, don't let them find us," he murmured, "don't let them find us!" Empty words ... He had to pull himself together, be strong for her and the child. There had to be an end to this ... pictures flashed, the blood mottled skin, life draining, how could it end any other way?

ɣɣɣ

Morning broke, clear and sunny, birdsong celebrating the dawn. He'd fallen asleep, back to the tree, rifle across his lap. She watched dappled sunlight trace patterns of chestnut fire through his hair. She remembered the first time she saw him, when they brought her to the camp, bedraggled and malnourished, a shadow of her former self. She'd wanted him even then, the smile, the bright eyes, the life in him ...

He stirred, a smile glimpsed, then faded. "We'll need food and water," he muttered, "best head towards the river."

⚥⚥⚥

Days turned to weeks. New blooms adorned the bank as bluebells relinquished their office to myriad hued cousins. Summer was on its way bringing plenty in its wake.

He'd that morning set off to the old camp in hopes of gleaning what they'd need for the birth. "It should be safe enough now," he'd judged, "the soldiers wouldn't stay." They had other "nests of traitors" to destroy. He'd left the pack, taking only his rifle and pocketknife. He said he didn't want to be loaded down, but he couldn't fool her ...

⚥⚥⚥

He edged towards the gully – all seemed quiet, the right kind of quiet. Birds flew hither and yon searching to placate growing young, insects hummed. The forest had resumed its tranquil cacophony of sound, proclaiming the absence of man. Relieved, but cautious, he crept forward. The smell became intense. The bodies were unrecognizable, gnawed by forest inhabitants, decaying from whence they came. Nature reclaimed its own. He tried not to look.

He was surprised they'd not torched the huts. Perhaps they were in a hurry? No matter. Their old lean to still stood. He ran his hands over the bullet holes riddling the frame. If they'd not gone foraging, if he'd not taken her along ...

Pull yourself together, get what you need and get out of here. Rummaging through the debris he found the big pot, blankets ... Thread, he must have thread ... No doctors, and no one to help them now when the time came. Glancing round he grabbed their winter coats, stuffing them into a blanket. It would have to do for now. He'd get more later he told himself, but in his heart, he knew he'd never venture back.

5

Hands full, view obscured, he never noticed the wire.

४४४

He won't come before evening, she intoned to herself, but as red deepened to violet the incantation ceased to comfort. What if he wasn't coming back? She'd never survive without him, let alone deliver a child. She lay quivering in the shelter, the fern bed an empty reminder. Tears began. She mustn't give up hope, give it time, give it time …

Time strode on, second by second. He didn't come. Perhaps they'd trailed him … perhaps they were even now searching for her. Stupid! She berated herself, stupid, stupid, they'd kill him straight off or follow him all the way. "Don't give in to fear". He'd told her that so many times, "fear paralyses you. You can't let it get a hold …" She tried to picture his face, the lean cheek-bones, luminous brown eyes, the unruly curls bound back with string. The vision transposed, eyes glazed, lifeless, chestnut diffused to another shade of red, browned skin paled in death … She mustn't think that way. He would come …

She heard a noise in the darkness. They'd come for her! They'd come for her! Scrambling, she crawled towards the back. *"Always have your escape planned, never get boxed in …"* A strange, distorted shape loomed before her. It called her name in the darkness.

It was Greg! It was Greg! Shadow yielded to moonlight as, dropping encumbering burdens, he opened his arms. Tasting salt in a hundred kisses, he hesitated.

"You thought I wasn't coming … I'm sorry, so sorry, I wanted to bring everything I could. It's summer, but winter will come. I brought the coats and the things you made for the child …"

She could say nothing, just cling, heart pounding.

"I thought … I thought you were dead … I …"

"It's OK. The forest is deserted. Anyway, I did come back. I'll always come back. You know that, right?" she nodded.

Holding her close, kisses transformed to something more urgent, desperate, as she fed of the life pulsing within him.

6

Sweat drenched them. They never undressed since that day, never dared be less than ready. Her hands took comfort in muscle like seasoned wood, supple, powerful, yet gentle, humble. There'd been better looking men at the camp, but it was him she wanted, always him. Life flowed richly through his veins, giving hope where there was darkness. In his arms she'd dared to dream, dared to live again. He'd welcomed the child, despite the difficulties, confident they could care for it, teach it to survive out here.

"Life must go on," he'd told her. "Life must always go on, or they'll have won!" Life had, for a while, a hard but happy existence. Feeding on his love she grew stronger, more resilient, but she'd never be as strong as him ...

Love climaxing in exhaustion they clung together in the darkness.

"I'll never leave you, never! I'll be there when the time comes, don't fear," he whispered as she surrendered to exhaustion.

℘℘℘

Deep in slumber, she knew nothing of the birds that roused him. A frenzied shaking awoke her.

"Get up! They're coming! God, I must have led them to you," his face contorted in guilt. "Quick, head across the river, I'll try to hold them off." She stumbled, brain numbed, through the back entrance. He thrust the pack into her hands, retaining the rifle.

"But ..."

"Go damn you! Take it with you. I'll stand more chance unencumbered!" With a rapid kiss he pushed her down toward the river. Stumbling, she pulled on the pack, thankful the tide reached but waist high. Once across she could ... what would she do? If they saw him cross, they'd follow ...

It was barely fifty paces, yet, as she gained the far bank, she heard gun shots. His rifle, but not from the shelter. Dogs howled. Her heart plunged. He wouldn't follow, he was leading them away. This was his way of saving them. A few shots were exchanged then a tumult erupted, ending abruptly and she knew he was dead. She gagged, clenching her fist to her mouth. Frozen in her hiding place, she watched. It was hopeless. Had he escaped they'd still be shooting.

A fierce defiance erupted, overpowering the grief, the fear. They'd not get his child! His life beat on within her. Turning, she edged from the river, marking the spot she'd last heard his rifle. She'd not leave him to rot, she'd come back ...

႘႘႘

She lay bundled in his blanket, inhaling his scent. There was time, she told herself. Summer was good for foraging, somehow, she'd survive. His last vestige lay within her and she must preserve it at all costs. Perhaps the child would be like him. She'd teach it as he'd taught her ...

"What of the winter?" The voice of foreboding echoed. There was no rifle, no Greg to set traps, the river would freeze. Trees and creatures would hibernate, life-giving sap retreat underground, plants die, berries cease, and she would be alone ...

She awoke, sharp pain piercing her exhaustion. Drawing up her knees, she gasped. There it was again. No! It couldn't be! It was all she had left. Agony rolled in, intense, excruciating, engulfing her. No! No! She mustn't lose it. It was too early. It would die, as its father had died, as she would die, alone in the wilderness. Better that way ... they'd be together, together in whatever lay beyond, if anything lay beyond ...

A tide swept between her thighs. She screamed. Again, and again, she screamed. They'd hear her! It didn't matter. Nothing mattered any more, nothing ...

2

Something cold touched her leg, recalling her from darkness. Yelling, she sat up, head spinning. It scuttled away. There was something squishy between her thighs. Amid the blood and

8

mucus lay a tiny form, barely the size of her palm, perfect in miniature. Perfect, but dead. She sought to wrap it in the blanket to keep the foragers away, but she slid back into oblivion.

Again she regained consciousness. It was still there ... Edging it out of the gore onto the blanket, she pushed away from the mess, inch by inch. The bleeding had eased, but she couldn't sit up. She clung to her bundle, too weak to bury it, as darkness overtook her once more ...

She awoke to an empty stomach and burning thirst. The pack lay close. Dragging herself towards it she grasped the flask. It was full but wouldn't last. She must bury the child, return to the river, but she'd not the strength. Perhaps she could take it, bury it when she was stronger? First, she must rest ...

She awoke next morning, strength sufficient to encase her bundle in the pack. She staggered up, dizzy and weak. She wouldn't be able to carry it, better to crawl and drag it. The land sloped down towards the river, she had only to follow ...

She rolled the pack, staggering after it from one tree to the next, cursing the dress she'd adopted when her pants could no longer accommodate her. The oak beckoned, she could see it now, its heart blasted, a yawning hole.

The hole! That was it, the place to put their child. The oak would keep it safe. She staggered on, collapsing at its feet. A little water eased her thirst, but she needed food. She needed to wash also ... Why bother? Greg was gone. His child was gone, what use to survive?

"Life must go on, otherwise they'll have won ..." His words no longer motivated her. Let them win. What did it matter? What did anything matter? But one thing did. She must bury him and the child. She'd rest a few minutes, then ...

Exhaustion kicked in. Her eyes drifted closed. When they opened night was coming on. She dragged herself up, peering into the crevasse of the oak. It was high enough to dissuade most scavengers, but she must be sure. Scooping leaves, she lined its base. The blanket wouldn't fit through, anyway she'd need it. Rummaging through the pack, she found an old T-shirt used to clean the rifle. Its pungent smell reminded her of him. It was dirty, but that didn't matter. It was Greg's, perhaps it might lead the child to him ... Don't be ridiculous she chided, yet somehow it helped ... the idea that they were together ... somewhere.

"I'll be joining you soon," she whispered. Gathering sticks and pebbles she barricaded the hole. Nothing would get in there. "Take care of her for me." She stroked the bark of the broken giant and curled up among its ancient roots. The blanket was stiff with blood, it didn't matter, it was their blood ...

Morning dawned, with it a determination to reach the river. It wasn't far now, but her belly ached with pain and hunger and the bleeding continued to weaken her. Downing the last of the water, she kissed the rough bark in farewell to the child within and, tears streaming, set her jaw. The pack was an encumbrance, but in it lay her means of survival, fishing gear, his Swiss army knife, a pot, what else she didn't know. They were his things, his legacy for her. After a while she heard the gentle lap of water, glimpsed its twinkle between the trees. Perhaps they were still there, waiting? What did it matter? She'd die anyway without food and water ...

She'd made it. The sun was high now. She reached a hand into the water, its freshness reviving her. She splashed her face, a dirty, blood smeared visage of blanched skin and matted hair glimpsed among the ripples. Later, she told herself, later she would wash. Food and water came first.

She lowered the flask into the flow. They'd drunk from this river before, when they first came and couldn't risk a fire. Greg said it came from the mountains ...

She rummaged in the pack arraying the precious items beside it. There it was – fishing tackle, several simple lines and hooks. A few yards down a tree hung over the water, she could attach lines to the branches. She rummaged further, his bait tin. The worms were dead, but the movement of the water might work ... She'd never been as good as him, but he'd taught her the basics.

Lines rippling, she looked around for forage. Plenty of nettles!

Not to her liking but full of iron. Her exertions had brought on the heavy bleeding again. Matches? Yes, he still had the matches. Greg used flints, but she'd yet to master the art. Thankfully this area abounded in fallen wood. She knew the smoke could draw them, but she no longer cared. Setting the kindling at the heart, she gently blew on the flame. The familiar crackle of wood sounded as she fed the blaze, setting the small pan to balance on two stones. Greg would have made a support, hung it from its chain ... but Greg was not here ... would never be here! Hands protected by the blanket, she cut the nettle tops, setting them in the warming pot.

It was not till late afternoon she saw a pull on one of the lines. Scrambling she glimpsed a flash of silver. It wasn't large but would sustain her. She'd washed the worst of the blood from the blanket and cleaned herself best she could, improvising pads from a roll of bandage she'd found in the pack.

Her clothes and blanket were damp as she lay down to sleep ... it didn't matter ... He lay undefended, meat for any forager. She chewed her fist, tears streaming.

It was several days before she was strong enough to cross. There'd been no sign of troops. She subsisted on fish and nettles, nourishing, not appetising, but she wouldn't have tasted the most succulent roast – he was gone! She was alone!

Grasping the stick to steady herself, she swayed under the weight of the pack. The water was cool and refreshing, pulling at her skirt. She struggled on, scrambling up the far bank. Tossing off the pack, she lay gasping, gazing up at dancing clouds.

She found the place mostly by smell. First a trace on the breeze, it turned to a nauseous stench as she drew closer – the smell of death. She'd not encountered it before. Her stomach clenched; nerves faltered. She couldn't do it, couldn't look on what he'd become ...

ℇℇℇ

"He's calling for her again," Ma said. Chad positioned the gun in

11

its usual place and scooped a bowl of water from the bucket.

"Did he say anything else?"

"Nothing."

"Fever still high?"

"It is that, and no surprise the state you boys brought him in. It's a wonder he's not dead."

"Might be yet. Sorry Ma there wasn't much time, did the best we could."

Ma clicked her tongue. "Just so you boys get back safe. Leave the doctoring to me."

He gave her a peck on the cheek. "You're the best Ma. At least he stands a chance. Shame, a few minutes earlier and we could have saved him."

"You do what you can son. I know that." Ma looked affectionately at the mountain that was Chad. At six three he towered over her, ex-marine, special forces, tough as nails, but underneath a heart of gold. He'd cared for her ever since their Sally died, he didn't have to do that, there's many that wouldn't. She wasn't much use, couldn't fight, could hardly shoot a gun. Instead she'd found her niche cooking and caring for them all, especially the injured. She was a tough old bird, had taken bullets out of a fair few of them, including the skinny specimen on the mat. The boys all called her Ma, not just Chad. God knows there were few enough women, only Annie left now, and she handier with her old AK47 than a cooking pot. Annie had seen her kids killed, that twisted the heart out of a woman ...

The lips moved, the name scarce more than a breath.

"You fight for her lad! Come on fight!" encouraged Ma lifting the cup of "medicine" to his lips, but he didn't drink.

☙☙☙

Bodies lay at intervals, once crisp camouflage fatigues gnawed and sullied, faces unrecognisable. She paused, gagging. He'd used his bullets well ... perhaps, just perhaps ... She saw jeans peeking through the bushes, a foot at a monstrous angle. Her guts heaved, spilling vital nutrients on the forest floor.

It took some moments to pull herself together. This was why she'd come. The scavengers had had their way, but no more, but there was no obliging oak to receive this charge. She couldn't carry him, had neither strength nor tool with which to dig. Perhaps the leaves ... leaves and branches ... at least his demise would be hidden away?

She seized an armful. They fell, evasive, through her fingers, twirling to nothingness. She dragged out the blanket. She needn't look, just empty the bundles, last year's debris, death camouflaging death.

Surely enough now? Pausing, she glanced down, the worst was already hidden. Bristles protruded, hedgehog like, in defiance of the decomposing leaves. She gasped. Brushing them aside, her heart leapt. No long brown locks lay blood caked beneath her gaze. It wasn't Greg! Ignoring the gore in her frenzied quest, she uncovered the legs – patches at the knees, patches she'd sown herself – His clothes, but not him? He'd survived? ... but why had he not come?

One by one, she checked the bodies, searching for clues. Perhaps they'd captured him, but why the clothes? He'd faked his death to evade pursuit, but why had he not come? Perhaps he couldn't find her, perhaps he was still searching? She remembered that night, her screams. He would have heard? There must be something more ... perhaps he was injured, perhaps, perhaps, thoughts flew in her head. Exhausted by her ordeal, she staggered back to the river away from the stench, away from death. Tomorrow she would search, but today she must eat, replenish what she'd lost ...

ชชช

Searching proved fruitless, she could only wait and hope. Hope he'd not been captured, that his body didn't lay someplace beneath the ferns ... but ... if he came ... how could she tell him about the baby? He'd so wanted a child. Perhaps it was just as well, what kind of life was this for an infant? Death was seldom far away.

She remembered her own escape, the guns, the carnage. She owed her survival to the depravity of the officer in charge. He'd taken her alive, for a little "fun" before execution. She'd used his games to escape. Her mind recalled the horror, his naked body drenched in blood. Engrossed in his perversions, he'd left his belt on the floor where she'd wantonly undressed him. Fool! Did he think she'd want a man like him? She'd noted the knife ... She felt guilty sometimes. She'd never killed before, but what choice had she had?

She'd used his uniform to escape – no one eyeballed a senior officer and it was dark – driven the jeep till the gas ran out then taken to the woods. They must have come after her, but they'd never found her. She'd survived a while on the jeep's emergency rations, but hunger eventually forced her to wonder the forest in search of food. She'd have died had Greg's comrades not found her ...

ꙮꙮꙮ

The face was there again, brash, ugly, peering down at him. Who was this fiend who tormented his dreams? The other face was old, haggard, but bore a motherly smile. Today it was the fiend again. He tried to move but he was too weak.

"Emmie, Emmie ..." he whispered. Why did they not understand?

"He's calling for her again," Chad turned to Ma with a sigh.

"Did you check around? Could there have been someone else there?"

"Not that we could see. Couldn't stay long," He looked dejected at the floor.

"You did your best Chad, can't go risking lives."

Ma placed a reassuring hand on his shoulder. "You can't save everyone Chad."

"Yeah, some I could."

"It weren't your fault about Sally, 'twas the sickness. It's a hard life out here for a woman." She'd often pondered why it had taken Sally and left her. God knows she'd have traded places.

14

She knew Chad blamed himself, blamed himself for every death, but what else could he have done?

"You're a good man Chad," she brushed away the tear he tried to hide. "I know how much you loved my Sally. You'd have done anything for her."

"Anything but murder kids ..."

"Yeah, not that. You know my Sal. She'd not condone that. She was proud of you Chad, right proud!" He squished Ma against his barrel chest.

"I know Ma, I do it for her, you know that," he choked.

"Yes, I know, and I reckon she's looking down, right proud."

Chad doubted that. He'd seen too much, but if it comforted Ma ... Ma believed the "Supreme Leader" was the devil incarnate. He didn't blame her, especially since the lightning strike of five years past that had left the Eastern Seaboard an atomic wasteland. He'd wiped them out indiscriminately, good and bad, even his own followers, nullifying the last major resistance and establishing the new economic system worldwide. Till then even Chad had been deceived by the promises – food for the poor and starving, justice, the destruction of the big multinationals and their cut-throat exploitation of mankind. Even after the collapse of the US government, he'd wondered. Maybe it was worth the cost? Like everyone, he'd been given land, a fair income, free Medicare, there was even a pension for Ma. TV had shown footage of the rescue of the poor and starving (it had been bad enough in the States, in third world countries it had been far worse!) It seemed right in a way and for a while things had seemed better.

Then the new "special ops" started. Chad's allegiance was transferred to a new elite, and he was called upon to enact its destruction of any who dared question. The hitherto voluntary economic identity mark had become obligatory ... He gazed down at the small scar on his palm where he'd dug out the chip. He knew they used it for tracking.

He'd refused to be the tool of such a regime. That decision had cost him everything, cost him Sal. Her face haunted his dreams, pale and sickly. He'd brought them north to Wyoming, away from people, away from the regime. Sal had never been strong, and the miscarriage weakened her. They'd done all they could, but Ma's herbs could only go so far. When the fevers came, she'd died as she'd lived, in his arms. There'd never be another like her, one who looked through the rough exterior, the broad unpretentious face and saw his heart. He couldn't have that again, but he could help others survive. He'd turned vigilante, started to watch over the small enclaves of fugitives finding refuge in the wilderness. Many had similar stories, even those of his division who chose to stand with him – special ops. They'd brought with them the tools of their trade, most importantly their experience.

❦❦❦

She woke in a cold sweat, faces of death dancing in the darkness. The nightmare repeated itself. She sat up, breathing cool night air, wrapping the blanket around her. The darkness was still, quiet. Comforting woodland sounds blurred the images in her mind, blurred but not erased. Like the commandant's body they remained with her, buried deep.

She listened as the breeze stirred the leaves. Out here it seemed so simple. Life went on he'd said. Yes, life went on. Day by day she grew stronger, blowing on the shred of hope that somewhere Greg lived, someday he'd come for her.

She should return across the river. He'd look for her there. If he lived, he'd come, he'd promised. God let it be before the winter! The thought of winter scared her. She'd salvaged the coats and blankets from the lean to, but she dare not live there. Better across the river. She could build something to keep off the rain and snow, but what of food?

❦❦❦

It was over a week before the fever broke, leaving him weak as a kitten. He gazed into the wrinkled eyes he'd seen so often.

"Emmie ..." His mouth shaped the word, but no sound came.

"Rest, now lad. Drink this." Ma propped his head towards a

16

foul-smelling brew. He tried futilely to push it away.

"Emmie ..."

"Now listen to me! Ain't no use you calling her name, we don't know who or where she is. You just swallow this and get your strength back, then you can go looking." Ma glared belligerently. Yielding, he opened parched lips, choking on the concoction.

"I know it tastes bad, but you lost a lot of blood and that fever sapped whatever strength you had left. I ain't no doctor, but I'm the best you got. 'N I ain't nursed you back from death's door to have you refusing your medicine, you hear me!" Inclining his head, he sipped reluctantly at the brew.

"That's better. Take more later. Rest now, give your body a chance to heal." He collapsed back onto the pillow. Awake, alive, but trapped in a body that would not obey. The old woman was right, he must regain his strength.

That evening the other face came – so he'd been real.

"Emmie ..." It hung in the air like a whisper.

"I'm sorry man. We looked, didn't see another soul. We had to pull out. We thought it was just you." The giant sat beside him, eyes sad, so sad. "Look, I know how it feels. I lost someone too. You get your strength up and we'll go back, search for her, OK. But we need to relocate. We didn't dare move you, but now it's past time ..."

ॐॐॐ

He woke on a stretcher of sorts, a blanket nailed to two poles. He noted the men, rough types, toting oversized backpacks and various types of automatics, government issue by looks of it. The old woman rode alongside on a nag that had seen better days. Before her sat another woman, mousy hair dragged back, face like stone. What was she doing here, or the old one for that matter? They were obviously rebels, but some sported government uniforms. Too weak to ask questions, he let his consciousness drift. Whoever they were, whatever they were, they must have somehow rescued him.

He had the story a few days later from the big one they called Chad.

"Reckon you want to know what happened?" He nodded. "We've been keeping an eye on you folks for a while now, leading the soldiers off when they got too close. We got wind of a big movement. Vince tried to warn you, but he was too late. By the time he got there the camp was surrounded. He couldn't do nothing but watch and look for survivors."

"Did ... you ...?" His voice petered out.

"Did we find any survivors? Yeah, we found two, pretty shot up but alive. Took them to a couple we know. Don't know if they made it or not ..."

"We decided to go back once things had died down, see if anyone else made it out. That's when we heard gunshots. There weren't more than five or six of them and you'd already winged one. We had the high ground, didn't take much, like shooting rabbits. I dressed one in your duds, let 'em think you'd killed 'em. He chuckled. "We stay on the move mostly, out of sight, there's not enough of us to take on a serious attack. We do what we can." He bit avidly into the meat bone in his hand. He noticed the glance. "Now look I'd give you some, but Ma would skin me alive, says you can't eat more than broth to start. Look at you, you look like a rat, all skin and bone and not much of that either." He laughed. The name stuck.

3

Autumn was here, the wind colder. She cowered in her dilapidated lean to, damp and musty from the previous day's rain. Berries were abundant, a change from her fish and forage diet, but soon the river would freeze, the berries be consumed. Still he hadn't come. The flame of hope flickered, a candle in the wind. Tears came easily. She brushed them away as she edged to adjust her lines, fingers numb.

A bird flew upward squawking, branches parted, startled eyes met her own across the water.

"Well look what I've found!"

She watched in horror as two more shapes emerged from the foliage. Senses kicking in, she scrambled from her perch, dashing into the undergrowth. Splashes resounded as they surged after her. No sense trying to bluff it out, once they saw she had no trading mark they'd know. Gasping, she sped through the forest, mud splashing as she slipped in the wet ground. She was stronger now, but not strong enough to outrun them. She must find a place to hide. She glanced frantically at the surrounding trees. The oak loomed before her but offered no refuge. She heard the crash of boots pounding behind her ...

There! That one! If she could grasp the lower branches, she could hoist herself up. Hands torn and bleeding, she scrambled higher into the foliage. Just in time! A man burst through the thicket, tall, broad chested, young face red with exertion. Plunging past he dashed off followed by a second, bearded, in an old leather jacket. No sign of the third. Breathless, she listened to the echoes die away. She'd wait till they were well gone then head back across the river, mask her tracks. Thank God they had no dogs, probably out for a day's fishing in the hills, simple lowlifes. Still they'd know about the reward ...

A rustle alerted her. The third, older than the others, came panting, following the engraved boot prints of his companions. Exhausted, he collapsed in a heap, his back to her tree. Did he know? Had he seen her tracks? Voices echoed through the forest.

"We must have lost her! damn it! There goes our money!"

"I'm sure she came this way. Don't see how she could outrun us, a little thing like that. Keep looking!"

"Where the hell is Ed?"

"Can't keep up with that beer gut of his."

"I'm back here Sam, giving my legs a rest," sang out the huddled figure below her. "Come, I've something to show you." Her heart froze.

"Never mind that. Come and help damn you!"

"No need. You guys need to use your heads."

She heard the muttering of the returning men. Angry and impatient, the big one strode towards them.

"What the hell you on about?" Ed nodded upward. "What?"

"Use your eyes. Look there!" Ed pointed to the ground beside him. "Those ain't your tracks! She's gone to ground up there." A look of incredulity spread over the young face as Sam also approached.

"She's up in the tree," he yelled grinning as he spotted her. "Whose gonna get her down? May as well have some fun before we turn her in, looks young and fit, if a bit scrawny."

"Well as not," drawled Ed.

"The one as gets her down goes first!" said the younger man hitching himself up into the lower branches.

"Fair enough," said Sam, "just as long as I gets a turn." She tried to scramble higher. It was no use. He grabbed her foot, pulling her down towards him. Writhing to escape she landed with a thump, winded and her ankle throbbing.

"Leave me ... alone!" she gasped. "I've ... done nothing to you!"

"Not yet you haven't, but you will!" Sam smirked, grabbing her arms as her tree hunter swung down to pin her legs open.

"Me first, remember!" Rummaging at his fly he thrust into her. Slobbering, his tongue violated her mouth as he invaded her body, silencing her cries. Finished in moments, he swapped positions. She begged and screamed curses at them, pain and terror engulfing her beleaguered senses. Unperturbed Sam took his time. At least the first had been quick ... The old man sat under the tree watching.

"Come on Sam don't take all day. We need to be back by sundown and you boys is giving me the itch."

"What? You want a go grandpa? Thought you was too old for that," laughed Sam.

"I ain't that old, and I ain't no gramps. I can still get it up went opportunity comes."

He was the worst, grunting and groaning, groping and licking like an animal in his attempt to gain release. This couldn't be happening, but she knew it was just the prelude to something far worse. Finally, berated by the younger men he gave up, muttering about needing to get a move on.

Hauling her to her feet, only to have her collapse with a yelp of pain, they finally realized her ankle was swollen.

"Should have been more careful getting her down, now we'll have to carry her," Ed muttered.

"Too much of a hurry. Young men are all the same!"

"You didn't even try to get her. You're one to talk!"

"Without me you'd never have found her!"

"Makes no difference. What's done is done. Let's get on with it. I want to be out of these woods by nightfall and on the way to claiming our reward," saying which, Sam threw her, sobbing, over his shoulder and stalked off. The others followed.

Nearing the forest's edge, they were alerted by the sound of tumbling pebbles. They stopped, peering into the gloom. There was no one in sight, instead the pebbles grew in vibration as the ground beneath their feet began to tremble.

"Quake!" one yelled. Tossed to the ground as they took to their heels, she grasped at a pine trunk. Earth slipped away, as if some giant wave sucked sand from beneath her feet. She screamed.

The ground rose and fell as she clung with all her might, body sloping down towards she knew not what. Rocks and soil came tumbling from the ground above. She cried hysterically over the tumult, arms aching.

"For pity's sake, someone help me!" There was no one, but a strange calm encompassed her. She closed her eyes and reached towards it.

Somehow, she survived, sobbing quietly as the quake subsided and the ground stabilized, arms still coiled around the pine. An unearthly quiet followed. Trees lay tossed, twisted, broken roots a testimony of the forces at play, but her tree stood, clinging to the earth.

Without it she'd have gone careering down into the shadows that lurked beyond. She hoisted herself up to straddle its base, wincing at the pain from her ankle. Crawling, she found a small space of level ground. Better to wait for morning, no knowing what holes or crevices she might blunder into in the dark ...

Daybreak came sunny and warm, comforting after nature's tirade. She examined her ankle. The swelling had gone down somewhat. She couldn't walk on it, but she might get along with a stick. She needed water, and her belly ached with hunger. Her arms and legs were bruised, her ankle hurt, but she was fortunate to be alive. She'd not have lasted long in custody. Doubtless there would have been the usual "preliminaries" with some sleazy official. No one cared, she was worthless to them. Last time she'd gotten away. This time she'd not been so lucky.

No, she reminded herself, she was lucky. She was alive, and she was free. Life, so nearly lost, was precious! Now to find water and hopefully some of the last berries ... What she'd eat after that she didn't know. She surveyed her new domain. Better to go up she reasoned, hopefully from there she could get her bearings.

She stood astounded. Beneath the slope she'd scaled the land dropped some hundred feet. Buried beneath a heap of red earth lay a small town, or what was left of it. She steadied herself.

Truly she'd been one of the lucky ones! Devastation lay all around, above and below her. What of her persecutors? Had they made it out alive or were their bodies buried at the bottom of the cliff? She'd never know. Now she must find water ...

ⵣⵣⵣ

Rat awoke from a violent dream, guns blazed, she was calling him ... Another week Chad had said. He knew he was right, but balked against the delay, afraid of coming too late. He knew why Chad delayed – he thought she was dead, had from the beginning. Rat couldn't blame him, there were others to watch over, others they might save ... and they had. He'd seen them come, blurry eyed and desperate, snatched from the hunter's maw. Raids were increasing. Chad saw his quest as a fool's errand, none the less he'd keep his word. Just a few more days ... Rising from his mattress Rat worked his muscles, pushing himself. It took time, time he didn't have ...

She stared at the devastation below. What other option was there? Any food remaining had been devoured. The pack, her crucial survival tool, was probably buried beneath the debris – even if she could find her way back. It was this or starvation. She must take her chances.

She began the descent, skidding on her posterior, skirts catching on protruding branches and brambles. Sheets of dirt and pebbles, disturbed by her passing, sped ahead. There'd be no going back. Scraped and disheveled, clothes ripped and stained with the blood of multiple grazes she arrived at the base of the incline. A mangy hound took to its heels at her approach. She'd never felt so alone ...

ℰℰℰ

Rat urged the nag on, finding its pace exasperating. Chad glanced back from the top of the rise; expression anguished. Something was wrong, horribly wrong. Before them lay unrecognizable devastation. Once familiar woodland lay buried in rock and soil, branches protruding like a vast forest of brambles, impassable.

"My God!" Chad breathed, "Lord help anyone caught in that! Sorry man, I should have come sooner ... I should have ..."

"Not your fault Chad!" Rat growled. "Let's go in on foot." Chad said nothing. There was desperation in Rat's eyes. He'd seen it before. The girl was doubtless old bones. He'd hoped the trip would help Rat accept it, now this!

Tying the horses, they skirted mangled groves of writhing branches, ghostly fingers seeking to escape their fate ...

ℰℰℰ

Exhausted, they huddled in their blankets. The search was fruitless, as Chad knew it would be.

"We tried," he muttered. "She couldn't say you didn't try ..." Rat remained speechless, tears rolling, defeated. It had all been for nothing. He may as well have died, at least they'd be together. There wasn't even a body to mourn. Doubtless she lay somewhere, buried by nature itself, her and the child within her.

⚡⚡⚡

"Sun's up. Time to go man." Rat shook his head emphatically. He couldn't leave, he'd stay here, continue searching, maybe somewhere ... He knew he was fooling himself. The quake was old, if she'd been buried, she was dead by now. "Life must go on, he'd told her." What a fool he'd been, deluding himself.

"You can't stay here Rat. There's nothing to eat, even the water's fouled. Stay here and you'll die!"

Rat shook his head.

"Listen!" Chad glared, frustrated. "So, you lost someone! We all did. Do you think I don't feel it every day? I do this for her, OK. I do it so maybe, just maybe, someone else doesn't have to suffer what I suffer. Be a man. Stop thinking about yourself! So, life stinks! I know it, but for God's sake don't wallow in it. We need all the help we can get. You can use a rifle. You know the woods, the wilderness. Don't throw your life away when it's valuable! Maybe you can give someone else a chance at life, even if yours is gone!"

Chad turned and pulled on his pack. "Now, come on man." He kicked out at Rat hauling him to his feet, pulling the pack over drooping arms. "Come on!" Chad dragged him along, unwilling, a few steps before giving up on his endeavour.

"Go to hell then, you selfish bastard! Waste your life wallowing!" Abandoning the struggle, he strode off.

"Chad, Chad wait!" Chad smiled, his gamble had paid off, Rat was coming.

4

The basement would suffice till she put something together, but it was dark and damp and if there were another earthquake ... She surveyed the food, only the corn beef was openable. She had no can opener and the other food was spoilt. The dog had led her to a smashed window submerged under the debris. What it fed on there she dare not think – the smell of death hung over the entire region. The garden tap, pumping fresh water from some far-off station, was her own discovery. Somewhere life continued ...

Clambering over earth and shattered concrete she watched for signs of life – for the dog, it might have other feeding places ... Nothing! A rat scuttled at her feet. Yelling, she jumped as it scampered away disappearing in the cracks. What was the use she asked herself? Food for one more day, one more day ... for what? *Maybe he'll come back?* Even if he did, he'd never find her here, her mind responded mercilessly. Only the pains forced her on, hunger was not a fast way to die ...

Another day, another night – she stared at the cans, food tantalizingly beyond her reach. If only she had the army knife. She tried again with the stone, but the can only buckled. Frustrated, she hurled it down, sobbing. Curling up for warmth, she succumbed to exhaustion.

ɤɤɤ

She didn't notice till the sun glimmered on the broken letters. Her heart pounded as she clambered towards it, cautious of concealed chambers beneath the debris. She scraped at the soil. Yes, somewhere below lay a supermarket. Another rat grazed her feet. She sprang back banging her ankle, healed but tender. Ignoring the pain, she watched it traverse a crack. She followed, cautiously pulling aside a slab of plaster board. A stench assailed her nostrils. Stomach heaving, she focused. She could do this. There was food down there.

A slab of concrete bared her way, but the soil beside was soft. A tiny tunnel showed where the rat had descended, breathless, she pulled at the earth. Another slab of plasterboard obstructed her. Frustrated, she heaved till it finally broke away. Weakened by its collapse, earth tumbled, subsiding beneath her feet.

Scrambling to grasp onto something, she was propelled downward. Panic engulfed her.

She was plunged into darkness. As her eyes adjusted, she perceived shapes, and the hole looming above. Desperately she tried to climb back to the light only succeeding in widening the hole.

"Stop it! Stop it!" she admonished herself. She'd bring the whole pile down. She closed her eyes, taking deep breaths, to calm down. *Maybe there's another way out, stay calm ... don't panic.* If she panicked, she was done for ... She opened her eyes, continuing the deep breaths. Around was chaos, shafts of broken sunlight revealing shadowed glimpses of collapsed shelves and broken freezers. The floor was littered with packs of putrid flesh, rotten meat, but not human remains. No cans here though, nothing she could eat. She noticed a darker triangle, groping her way toward it. Peering through the hole she glimpsed a dim light. Where there was light there might be an exit. Dare she? What other option was there? Heart thumping, she stumbled over piles of concrete and chipboard edging her way toward the light. Something fell tumbling at her feet. There was a momentary glimmer of light. Matches! They were matches. Groping, she scraped them into the box, igniting one of the remainder. It didn't give much light, but it was better than darkness. One by one she lit them investigating the collapsed shelves around her.

There! There they were! Placing the matchbox at her feet she pulled frantically at the plastic wrapping. Batteries? Yes, there were batteries. A beam of liberating light shot into the darkness. She gasped! It was huge, a great empty cavern. Aisles of produce, much rotting and fermenting, stretched before her ... but was there a way out?

ϪϪϪ

Pockets stuffed with sardine and corn beef cans, she edged towards the glimmer of light seeping through a mess of trolleys, baskets and debris. She shone the torch upward, relieved to see the roof area intact. Scaling the pile, bit by agonizing bit, she eased the all invading soil, plaster and chip board away. Trolleys had been pushed into the entrance by the landslide, their metal framework limiting its intrusion. She prized the first out, setting off a landslide of soil. Something hit her leg. Her eyes caught a glimmer of chrome. Could it be? Not a tin opener, but an equally useful item, a small saucepan. If this was the kitchenware section surely tin openers would be close by? Never mind. First dig herself out!

As more and more debris was cleared, the light became stronger. She no longer needed the torch. A gap appeared beneath a trolley – daylight! She didn't want to risk moving it, instead crawling between the wheels. She emerged in a semi collapsed car park. Steps led upwards. Scrambling to her feet she ran up, increasing light hurting her eyes. She was free! She'd made it! Her heart pounded with relief.

ɤɤɤ

She went over the list in her head. She'd vowed never to return, but reason had kicked in. Her supplies wouldn't last and who knew how long the roof would hold. She must return. This time she'd be prepared, know what to look for.

Edging down the steps, torch in hand, she descended. What had appeared light to her darkened eyes, was dim and shadowy. The trolley stood as she'd left it, guarding the way. Though covering a large area, the debris was not particularly high, emanating from the smashed corner through which it had poured. Reassured, she worked at enlarging the hole, pulling out the trolley through which she'd crawled, clearing the resulting fall of debris.

At last, entrance cleared to her satisfaction, she ventured in. The smell was foul as ever, but she didn't care. She began to accumulate a pile of items outside the hole: a bigger pot (stuffed with candles), knives, a stack of filthy, but usable, plastic bags, and the all-important tin opener. Grabbing a bag, she returned to the canned meat section, using the torch to check the labels.

Bag full, grabbing another, she searched for beans and veg. Staples were harder to find, requiring a little digging. She grabbed a couple of bags of rice, the only things visible. The roof moaned under its load and she wanted to get out in the sunlight.

Passing back through for the last time, she heaved a sigh of relief. Gazing down at her hoard, she began double bagging the treasures. She'd need two trips at least.

That evening she feasted, stomach full of rice and tinned meat. She'd make a couple more trips, if she dared – she must dare! Then she'd build a shelter. She hated sleeping in the cellar, but it was too cold in the open, even with the jacket she'd salvaged. She needed warm clothes, blankets and a safe place to live ...

ɤɤɤ

Rat gazed through the binoculars. There must be hundreds! Lines of vehicles, like multicoloured beads, dotted the highway below. Not the usual troop movements ... these were civilians ... refugees? He must tell Chad. Turning, he slipped off through the forest.

"How many?" Chad queried.

"Hundreds, loaded down with baggage."

A mass exodus? What could it mean? Something must have happened. He remembered the massive destruction they'd seen looking for Rat's woman. If so, most would head east towards the cities of the plains.

"We'd best send scouts and warn folks to be on their guard." Rat nodded. "We set out at first light. You in on this?" Rat nodded again and headed for the lean to.

"Want some food?" Annie thrust a bowl into his hands, eyes skimming his recovering physique. He knew what she wanted, knew she and Chad sometimes bunked together in an attempt to ease the pain. She wanted what he could no longer give – hope, but hope had died on a tree strewn slope, buried beneath the debris. He grasped the bowl avoiding her eyes ...

They set out early, he and Chad teaming up as usual. Chad was keeping an eye on him – he knew that. Little was said as they passed through the forest. Guns and packs on their backs, Chad in his worn Government fatigues, Rat in the oversized pants of his nemesis, and a purloined black sports jacket, they made a strange pair.

Ears attuned to the forest, Rat heard them first. Signalling, they crept toward the sound. Whoever it was had no idea how to survive out here. Raised voices broke the silence as they approached. Someone was clearly drunk.

"An' I say it was aliens! What else could it be?"

"Sober up for God's sake. You're embarrassing. You know that?"

"He's always believed in the little green men, Bart has. Too much tequila when he was down in Mexico." Raucous laughter followed.

"But I tell you I saw them!"

"Yeah, and pink elephants too!"

The banter continued as Chad and Rat slipped closer. Two Harleys blended oddly with the trees. Bikers! What were they doing out here? The owners, leather jackets emblazoned with skulls and eagles, passed a bottle across an ill made fire. Chad motioned to Rat, who sunk into the shadows, sights set. They were all half drunk, shouldn't be trouble, but you could never tell. Chad strode forward, gun swinging casually from one hand.

"What are you doing out here?" His voice was neutral, commanding, but not threatening. He'd done this before both in the forces and since. They looked up startled.

"Thought we'd do some hunting?"

Chad took in the scene. "I don't see no rifles ..."

"Trapping." The older one cut in. "Came mostly to get away from the wife." He joked offering the bottle. Chad shook his head. Obviously they were lying, but it was no concern of his.

"Look, I'm just after information. I saw a slew of traffic heading east back on the highway. What's going on."

"Ain't you heard?" The older man looked suspicious.

"Radio's out," Chad improvised.

29

"Hell, don't you know? California's gone!" the first sang out.

"It was those damn aliens!" Bart yelled, voice seesawing on a tide of alcohol.

Placing a restraining hand on his shoulder, the older one continued. "Huge earthquake, massive! Then a tidal wave, engulfed everything. Never seen anything like it!"

"It came out of the sky I tell you! It was aliens," Bart slurred, attempting to get to his feet, but failing.

"Looked like a meteor," the first continued. "Must have set off the quakes ... Everyone's fleeing east. There's been aftershocks and meteor showers, and not just in California."

"Yeah, there was a bad one not far from here a while back." Chad answered. "So where are you guys headed?"

"Don't know yet. Thought we'd get us a bit of peace out here."

"What about your wife?"

The older man, who'd been edging back, made a sudden dash for the Harleys, followed by his companion. The bikes pulled away in a trail of dust. Rat raised his rifle, but Chad waved him to stop. Petty criminals probably, they'd not stay now. The drunk looked around incredulously, too tanked-up to follow.

"The aliens will get 'em anyway. Wanna a drink?" he gleefully waved the abandoned bottle."

"I think you've had enough for one night." Chad responded, grabbing it from him. The face sank in disappointment. "Might as well be drunk when they come ... ain't no use trying to fight them."

"Fight who?"

"Them! ..." His eyes widened before dimming back into distraction.

It was getting late. After a brief discussion, they decided to use the bikers' camp and wait till their companion sobered up to see what other information they might glean.

It was unbelievable – California gone? Perhaps they made up the story, but surely they'd have made up something more plausible. After the east coast anything seemed possible. It would certainly explain the trail of refugees.

California was the power base since Washington went down. Angry at the US Middle East raids that almost assassinated him, the Supreme Leader had annihilated the eastern seaboard and all power related structures, setting up his leadership as far from the nuclear drift as possible. From there his envoys had enacted an iron grip upon the populous. Liberating the poor from enslavement by the big multinationals and their government puppets, they initiated their own brand of domination. Most folks went along with it, what choice did they have?

❧❧❧

Bart bewailed his fate. Not only was his head pounding, but his wrists were tied securely to the tree behind. Rat set a plate of food before him, reaching to untie his hands. Chad stood; gun casually directed in his vicinity.

"Don't get any ideas of making a run for it," he intoned. "We could easily have shot your mates if we'd wanted." Bart glared and rubbed his sore wrists.

"What do you want from me?"

"Information. After that you're free to go."

"Not much use now. I lost my ride." He jerked his head toward where the Harleys had stood.

"Not much in the way of friends to leave you behind."

"Naw not much! So, what you want to know?"

"What went on with California and where folks are headed, especially if the government went down with it?" Head clearing, Bart was beginning to catch on. He eyed Chad's uniform, noting the faded knees and collar.

"You're not government, are you?"

"You got it!" Chad smiled.

"So, what are you guys? Rebels ...?" Bart drew out the word sarcastically.

"Let's say vigilantes." The smile grew bigger.

"So, you an' me we're much alike ..."

"I think not." Chad frowned. "I know your sort. Now are you going to tell us what you know, or shall I tell Rat to tie you back

31

up and forget breakfast."

"No need. I'd be happy to tell you all I know. Got any water? My throat's parched as a desert." Rat threw over the canteen. Bart began his story interspersed by chewing.

"So, the new government went down with the ship, huh?" Chad prompted.

"All happened so fast. Don't see how they could have got away. We only made it 'cause we was on our way to Nevada … Even then it was some ride, mudslides, ground opening up and all. I've seen some scary stuff, but nothing like that. There was fire raining down on us, and great cracks all over. That's how I lost my bike, couldn't stop in time … Like some big death star in the sky it was, coming straight at us." Bart paused. "We were half-way up the mountains when it hit. There was like this huge impact, even that far away the shock wave hit us, and the ground started shaking. Ain't no one made it out of that! We just kept going, heading for high ground. Mike said that was the safest place and he was right. The wave hit a while after … just swallowed up everything!"

"So, those folks on the road, they're not from California?"

"Naw! Nevada and Arizona mostly. That thing weren't the only one, though it was sure the biggest. There was others hitting. Folks didn't feel safe. Power lines were down, water flooding, electric cables jumping around the place. Us, we just kept going, only stopped for gas and food."

"And alcohol," Rat chimed in.

"Listen, if you'd been through what I have, you'd want to wet your whistle!"

"So where are they all headed?" Chad steered the talk back to essentials.

"Don't rightly know. Different folks going different places, where they got family and so on. We've hardly been chatting down there."

"What about you guys, where were you headed?"

"We figured we'd come far enough for now. No point heading too far east."

"Well I reckon your friends are gonna head a bit further now."

"So, what you gonna do with me?"

"That depends. Once you've told us all you know you're free to go ... unless you want to hang around?"

"Join your vigilantes?"

"There are worse things you could do."

"Like hike down to the highway and try to thumb a lift, like that's going to work!"

"If you stay, you'll have to get rid of that thing." Chad motioned to the scar on Brad's hand. "It's also a tracking device."

"Figured. How do I get rid of it?"

"Have to dig it out." Bart pulled a face.

The chip gleamed in Chad's hand, encased in its bloodied silicone sheath.

"Nasty little buggers to get out," he announced. Placing it on the stone they'd used as an improvised "operating table" he smashed it with the blunt end of his knife.

"You ain't kidding there!" Bart nursed his hand in his T-shirt. "If I'd known it'd be that bad, I'd have changed my mind!"

"Too late now," Chad grinned. "You're one of us, for better or worse."

"Couldn't get much worse!"

They laughed. Rat joined in momentarily before reassuming his deadpan expression.

"What's with smiley?" Bart hissed, as Rat began to gather together any useful stuff.

"Lost his woman, killed a while back, a child too ..."

"Hell, that's bad man! Ain't never had a woman of my own, not for more than a few weeks at any rate. What about you? You got a woman?"

The laughter died in Chad's eyes. "I had one once, best woman a man could have. She's dead now, been dead a while." Bart fell silent, knowing he'd hit a nerve. "That's why I do this, for her, ain't no good grieving ..." They packed up in silence, shouldering the gunny bags.

33

"So, tell me, Bart, what's all this alien crap you were going on about last night?" Chad muttered. Bart glanced back as they trudged along between the trees.

"You really want to know?"

"Nothing else to do, but keep your voice down."

"You don't want anyone to hear about the aliens?"

"No. I don't want a bullet in the back 'cos you're too damn loud." Bart looked around furtively, attempting, unsuccessfully, to adjust his tread along with his voice level.

"Well, I saw one," he hissed. "No one believes me, but I did. And before you say it, I'd not had more than a couple of beers."

"What do you mean you saw one?"

"It was like a big circle of light, went right above my head – scared the life out of me!"

"Could have been a plane or a 'copter ..."

"Not at that speed and for sure not that low. It came in under the trees."

"Firework maybe?"

"Ain't no firework like that! Big oval of light it was – changed course when it saw me. Ain't no firework does that!"

Chad remained sceptical, "probably an optical illusion, or one too many beers."

"Told you I only had the two, two ain't nothing. But you don't need to believe me, you'll see when they come!"

"So, you think it was aliens sending that meter shower?" Chad muttered. Did they really want this guy on the team?

"It was around just before it happened ... Maybe they weren't meteors. Maybe they were some kind of weapon ..." Chad sighed, what had he gotten them into, still Bart was a useful kind to have around ...

5

The dog was there, not the mangy specimen she'd followed through the window, but a terrier she'd seen sniffing around several times. Only now it wasn't sniffing, but barking, running back and forth to get her attention. It looked like rain, still, dogs sometimes meant food, and this looked well fed. Huddling into her jacket, she stumbled towards it. It wasn't a vicious animal. She'd petted it a few times, noting the neatly inscribed name at its collar – "Jack" – odd name for a dog?

Jack dashed off, turning, barking, waiting for her to catch up, then off again. Obviously, it wanted her to follow, but why? If there was a chance that someone was alive ...

Scrambling between the piles of tumbled stone and earth she followed. It must have been a good mile when, half hidden beneath rubble and fallen trees, a farmhouse appeared. The barn had collapsed, but the house itself remained mostly un-scathed, though partially encased in mud.

Jack scratched at the door, barking. She followed. Something was blocking the entrance. Was someone in there? If so friend or foe? Her last brush with humans came to mind, suppose, suppose it was a trap? There was a scuffing sound from the other side of the door. A voice cried out, ragged with pain. Seizing a thick stick from the debris she pushed hard. Squeezing through, a nauseous smell assailed her. On the floor lay an old man, dressing gown and pajamas soiled with vomit. She dropped the stick. The dog crouched, licking his face, tail wag-ging prodigiously.

"Down Jack, down, damn you!" A withered hand waved inef-fectually at the beast. The voice, rough and laced with pain, was the sweetest sound she'd heard since the day Greg had been there, since they'd all been there.

"You're alive! You're alive!" she sobbed, tears streaming.

"Of course, I'm alive, damn it! What did you think, I was dead or something?" She nodded, unable to speak. He softened.

"It's just this danged ankle ... that on top of the cancer."

"You ... have cancer?" She covered her face, turning away.

"Yeah! What of it! Seems like we're all gonna die anyhow. How crazy is that, the damn quake got Bessy and left me, me that's going to die anyway. At least I got to bury her." He glared defiantly through welling eyes. "Ain't no one to do as much for me."

"I ... I'll bury you ... I promise." She turned to face him, "and you're not dead yet! Let's get you cleaned up and see to that ankle." Her old training was kicking in. "Do you have clean PJ's?" She tossed off her jacket and rolled up her sleeves, glaring down at him. The old man smiled a slow smile.

"You gonna boss me around like Bessy?"

"You bet I am! Now where's those pajamas?"

"In the airing cupboard, top of the stairs ... I don't usually mess myself like this. It was just the pain when I did it ... you might want to get some underwear too ... I got the door open for Jack, but I couldn't do no more ..." His voice trailed off ashamed.

"How long you been lying here?"

"Since last night ..."

"I reckon you've got an excuse then. What you really need is a good hot bath, but I don't suppose that's working now?"

"Not anymore, but there's a pump in the yard and a kettle on the stove. Don't seem right though a young girl like you, a stranger at that, having to clean up an old cogger like me."

"I was a nurse ... once ... a long time ago. Believe me, I've dealt with worse!" She laughed. How odd it seemed to laugh ...

"That makes me feel a whole lot better. Bessy moved my bed downstairs. If you can get me cleaned up and in there, I'd be right grateful ... There's a first aid kit in one of the cupboards in the kitchen, don't know where Bessy put it. It might have something for my ankle ... don't think it's broken ..."

"Looks like a bad sprain. We'll see to it when we've got you clean and warmed up." She dashed off to get things together.

Daniel stroked Jack's head.

"You knew old boy, you knew. Even in all this mess you figured where to get help."

How strange it seemed. Strange, yet familiar, kitchen shelves, a spice rack, stove, washing machine ... There was no power of course, only the bottled gas for the camping stove perched on

36

the counter, out lasting its modern cousin. She slid her hand along the table, soiled, but intact. It had been so long – it all seemed a dream. Curious, she opened cupboards and draws – food! Not in great quantity, but food none the less, flour, oats, spaghetti, sugar, molasses, and mouldy bread ...

Helping him to the couch, she sat him on an old bath sheet as she gently undid his robe and peeled off the sodden pajamas. He glanced down. Grasping her hand, he turned it over. They both knew what he was checking for. She looked up in alarm.

"Don't worry girl," Dan grinned as he patted her hand. "I won't tell if you won't! I didn't hold with making it mandatory. A man has a right to choose. Had to get mine, see?" He held up a wrinkled hand showing the obligatory scar. "Couldn't get pension money without it, an' me being diagnosed with cancer and all. Don't seem to matter much no how. It's not like anyone's gonna come sniffing around here, not after what happened to California."

"California?"

"Yeah, heard it on the radio – massive meteor shower, earthquakes, tidal waves, you name it, first the eastern seaboard, now this! Seems like nature's decided to get its own back." He chuckled.

She paused, sponge lifted, water trickling back into the bowl.

"California? ... how bad was it, what cities did it hit?"

"All of them child. There ain't no California anymore, it's gone, underwater they say, parts of Nevada and Arizona not much better."

"What about the government?"

"Obliterated! For now, anyway. Doubtless they'll fly more in. They're talking of setting up a base in Lincoln, but it's too early to say. Least ways they won't be going about rounding up folks that don't have no trading number."

She began to rub vigorously with the sponge, fighting emotions.

"You can stay here if you've nowhere to go ..." Dan muttered, "Take care of me for a bit and you can have all this, such as it is.

Our son and daughter were killed when the east coast got it ... ironic that. They were followers of his, always on about his new economic system, saving the poor and stuff – look where it got them." He laughed, but there was no humour, just a bitter ring. She paused, fist to mouth to stifle the sob, all those people dead, death everywhere! Placing the sponge in the bowl, she wrapped Dan in a clean towel seeking relief in action ...

Mission accomplished, she tucked him up in bed clutching a hot water bottle and sporting an elastic bandage on his ankle. His pain killers, she noticed where running low ...

"Thank you." He clutched her hand as she got up. "You can find a place to sleep upstairs. Not the first door. You don't want to go in there. I keep it closed." Tears welled in rheumy eyes, "The other rooms are usable, bit cold, but better than sleeping rough." She nodded gathering the soiled clothes.

"You can throw out them PJs and the undies, I got plenty, but the robe I need ... if you could ..." His voice trailed off.

"No problem, I'll do it outside under the pump."

She stood; hand poised on the door handle. *I need to see all the rooms,* she told herself, *there might be stuff we can use and anyway I need to check it's safe.* She knew it was an excuse. The door slid open revealing a mound of mud and stone spilled from a ruptured wall and window. Glancing at the bed she felt sick. Across it lay a heavy wooden beam crowned with a pile of plaster and dust, some scraped away revealing a large red stain ...

She'd seen bodies, some half decomposed, but the stain was somehow more moving. She hadn't known them, hadn't observed their methodical housekeeping, felt empathy, a respect for their sacrificial care of a loved one. Stifling her sobs, she closed the door of Bessy's memorial.

Next was a girl's room, all fancy picture frames and clutter, but the broken, mud drenched window reminded her of next door. The last was a young man's. Photos lined the wall. The window was intact, the view, though menacing, unobstructed. She sat on the bed ... damp, but comfortable. How long was it since she slept on a bed? She'd bring the mattress down by the fire to air it out a bit she decided ...

Candle in hand, she surveyed her domain. She was exhausted but couldn't sleep. She kept thinking about that other room – wished she hadn't opened the door ...

Books! She'd noticed the bookcase earlier but been too busy to check it out. There'd been few books at the camp and none since. Most were college tomes. He was reading law it seemed, not exactly light reading! Her eyes lit on a large scrapbook; thick black covers embossed with stickers. Inside lay a world long passed away. Evading party stickers and slogans, her eyes lingered on more personal renderings. A prom night photo with the words, "Susie has great eyes!" a football photo, purple squiggles surrounding a crouching player – that must be him! Peering by candlelight she could barely make him out. It was the words that grabbed her though. Scrawled across an old clipping of the supreme leader were the words, "I pledge my life to the deliverance of the United States from the oppression of the capitalist elite!" A wet spot enlarged, blurring the text. She rubbed her sleeve across her eyes. Like her, he'd been an idealist.

Her mind slid back over the years, she remembered the protests, the hustling throng, the armed police. It had seemed right back then, what other way had there been to evade the strangle hold of the corporations, the mega giants of commerce? People were dying, poisoned and enslaved by corrupt governments, little more than puppets for the demigods behind the scenes – the financial elite. She'd had her own book, different, but with similar ideology. It had been a craze for a while on campus. All propaganda, she realized now. One evil system had been replaced by another, even worse. Only in the forest with Greg had she been free ...

Light broke into her dreams, reminding of new obligations. Sliding into her clothes she noticed a distinct odour. It hadn't mattered before, but now ...

Dan was awake, propped on an old walking stick, edging toward the kitchen.

"Dan! Stop. Back to bed this instant! I'll do it ... I'm sorry, I slept late."

"I need ... my tablets ..." his face was contorted with pain. She remembered she'd set them on the counter.

"I'm sorry Dan, so sorry. I'll get them."

His fingers shook as he swallowed them.

"Do you have more?" she asked. He shook his head.

"Last bottle." She counted the tablets, enough for two to three days max.

"I'm going to need to get you some more."

"Like at the local drugstore?" His tone was sarcastic. "Look do me a favour, when those run out just smother me OK?"

"No way I'm gonna let you off that easy. Listen, the big supermarket in town, did they have a pharmacy."

"Why do you ask?"

"Because I know a way in."

"Yes, just round from the car park entrance on the right."

"OK, I'm going to get you some more, or at least something similar."

"Don't leave me now ..." his eyes pleaded. "I couldn't stand to be alone again. At least today, stay with me."

"Alright, but tomorrow I must go. I don't recall a pharmacy; it might be buried. I might need to try some other place." He nodded.

"Now, what about some porridge for breakfast? I haven't had oatmeal in years!" She put on a cheery smile, he smiled back grimly. They both knew they were fake, but it didn't matter.

ƔƔƔ

She squeezed through the entrance; this time equipped with a large backpack. She'd stock up while here. Shining the torch to the right she looked in vain for the pharma. Wheedling her way between tumbled shelves and mounds of fallen items, she spotted broken glass amidst the rubble. Cough syrup, the torch confirmed. It must be here somewhere. A creak from the roof chilled her soul. *The strong stuff will be prescription only,* she reasoned, torch beam scanning the debris. A shattered door lay diagonally across the pile. The door to the backroom? It had to be. Gingerly she dug beneath, gently easing away rubble, one eye on the roof. Shining the torch through the gap, she was relieved to see a small space within. Heart pounding, she wriggled through, abandoning the pack. Inside all was confusion. She grabbed at box after box examining the labels. At last she found it, not the same dosage but she could figure it out, she stuffed her pockets with as many as she could see, that ought to do it for a while ...

Wriggling back through the hole, she grabbed the pack. She wanted to get out of there. *Calm down.* She told herself. *You won't be coming back.* She remembered the batteries near the check out, grabbed tins of beans and veg. She didn't want to go back to the tinned meat section, couldn't. The roof groaned again. Plaster fell, echoing in the empty vault. She headed for the hole, pausing one moment to grab something, before blotting through and up the stairs. The creaking continued followed by a rush of air. Something had fallen. She had to stop, to breathe, pulse racing too fast to continue. Carefully she retraced her steps over the debris, aware there may be new perils lurking. She passed the place she'd first entered. The putrid smell was vanquished, instead, a vast dip lay before her. How much had collapsed there was no way of knowing. Thank God she'd not gone for the canned meat, had gotten out when she had. She'd never go back, never.

Jack was clawing at the door hearing her approach. She strode in, fighting off his greeting while dumping the pack on the table.

"That you?"

"Yes, Daniel. I'll be through in a minute." Pulling off the old boots she staggered into the bedroom collapsing on the armchair.

"You look done in."

"I feel it. That stuff's heavy."

"Did you ... er ...?"

"Yes, I got them. Better be enough, there's no way I'm going back, the roof's starting to go."

"Thank you." Deep old eyes expressed what the voice could not. "It can't have been easy."

"No, it wasn't, but guess what I grabbed coming out?" She found a smile from somewhere. "Coffee, fresh ground coffee, for that old machine of yours. Tomorrow we'll have coffee with breakfast! I got batteries for the radio too, so we can stay in touch with the outside world, or what's left of it."

"You're a wonder, you know that? You and me we'll do alright for ourselves, you'll see."

ଧଧଧ

Bart seemed to be fitting in fine, much to Chad's relief. No more was said about aliens and he turned out to be a natural with a rifle. The stream of refugees continued, heading east.

The night sky was peaceful. Rat sat brooding, eating alone as he often did these days.

"Need some company?" Annie sat down beside him. He said nothing, continuing his meal in silence.

"You never quite get over it you know," she ventured. He pulled a face, didn't want to talk.

"Maybe it might help if ..."

"No!" He cut her off. Why couldn't she just leave him alone?

"Sorry I asked!" she hissed angrily, taking her food to join the others.

"He doesn't seem much for company," Bart jeered.

"'Bout as friendly as a rattle snake!" Annie spat out. "Just trying to help and he bites my head off."

"He's still coming to terms with it," Chad defended. "I seem to remember you weren't so all fired friendly when you first came." "Still not ..." He whispered to himself. Their couplings had all the tenderness of a pair of ravaging wolves. It wasn't like it had been with Sal. He knew he was being used.

42

Annie fell quiet. Bart, not realizing the underlying tensions, blundered on. "Maybe he just needs some space. I've been like that too sometimes."

"I think we all have. It's tough! Better to keep busy though." Chad added.

"Hey Rat, wanna come check the traps when you've finished, maybe bag a rabbit or two?" Rat nodded. He knew they were talking about him, knew Chad was trying to help, but nothing could fill the empty void inside.

Bart glanced over to Annie as Chad and Rat walked off.

"Hey, if you're looking for company, I'm always happy to oblige," he raised an eyebrow questioningly. Annie glared. Picking up her dish she stalked off.

6

Propped up with pillows, Daniel rested the photo album on his lap, reminiscing. Emmie sat beside him taking in the photos. He reminded her of her father, comforting, despite his gruff demeanor – maybe even because of it.

She needed comfort tonight. She could no longer lie to herself. She hid the nausea, didn't want to worry him. Her breasts were tender, food tasted metallic, as with Greg's baby. Whose child was this? Faces swam before her. She found it hard to concentrate on what Dan was saying.

"Is something wrong girl? You can tell me ..." She shook her head, but tears escaped, betraying her. She went to go, but he held her wrist. "Tell me!" he ordered. "You ain't going nowhere till you tell me what's troubling you."

"I was thinking of Greg," she lied, shaking him off.

"And?"

"I just miss him ..."

"Now listen," he said, twisting painfully to face her. "You can trust me, OK? Don't go thinking I can't handle stuff, 'cos I can. It's just this old body that's ailing, this is still OK." He touched his forehead. "Now, out with it. Don't think I haven't noticed the smell in the bathroom of late. I know vomit when I smell it. What you got? Is it something long-term?"

"I ... I'm not sick ... I'm pregnant ..." It burst out.

"Ah! Honey, that's nothing to worry about. Why I was with Bessy when we had our two. I know a bit about it. You'll have something of Greg to keep always. You won't be alone when I'm gone."

"I don't want it! It's not his! Don't you see! I was raped! I ..." The story came heaving out, like bile too long contained, globs of pain and anguish. He set a fatherly arm around her shoulders, rocking gently as with a small child, just letting her get it out, silent but for soft, inaudible platitudes.

"It's going to be alright, you'll see," he muttered. "Even if it's not his, it's a part of you."

"It's not! It's not! I don't want it! I can't bear the thought of it inside me." She pulled back, glaring at him.

"Hush now child, hush. They'll not hurt you ever again. You stay here with me. They're dead ... all dead, I tell you. You're with me and Jack now ... we'll take care of you ..." He held her, sobs shuddering through her broken heart, till, exhausted, she fell asleep. Moving towards the side of the bed he winced as he moved his ankle.

"God damn them!" he muttered looking down at her ruffled hair and red, swollen eyes. "Men like that aren't fit to live!"

She woke shortly before daybreak. For a blissful moment she thought Greg was beside her ...

Reality dawned. It was only Dan. She'd fallen asleep on Dan's bed. The nightmare was real. She edged away re-tucking the quilt he'd pulled over her. She crept upstairs, thoughts and fears crowding in. She couldn't sleep. Stars beckoned from the window. Wrapped in her quilt she gazed out. Devastation swallowed in shadow, as the moon beamed down serene, untouched. Far above it all, peace reigned, a comforting thought. The stars were there long before her time and would continue after she was gone. Infinity dwarfed her pain. There was a dazzle of movement on the horizon – a shooting star, or was it a comet? Could it be a sign of better things to come? Would there be an end to all this hate and pain?

ɤɤɤ

"Ah there you are!" Daniel smiled, inhaling the smell of fresh coffee, as she set the tray beside his bed. "You're looking more cheerful this morning. Have you had yours?"

"Yes, I was up early. Thought I might try and have a bath. I saw an old tin tub out back. Needs a scrub but, I was looking in the mirror this morning ..."

"Good idea. If you explore the bathroom, you'll find all kinds of stuff, course you'll have a job hauling the water up there. It's a bit cold too!"

"I was thinking to stoke up the fire and have my bath there if you promise to stay in bed."

"I ain't no peeping Tom! But I fancy trying to get the news later, can you bring the radio through, so I don't need to disturb you?"

It seemed impossible to warm the ice-cold water, even using the kettle and big pot. Regretfully, she drew some out and decided on a wash down. Clean clothes from his daughter's room, and a plump towel and dressing gown, winked beguilingly at her from the chair as she stepped into the water. At least the big sponge made it easier. Seizing the nail brush, she began to scrub at the grime and dirt. When had she last had a proper wash? Not since summer when she and Greg had ... No! She wouldn't go down that path ...

Bath emptied, mission accomplished, she went to give Dan the all clear. He could hobble to the bathroom on his own now with the old walking stick.

"You cut your hair!"

"Couldn't get a brush through some parts, even with gobs of conditioner. Greg always liked it long but ..." Why did the tears come like this?

"I'm sorry Dan. I'm not usually ..."

"It's alright, I understand. You've kept it bottled up so long, it's all coming out now. It's OK. I don't have no one to take care of since Bessy went, even then she was pretty much taking care of me at the last." She set the food on the bedside table, pulling up a chair.

"You know you're a right pretty thing when you're all cleaned up ... Looked like a bit of a rusti before." He laughed. "We'll just do the best we can for as long as we can, OK?" She nodded. "And maybe, one day, that man of yours will make it back."

"You think he's still alive?"

"I don't know child. Don't know anything nowadays. It's getting so I don't want to turn on the radio anymore."

"What's happened now?"

"Red tide. They reckon it was the quakes and landslides in California that caused it, all that stuff going in the sea. Half the Pacific's blood red, fish are dying like crazy."

"A red tide?"

"It's some sort of algae, start multiplying like mad, killing everything. They used to get them down in Mexico sometimes, but this is spreading like crazy."

ೱೱೱ

Emmie checked the kitchen clock, barely 2 p.m.? Yet the light was dimming. *Hope it's not a storm coming,* she thought. *I'd better get more wood together.* Outside, heavy clouds were rolling in. She stopped to watch the shadows traversing the mountains. Rushing her bundle inside, she returned to gather more. Dan was calling.

"Be there in a minute!" she yelled. It was growing darker by the second. Depositing the branches by the hearth she hastened to Dan's room.

"What the hell's going on?" Dan was groping for his glasses. "Is it me or is it getting dark?"

"It's not you Dan. We might be in for a storm. You should see the clouds gathering over the mountains!"

"That's a relief, I thought maybe my time had come early."

"Sorry Dan, I was getting wood in incase we're stuck a while."

"Well I'm always stuck here, but at least I got me a pretty nurse." He winked. "You might want to check the oil lamp is filled, it sure is getting dark!"

"Here, I'll light your candle."

Lamp in hand she watched shadows race towards them. Oddly there was no rain, no thunder or lightening as she'd expected, even the wind didn't seem that intense.

Dan was staring out of the window.

"Can't see no light at all," he said. "That cloud must be pretty dense! Ain't never seen anything like it in all my days."

"I was wondering ... remember the ash clouds when they nuked the east ...?"

"You could be right. Better check all the windows and doors, don't want no bad stuff in here."

"You don't think ...?"

"Likely not, maybe it's something to do with California, but best not take any chances." She went to check the windows, remembering the winter when the bombs had fallen. There'd been no spring that year, even the grass had withered and died. Slowly the skies had cleared, grass grew back, and the trees that survived recovered, but the memory remained. God help them if it had come again!

෴෴෴

Emmie helped him into the armchair and passed the tray.

"It's been a while since I sat by the fire." He smiled up at her, tucking in.

"Couldn't leave you to eat alone in the dark." Emmie smiled a false smile.

She turned her eyes to the bowl of vegetable stew on her lap. Despite morning sickness, her appetite remained keen. She'd taken stock of the kitchen shelves and found more in the cellar, rediscovering tastes she'd all but forgotten. The orchard was buried under mud and rubble, but the apples remained, stored away, a legacy of Bessy. There were potatoes, onions and carrots also, and more to be dug up before the frosts came – the kitchen garden was unharmed.

"I've been thinking," Dan said between mouthfuls. "You're going to need things for the baby, blankets, clothes etc."

"No way am I going back in that store. Besides, I don't think they had stuff like that."

"No need. Are you handy with a needle?"

"Not really, but I could work on it."

"Well, there's extra sheets and blankets in the airing cupboard. You could make some nighties and stuff for the baby, should be simple enough ..."

"I don't want the baby!" She glared, but Dan was not to be silenced.

"Well you're going to have it anyhow! What are you going to do, just abandon it to die?"

That was exactly what she planned. She couldn't bear the thought of touching it even, but she couldn't confess that to Dan.

"There's plenty of time. Winter's coming on, I need to get the other veg dug up and stored and we'll need wood for the fire."

"You're right. You're going to need warm clothes, and a coat too. Bessy has a couple in her closet. They'll be four sizes too big for you, but maybe you can belt them in or something."

"That'd be great, there's not much in your daughter's room, but won't it be hard for you, me wearing Bessy's stuff?"

"Well she can't use it no more. She'd want you to have it." He reached out to take her hand. "She'd have taken care of you if she was here, she was like that, and there'd have been no nonsense about the baby. My Bess would have known what to say ..."

She doubted that. Nothing could make her keep the child, nothing! She just couldn't. She sat, holding his hand, looking evasively into the fire ...

"Isn't it news time?" she interrupted the silence, wishing to get away from things she didn't ... couldn't, think about. Reaching out she turned the dial, seeking. The usual party propaganda was interrupted by news.

"We have unconfirmed reports that a large meteor impacted northern Kakastan around five thirty this morning. First thought to be a comet, the meteor was clearly visible over Europe, its tail emitting clouds of ash and vapor as it plunged earthward, narrowly missing highly populated areas of eastern Europe. Stories and sightings abound, fanatics terming it a 'death star', predicting the end of the world. Our scientists confirm, however, it is merely another meteor, like those causing the catastrophic quakes in California, originating from an unforeseen planetary disruption. These meteor showers appear to be coming to an end, as an unnamed planet moves further from our orbit. There is no cause for concern. I repeat there is no cause for concern."

"No cause, my arse!" Dan bellowed. California gone, meteors crashing into the earth and they want us to believe there's nothing to worry about! I remember back in the 80s there was talk of some planet coming. They were all freaked out about it. Then, suddenly, it went quiet. Bet they were busy building their bunkers, where they'd be safe and sound, while the rest of us ..."

"Dan, don't ...!" He fell silent. "I'm sorry ... didn't mean to scare you. God knows we've got enough to worry about with this infernal dust cloud or whatever it is."

"Let's talk about something else. Maybe you could finish showing me the photos?"

"Sure, go get me the book."

Emmie woke sometime during the night. Her legs had gone to sleep, and her neck ached. They must have fallen asleep on the sofa. The oil lamp seemed to be faltering. Something was different? She couldn't place it till she noticed a gleam from the curtains. Opening them, she took in the full glory of the moon, serene, calm, reflecting hidden sunlight. Around it gathered a host of stars, gleaming in the darkness. Gently, she shook Dan's shoulder. "Dan, Dan," she whispered, "look the stars are out."

7

Rat felt wretched. He knew he'd been obnoxious to Annie. She meant no harm, maybe even trying to help. He'd tried to explain, but she'd brushed him off. Why was it when you hurt, you hurt others? Maybe he'd talk to Chad, Chad knew her better ...

It's no good trying to talk," Chad said. "She won't listen. You sure upset her this time. What is it with you two?"

"She wants to make out, at least I think so, but I just can't, I ..."

"Wouldn't help her anyhow. God knows I've tried. She's like a wild animal sucking the life out of you ..."

"Are you and her ...?"

"Not really. Look if you want to take her for a tumble, I ..."

"It's not that. She wants something I can't give."

"Yeah me neither! Sex is one thing, but she wants more, and I can't give it. She wants someone to fill the pain inside. She doesn't understand it herself, but I reckon that's it, but you and I ain't free, not really." Rat nodded. "Look I'll try'n talk to her, but I don't promise anything."

ᛉᛉᛉ

"Almost there. Just as well, looks like a storm brewing, be good to have a roof over our heads."

"A roof?"

"Yeah! A real goddam roof!"

Having gotten nowhere with Annie, Chad had elected to bring Rat on his rounds to let things cool off. It had been a long haul, the terrain challenging.

"Is that smoke?"

"Sure is! We'll be warm and cozy tonight!" They turned their horses into the valley, weaving between the pines. The cabin was in a small gully hidden by redwood and cedars.

"I'm hoping there's someone here you know." Chad winked.

Rat stared, puzzled.

Rain started as they pounded on the door. It opened a crack. A friendly face thrust through.

"Why you must be frozen! Come on in. I'll see to the horses, come and get warm."

Inside was like a step back in time. A woman sat by the fire sewing, while three young children played on the rug. On the far side of the hearth an older man slouched in a chair. He looked familiar ... no it couldn't be! Chad's words came back, "we found a couple still alive ..."

"Bill?" Bill turned, a smile lighting his face.

"I can't believe it, you're alive!" stumbling from his chair Bill thrust an arm around Rat, voice husky. "I hoped you guys got away! But ... where's Emmie, is she with you?"

Rat's voice quivered, "She's gone. We managed to evade them, but I was fool enough to go back. They must have had it rigged. I led them right to her ... I ..."

"You weren't to know. It's not your fault."

"What about the other one," Chad interrupted, changing the subject. "We brought a boy, shot in the leg. Did he make it?"

"He did." Bill smiled. "Though he'll be using a stick a long while, maybe for good. He's in the back room." He turned to Rat, "Alice's gone," a cloud drifted across his face. "None of the others made it either, but I've still got Lenny. The roof collapsed on us. They didn't bother to check. One of Chad's guys came, heard Lenny crying and pulled us out. I didn't know nothing about it till I woke up here with a hole in my hide. Thankfully Liz here was able to fix me up." He smiled at the woman in the chair.

"It was Pete that got the bullet out," she offered. "I can't take credit for that. I hid in the barn with the little ones." She laughed.

"Not my finest hour." Bill interjected.

"I bet you guys haven't eaten?" Liz set down her sewing and rose from her chair. "Let me see what I can rustle up."

"We have foo ..." A nudge stopped Rat mid-sentence.

"We're talking real home cooking, boy," Chad hissed. Liz turned laughing.

"Don't worry Chad, I know you love my cooking. I've got some bean and onion stew left over, cooked with bacon fat and home-made bread to soak it up."

"Liz, I love you!"

"It's Pete who keeps the farm going, without that we'd be as hard off as most folks out here."

"Glad to hear you give me some credit," Pete chimed in, closing the door on the wind and rain. "My Pa started this place way back. He was a bit of a rebel, liked to be out here alone. My brothers took off, but I liked the life and I found me a good woman who liked it too." He bent to kiss Liz's forehead. They were an odd pair, Pete tall, lanky and several years older, Liz a petite, chubby little doll, but their love warmed Rat's soul, reassuring and infinitely painful ...

"You boys get off to bed and don't forget to say your prayers." Liz instructed the kids as she set two steaming plates on the table. Rat looked up in surprise.

"You're religious?"

"Yes," Pete responded. "Not all believers are like that demon mullah you know!"

"But I thought ..."

"Don't go listening to all that propaganda. Not all Christians go around shooting guns and bombs at people ..."

"But the anti-Muslim extremists ... the riots ... the mass shootings?"

"Oh, there were some, I don't deny it. Just played one off against the other, didn't he, that's how he came to power. They'd have done better joining with the moderates instead of driving them into the arms of that fanatic Mullah. How long did that last? Little more than three years and he turned on them too! The damned government sure gave them plenty of ammo for their propaganda machine, with their exploitive foreign policies and defense of the capitalist elite."

"You guys communists then?"

"Not when it's enforced with a barrel of a gun."

"I was communist once, like Bill here." He nodded toward his old companion. "I wanted justice for the poor, I swallowed the whole lie," Rat confessed. "Now I'm just confused."

Liz came behind to squeeze his shoulders. "Just keep living, keep loving, keep giving, as long as we do that they haven't won ..."

"I believed that once," Rat hissed. "It just made it worse, that's all."

"Ah! but we're not at the end of the story yet." Pete smiled.

"You mean the bit when we're all dead!" Chad quipped. He could see Rat was getting heated.

"We're not dead yet, and I reckon you guys have some good stuff due you," Pete answered, smile turning to a grin, "but let's not spoil our evening with politics, it's so rare we get to see you."

Rat felt bad, first Annie, now ... "I'm sorry Liz." he mumbled. "I didn't mean to snarl at you. I know you were trying to help. It's just ..."

"It's just you're hurting. I understand." She plopped a kiss on his cheek. "Now I'd better go chase up those scallywags."

Rat settled down to his food, it was not the only thing he was digesting.

Stomachs full and blissfully warm, Chad and Rat settled down amid quilts and mattresses in front of the fire.

"Boy this is living! I could stay here forever!" Rat breathed.

Chad laughed. "They wouldn't last long if we did! Last time we managed to lead them away."

"The troops?"

"Yeah! They'd like nothing more than to destroy all this. Pete's Christian through and through, Liz too, brought up with Mennonites she was. They'd never go along with his regime, nor would they defend themselves, pacifists, both of them ... couldn't imagine Pete with a gun ..." he chuckled to himself.

"Are there others like them?"

"That's for me to know. Better that way. What you don't know you can't tell. Those inquisitors can be pretty persuasive." Rat caught his meaning. "This much I'll tell you, this is the only farm I know of. The others are long gone ..." Chad rolled over curled blissfully in his quilt.

Rat lay awake pondering what Pete had said. For sure it was the unholy alliance of the Supreme leader and the Mullah, with his blue turbaned fanatics, who had swept him to power. Strange bedfellows, but united in their hatred for western corruption and the financial elite who held the world to ransom. Then again some of those same elite now held office in the new one world system.

It was more than he could ponder, but there was something about this place, a little spot of paradise amid hell. A place love survived, like Liz said. He could understand why Chad tried to protect them, but how long would it last?

Back home things were as before, save Annie had cooled. It seemed a dream, Pete and Liz, Bill and the children. Rat could almost taste the bread, the honey and fresh eggs, somehow the only real thing about the visit now. The rest blended to shadows like a fairy tale, yet somehow warmed his heart.

"You big, dimwitted, idiot! How you ever gonna catch anything that way!" Annie's voice cut the air, disturbing his thoughts. She was trying, in vain, to teach Bart the art of fishing. Bart took it in good part, chuckling and pulling a face at her. She laughed at his shenanigans. Rat looked up. He'd never heard Annie laugh before.

"Hey Pudding!" Chad cut in. Annie had coined the name. Bart was outgrowing it as short rations, lack of alcohol, and excessive vigorous exercise took their toll on his belly. Bart looked up.

"I need a couple of rifle men to go with me and Vince." Chad continued, "You too Rat. The old shooting lodge we winter in, Vince went to check it out and there's smoke billowing from the chimney. He couldn't see anyone, probably inside. We'll go calling in our uniforms, but I want you guys as back up." Then to Bart, "look, you're like a bull in a china shop, but you're one of our best shots so try to keep it quiet, OK? Maybe Rat can give you some tips."

Bart nodded. It was the first time he'd been on something like this.

"We'll go on foot. The horses won't manage all of us."

"Hey! I've been slimming down!" Bart objected. Though he joked it off, he didn't like Annie's moniker.

"Not enough for them! They're getting old."

Are we staying overnight?" Rat asked.

"No, reckon we can make it there and back if we get a move on, ain't that far from here. That's why I want to check it out, we might need to move camp." Rat sighed.

A plume of smoke rose from the slope below them. The immediate land had been cleared of trees, lending little refuge. Rat could see why Chad wanted back up. He motioned to Bart to take cover. Much of the undergrowth had withered away, but in some places ragged stems still carried remnants of summer's glory. Uniformed, Chad and Vince moved forward, guns casually in hand. Rat had seen Chad do this before, only last time it had just been Bart and friends ...

The door opened. A guy stepped forward, his size putting even Chad to shame. Military haircut and army pants contrasted the leather jacket and cigar. This looked like trouble. Rat glanced at Bart; finger poised on the trigger. They couldn't make out what was said, but the guy looked upset, pulling back the jacket to show the pistol lodged in his belt. Chad was talking and gesticulating. Rat's heart froze. Please not Chad! Not Chad! He had a clear shot of the guy's head, the rest was obscured. Could make the shot? Men were not deer or elk. He'd not let Chad die though, if he pulled the pistol, he'd let him have it! The guy was getting increasingly angry. Waving his fist, he began to bellow.

Chad and Vince gave a rapid salute, turned tail and headed back to the trees at an undignified pace. The giant lingered on the terrace, hand playing on the pistol. Finally, tossing the cigar butt, he turned to go in. Rat lowered his rifle. They edged back to where Chad had entered. Even Bart was silent.

Chad was leaning against a pine.

"Who the hell was that?" Rat hissed.

"Commanding officer, off on a little 'retreat'. If it hadn't been for Chad's fast thinking, we'd have been dead!" Vince explained.

"I had him covered. I'd have got him before he pulled the pistol."

"Maybe, but I heard voices and saw at least one other gun at the window." Chad gasped, breathless.

"How the hell did you get out of it?"

"He said we were in Nevada when the meteors struck. That we couldn't find our unit and were looking for a place to stay overnight."

"How did he react?"

"Swore at us for a couple of imbeciles. Ordered us to get the hell out and head for Denver. I think he was in two minds whether to pop us off to keep their little rendezvous hush, hush."

"Yeah, I saw how he was fingering that pistol."

"I was expecting a bullet in the back any minute! I think it was only our automatics that dissuaded him."

"So, we move camp?" Rat looked at Chad.

"You bet we move camp, just as fast as we can."

"But there can't be that many of them?" Bart ventured. "I mean we could clean them out, couldn't we?"

"And risk losing men? They have the advantage of cover."

"Plus, they're sure to have radios," Vince added.

"Exactly!"

As Rat predicted the move was far from easy. The weather was worsening and picked that day for a downpour. Wind whipped between the pines blowing canvas and tarpaulins as they fought to secure the ropes. It finally stopped at evening as they gathered round small fires to dry off. Ma took sick that night ...

୪୪୪

The room was icy as she slipped from the covers. Pulling her sweater on, she secured the oversized pants with a belt, throwing Bessy's coat over all. She felt like a dumpling and longed for her padded jacket buried among the tumbled trees.

Feeling for matches, she glanced at the window. Frost gleamed in the morning sunlight, bringing splendour even to piles of debris. She'd forgotten how beautiful nature could be.

Setting the kettle to boil, she began to kindle a fire, blowing on the budding flame, feeling the warmth reach out as it grew.

"You're an angel! You know that?" She looked up to see Dan. He could manage without the stick now. "That was my job every morning before we got the heaters installed."

"Not anymore. Now it's a nice breakfast in bed for you while things warm up."

"Come on, don't coddle me. I ain't dead yet. Tell you what. I'll take over the fire while you get breakfast going."

"Deal."

They sat beside the blaze, toasting their feet as they ate.

"Dan ... I've been wanting to ask you ... you know what you said about the underground shelters, is it true?"

"Can't say for sure, but I wouldn't be surprised. There were rumours of a big one under Denver air base. Of course, they'd never admit it. One thing for sure, the Mormons had one. Now what was the name ...? Anyway, they had a big one, all stocked up too. I thought they were nuts but looks like they weren't so crazy after all."

"I thought they were all sent to camps?"

"Some were, but most escaped. They tried to bomb them out, but you can't bomb granite. They just destroyed the main entrance, bound to be others. I reckon they're down there safe and sound, with plenty to eat. Not a bad idea eh! Wish I'd done the same," he chuckled.

"You really think they're alive down there?"

"I don't doubt it. Got their heads screwed on those guys. I had a couple of Mormon friends, even went to one of their parties. They're not the stuffed shirts they appear! I'll tell you a secret too." He leaned over as if to whisper. "Some of those guys still have two wives. Not legal of course, they preserve appearances. My friends pointed some out to me. Reckon they were trying to convert me?" He chuckled. "Might have done, if I hadn't met my Bessy." He sighed.

"I'm sorry."

"Give it no mind. I'll not be long following her. We'd take a nap mid-afternoon; I'd just gone down to put the kettle on when it happened ... You know what I think? I think one of us needed to stay ... for you ..."

"For me?" He reached out to take her hand.

"Yes, so you wouldn't be alone." Tears welled in her eyes.

"I'm glad you're here Dan, even if you can't stay long. I was going crazy on my own. I don't know what I'll do when you go ..."

"Now, now, I ain't going yet, I've got a few months in me. I've a mind to see one more spring. When spring comes it feels like anything's possible!"

ชชช

She sat, the pants across her lap, face lined with concentration – sewing had never been her forte.

"Shame there's no electric, Bessy's old sewing machine's still up in the attic. That would make it easier."

"Hell, if we had electric, I could Google and see if I'm doing it right." She smiled, these were her favourite times, sitting together by the fire, so "normal" she could almost forget the stuff outside.

"We could catch the news if you want?"

"No thanks. After that poisoned water in Europe, thousands more dying ...? I'd rather not."

He took her hand. "Look that was Europe. They say it was the gases in the meteor and that thing was too high over the US. Besides, we've got us ground water." He chuckled. "Ain't no falling star gonna taint what we've got."

A falling star ...? She remembered the night she'd seen a star and thought maybe it was a good omen. Instead, it was just another harbinger of death. She thrust the thought from her mind. She wouldn't let it spoil this time. Time with Dan was precious, every moment of it.

"Maybe we could listen to some music? I brought extra batteries."

"Music! Ha! You've got some hopes, all propaganda, every song is full of it. Besides we don't need no radio for music, reach me down my guitar from over the couch."

"You can play? I thought it was just décor."

"Course I can play. How you think I scored a girl like Bess? An' I can dang well shoot the rifle too. Well, least ways last time I tried I could ... it's been a while." He chuckled. "I wasn't always like this you know. I had girls eating out of my hand, but not Bess, no. I had my work cut out courting her, I can tell you. She wouldn't put up with any of my shenanigans." He smiled wistfully as he tuned the guitar.

"Now let's have us some real music!"

He played surprisingly well, though his voice was a little hoarse and his stiffened fingers fumbled sometimes on the cords.

"My voice ain't what it used to be, but I can still get out a song or two. Hey, why don't you give me some help?" It felt strange, she couldn't remember when she'd last sung, but as time went on, she abandoned her sewing to embrace the magic.

"Did you and Bessy have a favourite song? You know couples used to have 'their song'."

"Well, kind of, it's named after someone else you see. It's called 'Annie's Song'. Guess he felt the same about Annie as I did about Bess. We borrowed it."

His fingers picked gently at the strings, she listened mesmerized.

"You fill up my senses, like a night in the forest ..."

The music transported them to another place, another era, a time of peace and beauty. Tears trickled down Dan's wrinkled old face as he sang. It was not till she felt a drop on her hands, she realized she too was crying. Song finished; Dan plonked the guitar down. She looked up into the fatherly old face.

"You know, Bessy was one lucky lady."

"No, I was the lucky one. Now let's have something special to celebrate. In the cellar behind the mattresses, you'll see a shelf with a green storage bin full of newspapers. She nodded. She'd seen it when she'd sorted through.

Dan smiled, "Bet you didn't look under the papers. It's my secret stash. The doctors said I shouldn't drink with my medication, but a glass or two of wine now and then ..." He flashed a wink with the unabashed mischief of a schoolboy.

"Why you are positively wicked!" She bashed him playfully with her cushion. "I've a mind to tell Bessy!"

"Well, do you want some or not? Don't stand there lecturing me, go get it!"

"Only if you'll promise to stick to half a glass."

"That's all I ever take these days."

8

Chad looked down at the snow-covered mound of Ma's grave.

"I'd have liked to put her by Sally, but the ground up there will be like rock. Better here anyway where everyone can say their goodbyes."

"I'm sure they'll find each other," Rat muttered.

"You don't believe that rot, do you?" Chad snapped.

Rat reddened. "No, you know I don't, it just seemed like the right thing to say ... Don't even know why I said it."

"Maybe I shouldn't have taken you to the farm ... Makes you soft, that stuff!"

"Look Chad, I ..."

Too late. Chad had already stormed off. He'd been in a foul mood ever since it happened. Rat understood, felt the loss. He owed his life to Ma, as did others. It had been her nursing and tough love that pulled him through. Hell, she was better off out of it! He didn't know how she'd lasted so long out in the wilderness. He recalled her bundled up in the tent coughing and coughing, refusing to give in, till finally her lungs gave out. At first, she'd seemed to recover, then it came back, double force, little wonder with the weather they'd been having. If only they could have used the lodge ...

Chad had been gone awhile, no one knew where, only that he'd been in a foul temper. No one mentioned it, everyone knew. It wasn't till dusk he returned, speaking to no one, just dossing down in the tent. Next morning, he was up before the camp revived from their frozen nightly ordeal. Bart, taking an early morning leak, saw him stuffing provisions into his pack.

"Where you going man?" Chad ignored him. "Look, it's not for me to say, but everyone looks to you. They're worried sick. At least tell me where you're going!"

"The lodge!"

"The lodge? What the hell you gonna do there?"

"Check if they're gone. If I'd not been such a pussy, we could have had it off them and Ma wouldn't have died."

"So that's what's been eating you."

"What of it?!"

"Well, sure as hell you ain't going there alone."

"You can't stop me."

"Nope, but you can't stop me coming along, you're going to need a rifleman." Bart stood, arms crossed, in Chad's path.

"Look it's dangerous. I don't want to put anyone else at risk."

"You don't have a choice do you, 'cos I'm coming. Now I'd be a site better off if you let me go get my rifle and stuff." A smile cracked Chad's face.

"OK, you win. Go get your stuff."

The lodge looked ominously quiet. Though it was bitingly cold, no smoke billowed from the chimney. Chad motioned to circle round. A shattered door swung against the beams, but it was the figure curled at its foot that stilled their hearts. Face fixed in an agony of terror, body contorted, lay the guy they had spoken to before.

Warily Chad edged forward, Bart covering him from the trees. He bent to check the pulse. Unbelievably, it was strong and active. He kicked the prone form. Was this a trap? The body shifted but there was no reaction. Nodding to Bart he stepped inside, gun raised. He emerged a few moments later.

"Think you'd better come see this."

Bart emerged, feeling edgy. Chad's face was ghostly, and Chad didn't scare easy.

Inside lay others, same expression, same contorted form.

"What the hell killed them?"

"That's the thing Bart, they're not dead, not one of them. Feel their pulse and tell me I'm not hallucinating."

"My God man! What happened here?!"

"You tell me!"

There was a noise outside.

"Get down!" Chad pushed Bart to the floor. Signalling to follow, he crept towards the bedroom window. There was something in the bushes, something sniffing. Glimpses of mottled grey and black moved among the leaves.

"What the hell is that?"

"Dammed if I know. If it shows its face, shoot."

Bart nodded.

A head reared above the leaves, freezing fingers on the trigger. It turned, grinning. The face was not human, nose flattened, eyes large and rounded, a mutation of man and insect. It opened its mouth. Teeth gleamed, pointed and blood stained.

"Oh my God! oh my God! It's a bloody demon!" Bart drew back from the window.

"Shut up, damn you!" Chad hissed. "Whatever it is, we need a clear shot. Get back here with that rifle. I can't do it alone."

Bart cringed blubbering. It was too late. Flattened nostrils sniffed the breeze and eyes gleamed in their direction. Then it sprang! Chad's automatic blazed from the window. The shock brought Bart to his senses. Levelling his rifle, he gazed out. The creature had drawn back to cover but seemed far from dead.

"It's got armour," Chad muttered, "like body plates ... I only caught a glimpse of it. It sprang at me ... I hit it in midair ... It dropped with the impact, then scampered back in the bushes."

"It's still out there then?"

Yeah! Weirdest thing I ever saw, with this long, scraggly hair waving like a banner, and I swear it had some kind of wings sprouting out of its arms, like a bloody half human insect!"

"Look man, I'm sorry I screwed up back there ... I ..."

"It's OK. Just watch those bushes. It knows we're in here."

"Think it'll come again?"

"I'm sure of it! Close the door and set the chair against it. I wouldn't mind betting it's been in here before. The front door didn't hold it, but at least it will give us some warning."

"You think that was what got those folks?"

"Maybe."

The silence was deafening as minutes dragged by. A thud on the roof alerted them seconds before a hideous face swung down blocking the window, reaching in to knock the gun from Chad's hand. Bart shot, but it went wide.

"Run!" Chad screamed as it squeezed its way through the window frame, wings catching in shattered glass.

Bart needed no urging, pounding down the steps they sped outside. It was after them in moments. In huge leaps it plunged down on Chad. Writhing, he gazed up at open jaws, teeth gleaming. Then he saw something even more terrifying, whipping back and forth like a serpent, the spider like hook on the end dripping venom. He knew now what had happened to those folks.

A shot rang out. The head lifted for a moment in deliberation, more shots. Angrily it released its hold on Chad, springing toward Bart.

Everything happened at once. A dazzling sphere whizzed past at incredible speed amid a flash of light and the beast lay dead, steam and smoke rising from its charred body.

"What the hell ...?" Chad lay dazed. Bart watched transfixed, speechless.

"If that was one of them aliens you're always on about, I think they're on our side, and I gotta admit that one was real enough!" Chad was quiet for a moment. "You saved my life man ..."

"I had to make up for being a blubbering coward, didn't I? Can't let word of that get out."

"They'll never hear it from me." There was more to it though, they both knew. When it came down to it, Bart had what it took to defend his new "family".

They gazed down at the beast, its charred remains a ghastly epitaph to the terror of the last half hour. Chad turned it over with his boot, prodding the body armour with a stick. "Oh my God! Look Bart! It's not armour. It's bone. This thing has an exoskeleton!"

"Reminds me of a locust the way it jumped you."

"That tail or whatever it was ... That weren't like no locust, more like a snake or a scorpion's tail."

"You reckon that's what ...?"

"Yeah, that's got to be it."

"You think there might be more of these things about?"

"I don't know, but I sure as hell am not waiting to find out."

"What about those folks inside?"

"We ain't no medical unit an' they weren't exactly friendly. Don't see as they are our concern, nothing we could do anyway. It'll either wear off or not, at least that beast won't be back to feast on them later ... Just one thing." Chad turned. Re-entering the cabin, he emerged with two pistols stuffed in his belt and a lump protruding from his pocket.

"What's that?" Bart asked gesturing to the bulge.

"Radio." Chad answered. "Best we keep that to ourselves, OK?"

Bart nodded. "Whatever you say."

"Where do you think that thing came from, Chad?" Chad paused, dodging an overhead branch.

"I've been wondering that myself. Maybe it was one of those 'government experiments' escaped from the lab."

"They can do that sort of stuff?"

"You wouldn't believe what goes on under wraps. They've been experimenting with genes for years, looks like they've gone and created their own Frankenstein's monster. I just hope there's only the one."

"You don't think it was an alien then?"

Chad smiled and good humouredly cuffed Bart's head. "You and your aliens!"

"You seemed pretty convinced about the one that saved us!"

"Yeah well ..." Chad laughed, humour dispelling some of the tension inside. He'd been scared shitless. He'd learnt to hide it, but he knew if that thing hadn't come they'd both be trapped, encased in an unresponsive body. He'd seen the terror in their eyes. It was a horrifying thought. Maybe he should have put a bullet through them? It might have been kinder.

"What are you going to tell the others?" Bart ventured.

"The truth. Whether they believe us or not, they have a right to know. What if there are others out there?"

"Even about the spaceship?"

"Yes, even that, though I'm not sure it was a spaceship. What if they just look like that?"

"Must have been a spaceship. Did you see that beam they sent out? Like zap man! Zoom!" He waved his arm expressively, then, catching Chad's look, he sobered.

There were anxious faces as they staggered through the lengthening shadows.

"Where the hell have you guys been?" Vince intercepted them. "You know the rules, we always tell someone. We didn't know what happened to you."

"We went to the lodge." Chad said icily. "Not that it's any concern of yours."

"What the hell were you ..."

"It's good to have you back!" Rat cut in rapidly. "We were worried about you."

"Damn right to be worried, we were near goners."

"Those military guys still there?"

"No, worse, much worse, but you're not gonna believe what happened ..."

They sat in silence, not knowing what to think. It was too weird to be true. At first, they thought it a joke, but soon sobered. Chad wouldn't lie, and he was no one's fool. Still, the story was unbelievable.

"Does that mean you believe in little green men now, Chad," one of the men quipped.

"Look guys, you don't have to believe us," Chad retorted. "But I'll tell you, if you come across another of those beasts, you'd better hope those 'little green men' are somewhere close by, and they weren't green they were kinda white, just pure light really."

"Do you reckon they could be some secret government weaponry?" Rat interjected.

"They're always updating their technology, but I never saw the like. It moved with incredible speed and agility, almost as if it were alive. I could be wrong, but if so, why didn't it zap me and Bart? It seemed more like it was defending us."

Rat scratched his head. "Beats me." Monsters and space craft were just too much to believe, even of the rationally minded Chad. There had to be an explanation, there was always an explanation ...

A decision had to be made. Winter was here, they needed better shelter than the tarps could provide. Should they move into the lodge or remain here and build something more substantial?

"I don't mind as long as we do it fast!" Annie said, "Body heat will only take you so far!"

"Agreed!" Chad chimed in, "I was hoping we could use the lodge, but I'd sooner not be there if another of those things comes sniffing around. Plus, what do we do with the bodies? They're not dead, can't bury them."

"They're government. Just put a bullet through their heads. They'd do as much by you," Vince snarled.

"I tend to agree, but two of them were women, civvies by looks of it ..."

"Why not find a more sheltered spot and build our own lodge," Rat suggested. "There's plenty of timber and we have tools."

"I don't call a couple of axes tools to build a cabin. We've no

66

saws and hardly anything in the way of nails, and stuff."

"We don't need nails. Saws would be faster, but we have manpower. The old pioneers did it and we can too."

"And who knows that stuff? I say we go lay claim to the lodge, shoot those bastards and ..." Vince interrupted.

"I do." The group fell silent staring at Rat.

"You know that stuff?" Chad queried.

"Yes, in theory at least, my grandpa showed me one built that way in the backwoods. Besides I was training to be an engineer before all this happened, I'm good at figuring out how to build stuff." Chad looked at Rat with new interest.

"Why didn't you tell us this before Rat?"

"Well it's not rocket science. You cut long straight pines, plenty of those up here, and carve a hollow at each end, so the logs fit into each other. Hell, anyone got a piece of paper?"

An old notebook was brought, and Rat drew a simple diagram.

"See it's not hard, we just need one room really and a chimney, course the chimney will need to be stone and mud ..."

9

Emmie glanced out of the window.

"The snow's building up. Think I'll get more wood in. The stock's running low, I need to make another foraging trip."

Dan looked up. "There was a ton of wood in the barn, but I don't suppose it's reachable."

"I'll have a look."

"OK, but no crawling in any holes and stuff. I just thought if it's easy to get, it would save hauling."

"I'm all for that!"

Sadly, the collapsed barn showed no sign of firewood, though a large, broken branch added to her stock. Small stuff was around in abundance but didn't last long. She filled the pack, dragging the branch behind her. She'd used an axe in camp and would soon have it in suitable lengths. Hauling it round to the chopping block, she froze in her tracks. There were footprints in the snow, large enough to be cause for concern. Abandoning her quest, she headed indoors taking the axe with her.

"Dan, that gun, does it still work?"

"Why, you thinking of shooting someone?" His humour died as he saw her face. "What's wrong Emmie? If it's soldiers, hide in the cellar ..."

"It's not soldiers. There are animal tracts out there, weird ones I've never seen before, but big."

"You sure they're tracks?"

"Certain."

"Maybe I should go look."

"No Dan, stay in here where it's safe."

"We can't stay in here forever Emmie, sooner or later we'll need more wood."

"Let's make it later. Maybe it will go elsewhere. Meanwhile let's load up the gun, just in case."

She set her mattress near the fire. It was warmer down here, she told herself. The rifle propped beside her told another story. She didn't sleep much. Jack was restless, snarling at the door at one stage. There were flashes of lightning, yet no thunder, just one resounding crash.

"Are you alright Emmie?" she heard Dan call.

"Yes, I'm fine, but Jack's upset about something." Dan came waddling through in dressing gown and slippers, storm lamp in one hand.

"There's something mighty strange going on out there."

"I know!"

"Stoke up the fire, don't think we'll sleep much tonight." Dan picked up the rifle and sat with it across his knees. She joined him on the sofa, dragging the quilt with her.

"What do you think it is?"

"Damned if I know. I was having this dream of Bessy, then there was this bright light and a crash ... woke me up. I heard Jack growling ... thought I'd better come see."

"I'm glad you did. I was scared."

"No need to be scared, me and Jack will take care of you. Maybe I'd better teach you about the rifle as well as the guitar." She snuggled up to Dan's wiry old frame, it helped somehow, though what good he'd be if something broke through the door she didn't know.

"Greg taught me a bit, but we had too few cartridges for me to actually fire it."

"Well I've got plenty of shells. You can try your hand tomorrow."

"Don't know if I want to go out tomorrow."

"You can take Jack with you. He'll let you know if anything's lurking around."

Daybreak found Jack sleeping soundly by the glowing coals, residue of last night's blaze. She got up, carefully re-tucking the quilt around Dan. They'd used up most of the wood. She put on the remainder. There was nothing else for it. Checking the windows, she could see nothing. The woodpile was close to the door. She could do this, Dan needed warmth.

"Come on Jack, come with me." Jack stood, tail wagging softly from side to side.

Fresh snow had fallen, all but covering the tracks surrounding the perimeter. She filled her arms and dove back inside. Jack lingered, sniffing tracks and growling softly. Emmie stoked up the fire, setting the kettle to boil on the little camping tripod Dan had set up to save the precious gas.

Jack clawed at the door, apparently satisfied that all was as it should be outside. Dan slept on a while. She thought about putting him back to bed but didn't think she could carry him. She put his feet up on the couch instead, pondering in the chair as she ate.

By mid-day she'd summoned her courage. Jack had been out several times, sniffed around, and returned unperturbed. Dan passed her the rifle, now loaded.

"Take this, just in case. Most critters won't stay around if they see a gun. You don't have to hit them, just firing it is generally enough to scare them off. Anyway, like I said Jack'll smell 'em coming."

Knees shaking, gun and axe to hand, and Jack leaping at her side, she headed for the chopping block. Rounding the corner of what had been the barn, she gasped. Where a large pine had stood lay the charred remains of its stump. The tree, toppled from its dominion, lay part across the stump. So that was the crash! Seizing the axe, she cast one last look round and set to work ...

"Someone up there is looking out for us!" Dan cried as she explained her rapid reentry, arms full of rough-cut pine.

"It was struck by the lightning last night."

"Mighty convenient it should strike right there, don't you think?"

"I don't care how it happened, I'm just thankful it did!" She knew what he was thinking, that in some way Bessy had helped them." She didn't want to trample his faith. She knew the comfort of such thoughts even if she couldn't entertain them herself.

ЖЖЖ

Even bare logs chalked with mud and the tarps suspended above and across the door hole proved a far better shelter. Tomorrow he'd start on a chimney while the others cut a couple of windows and started on the roof. Rat's back ached, but he felt a satisfaction he'd not felt in a long time. Chad came and sat beside him, bowl in hand.

"Good job Rat." He nodded at the brown green walls. "I reckon we'll do just fine here so long as we don't need to move."

"God forbid."

"I wanted to thank you for your support ... You know, about building up here. I can handle most things, but that beast was like nothing I've seen before. Our bullets barely stunned it."

"Government experiment got out of hand?"

"That's my guess."

"Think there's more?"

70

"No way of knowing. God help us if there are."

"There must be a way to defeat them."

"Explosives maybe! This exoskeleton thing is tough as iron."

"What did it look like? I mean overall."

"You really want to know? It looked like a ruddy demon. I almost shit my pants when it leapt out at us."

"I had you pegged as the fearless type."

"I just know how to hide it ... fear's contagious, it incapacitates." Rat nodded his agreement. "But I tell you I'm scared if there are more of those things, there's no way we can handle them ..."

"Well I doubt they'd hang about here long, hardly bursting with food ..."

"That's the weird thing. It had made no attempt to eat its prey, unless it was leaving them as winter storage. It was more like a cat with a mouse. It seemed to be enjoying my fear."

"Doesn't bare thinking about! Still, I see no reason they'd make more than one, seeing as how they turned out." Chad nodded.

"I hope you're right ..." He broke off momentarily. "Hey, look at that! Those two are getting awful pally of late." He nodded to where Bart and Annie sat cuddled together warming their hands on bowls of stew.

"Well, it solves my problem. It'd be nice if Annie had someone. Bart's not bad looking now he's slimmed down a bit."

"It's not that, though it helps I suppose. He makes her laugh. That's what I reckon it is ..."

They were disturbed from their diversion as the lookout raced up.

"Chad, I think you'd better see this." The pallid face had Chad bounding after him, Rat followed. Diving into the lookout cover, they gazed down. A cloud moved across the valley, black speckled against evening shadows. Chad grabbed the binoculars.

"Oh my God!" He swore, passing the glasses to Rat.

"Is it ...?" the lookout stammered.

"Yes ..."

Rat gazed in horror. There were hundreds of them, swarms, only these were not bees, but something far deadlier.

"They're headed east," Chad muttered. "God help us if they come this way. If we'd bunked down in the lodge ..." Rat could say nothing. It was not that he'd doubted Chad, but there was something so ominous, so horrifying in the swarm below it had no reality till now ...

The roof was all but complete; a mishmash of stout beams, branches and turf, to camouflage it from government aircraft. Rat's chimney reared against the cabin wall, waiting for the adjoining hole to be cut and lined to make it operational.

They'd said nothing of what they'd seen. Why create panic? If the swarm came their way no preparation would help. Rat thought about Pete and Liz's family nestled on the slope across the valley and hoped their camouflage of redwoods would protect them.

There was nothing they could do. He punched his fist into the stone chimney in frustration, skinning the knuckles. Grasping the axe, he went inside to begin the needed hole, taking his anger out on the wood.

"Think it'll be ready for tonight's meal?" Chad interrupted.

"Not unless you want to burn down the cabin. Got to line it first, keep the heat off the logs." Chad leant against the beams.

"You OK, Rat?"

"Yeah! I'm OK. We're OK up here, but what about the folks down there?"

"Thought that was it. Thinking about Liz and the kids?" Rat nodded. Chad grabbed him in a rough squeeze as the axe fell with a clutter to the ground. "Nothing we can do. Let's hope they pass them by ... seemed they were intent on other prey."

"Yes, but ..."

"We can only do what we can Rat. As I see it, if we don't make it no one will ... at least we're unlikely to see any raids in the near future. Those things seem to have a taste for government troops." He grinned, slapping Rat on the back. "Let's get this stuff finished, huh? I'll feel better if we can cook inside. A good fire of a night would be nice too ..."

☙☙☙

Cabin complete, Rat turned his skills to beds, a frame to hold the cooking pot, benches. He kept busy, but his mind continued to stray. There'd been no further sighting of the swarm and the hunting team returned with nothing abnormal to report. He ached to find out if Pete's family were OK but knew Chad wouldn't send teams out. Perhaps Emmie was better off he thought. This was no life for a woman ... He was startled from his reverie by a goofy face.

"What do you think?" Bart's grin lit forth from a newly groomed exterior, shaved and hair neatly cut and combed. Rat was incredulous. Normally Chad and occasionally Vince were the only ones to bother shaving and that only in view of their government disguise.

"Annie wanted to smarten me up a bit."

"You and Annie ... are you ...?"

Bart winked, "you might say that ... Worth a bit of a shave and haircut." He chuckled.

"Good for you!" Rat pounded his shoulder. "I'm happy for you, really I am ... Annie too!"

"I've never had me a woman of my own Rat. I'm just hoping it lasts."

"Me too, Bart, me too." Rat smiled. Love bloomed in the oddest places, at the oddest times.

10

"Do you realize what day it is?" Dan asked. Emmie looked blank.

"December 24th!" The dazed look continued.

"It's Christmas Eve, damn it!"

Christmas ... Emmie's thoughts drifted back. Christmas was a dim memory, replaced by "Winter Holidays", replaced by nothing, at least in her life. Any December celebration had been banned at the formation the United States World Government as being mass materialism, the very epitome of capitalism.

Daniel was looking at her expectantly. "Don't you want to celebrate? We have decorations in a box in the cellar. We never got rid of ours."

"But it's banned?"

He laughed. "Little Miss law-abiding citizen without even a trading mark to her name, is worried about celebrating Christmas! Come on who's to know out here ...? This will be my last Christmas and I want to celebrate it. Me and Bessy always did, real quiet, so no one would know. Now we've got no nosey neighbours we can put up some stuff. It's in the box labelled odds and ends ... and while you're down there grab a bottle from my stash. Ain't got turkey or even a chicken but we do have wine!" She decided to humour him.

Emmie looked round, enjoying the scene despite herself. A small, plastic tree complete with baubles caught the firelight, and, together with the candles and oil lamps, added an old-world charm to the décor. Stew boiled on the stove containing the last can of beef salvaged from her old domain, together with their usual fare of potatoes, onions and carrots. Dan poured a glass of wine.

"You did a good job Emmie. Here, you deserve this. I'll have my half glass later with the meal."

They sat at the big table, having stoked the fire up well. Emmie spooned the stew into bowls.

"Cheers! Merry Christmas!" Dan raised his glass.

"Merry Christmas!" Emmie replied beginning to relish their "rebellion".

Food finished, Dan took the guitar, singing timeworn, half-forgotten songs and carols, evoking a past era, before families enrolled in re-education and propaganda filled summer camps. A time life was simple, before the new government, before even the economic crashes and take overs of the multi-nationals. They snuggled on the couch, watching the fire. Dan was like a remnant of a bygone age, what would she do when he was gone?

❧❧❧

Chad came to sit next to Rat, food in hand.

"You game for a trip tomorrow? Me and Vince are going ammo hunting and we'd like you and Bart along for back up."

"Are we that low?" There'd been no sign of the swarm for two months now, likewise no raids or government patrols, from which they generally replenished their ammunition.

"We have some, but I'd rather make this trip sooner than later."

"Where are we headed?"

"The army base, three days' journey from here."

"The ... have you gone suicidal?"

"If I had I wouldn't be taking no one with me."

"But ...?"

"I'm betting there'll be no opposition." Chad reached into his coat pocket and pulled out a radio receiver.

"Where the hell did you get that?"

"The same place I got the pistols. There's been no messages from the camp since the night we saw the swarm."

"You think ...?"

"Well, Lincoln is decimated. They hit them with everything they had, shells, bazookas, flame throwers. They managed to hold out till they dispersed, but casualties were high. Most messages are relayed from Denver now."

"And you didn't tell anyone?"

"No point freaking the whole camp out. I'm keeping it on a 'need to know basis'."

"And now I need to know."

"Yep!"

"But the guys at the lodge weren't dead. Suppose they've revived?"

"The lodge guys haven't, me and Bart went and checked."

"So that's where you guys were ..."

"Yep. So, are you in?"

"Nothing else to do."

75

There was an oddly emotional farewell as they set off.

"Now you take care, Bart! If you … if you … I'll bloody well kill you myself." Annie kissed him hard, then violently pushed him away, storming back into the cabin.

"Hey! Think she loves you man!" Vince elbowed Bart whose ear tips uncharacteristically reddened.

"Think so?"

"Well if that performance is anything to go by."

Rat had his own ideas but said nothing. He'd seen Annie throwing up outside the cabin. She'd avoided his gaze. It was her secret, not his. He remembered how emotional Emmie had been … He slammed the door on his thoughts. It was the only way to stay sane.

ꙮꙮꙮ

"Can you see anything?" Chad called up to Rat in his tree top perch.

"Not a thing. Seems dead as a dodo … just a minute. That looks like a jeep back there half buried in snow … I'm pretty sure that's what it is."

"Probably some poor bastards trying to escape," Chad muttered. Rat scooted down.

Jeep it was. The driver lay slouched, blood caked, over the wheel.

"Poor devil." Bart said.

"I think you'll find he was the lucky one," Chad replied grimly. Sure enough, three more "bodies" lay around, horror concealed under a blanket of snow, raised mounds the only evidence of the pulse that throbbed within. Vince took the pistol from his belt. Chad stopped him.

"Why not? They've got it coming."

"Because if there's anyone alive, I mean really alive, they'll hear us." Vince set the gun back in his belt.

Rat examined the jeep. "Minor damage, mostly bodywork. Might still work, want me to try?" Chad nodded.

"Hey! You said no noise!" Vince objected.

"This is different." Chad said. "With this we could drive right in. No one would stop us." Rat fiddled under the bonnet, then turned the key a couple of times, third time lucky.

"OK in we get," Chad seized the wheel. "Not you Bart, Annie wants you back in one piece, nor you." He gestured to Rat. "You don't have full uniforms. Me and Vince will head in alone, if, as I'm expecting, they're all comatose, I'll lower the flag as a signal to come help load up. Circle round to the main gate undercover, once you're in position we go in. Just keep an eye out in case we need to make a run for it.

The gates were deserted. Only soft, scattered, knolls gave evidence of former inhabitants. Most lay in the dorms, some still in bed, others contorted on the floor.

"Must have come when they were sleeping and taken out the guards." Chad ventured. "Let's hoist down the flag." Something fell with a clatter. Chad motioned as Vince slunk to one side to cover him. A harsh, hysterical scream rang out.

"That's no soldier or I'll be damned!" Vince hissed. "Sounds female." Chad charged into the adjoining room; gun raised. A woman shrieked, scrambling and clawing at the wall as if trying to escape. Chad lowered the automatic and took off his beret. The screaming continued.

"Look lady, it's OK, we're not going to hurt you." She cowered in the corner covering her head with her arms, making incoherent noises.

Chad grabbed her arm, turning it to see the hand. No mark.

"She must have been a prisoner." He said to Vince, who'd just entered.

"Look it's alright. You're safe! We're here to rescue you." It wasn't quite true, but they couldn't leave her here.

"The demons will get you too!" she screamed in their faces, eyes wild and crazed.

"Get the flag, Vince. We need Rat and Bart, it's the uniforms. She thinks we're government."

"I can easy convince her we're not!" Vince drew the pistol. Pointing to the nearest body he pulled the trigger. Far from reassuring, she began to scream again, and pull away. It was all Chad could do to hold her.

"Idiot!" he snarled. "Go get the flag down like I told you ..."

Vince waved them over at the gate.

"We need your help with something!" Rat and Bart exchanged glances. They'd heard the commotion.

"Rat, take her. She thinks we're troopers." Chad called.

"It's OK. I'm rebel too," Rat coaxed, showing his unmarked hands and slowly drawing closer. "We won't hurt you ... We've come to help ... We'll take you away from here, back to the forest ..." She glanced at him. "Come, you have to come with us. I won't hurt you. I promise ..." She calmed a little, sobbing and cringing in her corner.

"Take care of her," Chad called impatiently as he relieved his grip on her arm. "We'll load up the ammo and anything else useful. Since we have a vehicle we may as well use it."

Rat found himself alone with the woman. She watched them go, wide eyed.

"The demons will get them too," she muttered. "Serves them right, filthy pigs!"

"Did they hurt you?" Rat asked.

"They didn't hurt me, only the soldiers," she muttered, misunderstanding. "My angel kept me safe ... They didn't have angels, so the demons got them. Serves them right ..." Her eyes glazed, as if reliving the attack. Rat noted the crucifix ... Catholic probably. She was evidently in shock, perhaps mad.

He told her about himself, about the camp, about Bart and Annie, even about Emmie, surrounding her with comforting words. How much she understood he didn't know, but it helped her simmer down. Time passed. He gradually edged closer noticing as he did the blood-soaked pillow opposite, so Vince had got his way it seemed ...

"Bring her out to the jeep. We need to get going." Chad's voice erupted through the door, startling her. Slowly Rat held out his hand, coaxing her along, like a wild, scared, animal.

"We have to go now." Alarm sprang in her eyes. "Don't worry. I'll take you with me. I'll take you somewhere safe, away from the soldiers, where the demons won't come ... But we must go now!" Hesitantly she took his hand, following.

She stiffened as she saw Chad and Vince in the front seats. "It's OK, they're friends. They'll drive us somewhere safe ... They're not soldiers ... they're just dressed up like soldiers ... Look there's Bart. I told you about Bart ... Him and Annie are together, remember ...?" Bart smiled, then hesitated, uncertain what to do. Finally, Rat persuaded her to get in, sandwiching her between them. She made furtive glances at the front seat. Chad set off down the highway.

"May as well take the road a while, seems deserted," he replied to the inquiring gazes. "We can take to the woods pretty fast in this if anything comes. Keep an eye out guys."

"Reckon they're gonna stay well away for a while," Vince sneered.

"Maybe, but they might send in 'copters now things have quieted down. Don't think they'll re-staff it in a hurry though." Chad laughed grimly.

"So, do we take the jeep all the way?" Rat asked.

"No, but maybe we can shave a day off our journey. We can leave it someplace, but not too near camp."

"So that's why we're taking the road, plenty of tire tracks to get lost in."

"Smart boy! You catch on fast. I plan on taking the next well used side road, keep 'em guessing. I'm thinking no one will be worrying about us with those ... whatever they were ... on the rampage, but you can never be too careful."

Exhausted, her tear stained face sagged against his shoulder, the woman's eyes closed. Rat examined her. The long, black curls, crucifix and dusky skin spoke of possible South American origins, though her voice had been untinged. Her clothes were torn and dirty and she had no coat other than Bart's leather jacket he'd put round her. They'd probably sneaked her into the dorm for a little "fun" before sending her on. It was common practice from what Emmie had said, a perk of the job. Would this woman also recover? Emmie had not seen the monsters ...

Why had they not attacked her? Perhaps they only targeted men? No ... Chad had mentioned there'd been women at the lodge ... Whatever the reason, the attack probably saved her life.

"What are we going to do with her?" he whispered to Chad. "We can't have her at the camp in this state."

"Pete, I think, if anyone can help her, he can. He has this soothing way with him."

"If they're still alive!" Rat hissed.

"Guess we'll find out. First we need to get this stuff back to camp."

11

They returned to a warm welcome. The woman clung silently to Rat's arm, her refuge in a sea of humanity. Annie strolled out, playing it cool.

"So, you're back are you, Bart. You were gone long enough! Who's that you've got there?"

"She's with Rat," he hastened to explain, leaping aside like a scalded cat. A half smile flickered on Annie's lips.

"I can see that well enough. Where did you find her?"

"She's the only survivor of the camp. She's still in shock," Chad warned.

"Camp? What camp ...?" Realization dawned as she looked at the boxes of ammo. "The government camp ... the one full of troops!"

"Yeah! That camp 'cept they're all dead, or as good as dead. A bunch of those things Bart and I tangled with paid them a visit."

"How did you know that Chad ... you been holding out on us?" she accused, arms akimbo, blocking his path.

"OK, Annie. You always were the smart one, you might wish you didn't know one of these days." He pulled the radio from his pocket and made to pass.

"And ...?" Annie stood her ground, belligerent.

"And, there was a whole swarm of the damn things, headed east, almost took out Lincoln ... Gonna sleep good tonight Annie?" For once Annie was silent, standing aside to let Chad pass. Bart gingerly slipped an arm around her waist. She recoiled.

"Did you know and not tell me?"

"I swear, I knew nothing till we were underway."

"It's true, Annie. Me, Chad, and the lookout, were the only ones that knew. Chad didn't want everyone to worry." Rat interjected. "If they'd changed course and come this way there was nothing we could do ..."

"So that's why you were so damn uppity," Bart blurted out.

"Yes, that's why ... Now look, I need a place for her," he nodded to the woman clinging at his side, wide eyes assessing Annie.

"She's not going anyplace but with you by looks of it." Annie's face softened. "Take her in by the fire. I'll find her some blankets and food."

His charge asleep by the hearth, Rat escaped his custodial role, only to be accosted by Chad. "Did you get anything else out of her?"

"Only that her name's Sofia. I think she was a nanny. She was talking about a kid called Jemma, but most of it was babble about demons and angels. I just hope Pete and Liz are OK and can take her in. I wasn't cut out for this kind of stuff."

"The big question is, why didn't they attack her?"

"That's what I've been asking myself."

"Did she say if her 'angel' appeared like a globe of light?"

"Like the thing you and Bart saw?"

"Yes."

"She didn't say. It's hard to get anything coherent out of her."

"We can try tomorrow, after she's had some sleep. Vince can lead a team to get the rest of the stuff and we'll head out at daybreak. Hopefully we'll have a fire and home cooking at the end of our trip." His companion looked doubtful.

Rat was beset by fears. Nightmare pictures flashed, gleaned from a disturbed sleep. Liz and the children with that look of terror, Pete's bright smile stolen forever. He mustn't think of it or he'd go mad. Perhaps Chad was right ... perhaps they'd be waiting like before.

Annie came out with Sofia, clad in borrowed pants and sweater, with a blanket over her shoulders against the cold. The two had forged a tentative feminine bond. Only for Annie would Sofia relinquish her position beside Rat. He mounted up while Annie brought her over. Reaching down for Sophia, he whispered to Annie. "You need to tell Bart."

"Tell him what?"

"You know what."

He dug in his heels, pulling away from the cabin. The weather was calm and crisp, the sun out, a perfect day for travelling. Chad was in uniform – a necessary precaution, but one that precluded any communication with Sofia.

"Ask about the 'angel'," he mouthed to Rat. Not wanting another meltdown, Rat chose his words carefully.

"Tell me, what does your angel look like?"

"Beautiful!" her face glowed. "Golden hair, blue eyes, and a long white robe, so pretty!"

"So, you saw one?"

"Saw one ...? No. You can't see them ... they're invisible ... but I had a picture. My mother gave it to me ... She said to keep it always ... that it would keep me safe ... but, they took it ... they ..."

"But you're safe now, safe with us." Rat interjected quickly, "We're going to Pete and Liz, they'll help you feel better. They believe in angels too, maybe they'll have a picture."

"Pete and Liz have angels?"

"Yes, I'm sure they have angels," Rat reassured her, straight faced. Chad, who'd been avidly listening, rolled his eyes and moved back. He could see why his companion was finding it hard.

A plume of smoke wended its way between the pines. Chad reached out, squeezing Rat's arm in acknowledgement.

"I knew it, I just knew it …" There was a crack to his tone, emotion stirred beneath the granite frame.

Rat could say nothing, his throat was dry, feelings overwhelmed him. He'd been sure they were dead – worse than dead. The love he'd felt there couldn't have survived? It seemed unreal, but there it was, the tiny film of smoke, a defiant banner among the trees.

Pete took his time, as with a wild thing, slowly gaining Sofia's trust as the evening went on. For Liz it was easier, but most of all it was their little girl who won her over. Rat remembered about Jemma …

"She'll be fine with us," Pete whispered, as Liz led her to the children's room where she'd made up a mattress. "It'll take time … she's evidently been hurt a lot."

"It's not only that …" Chad pondered how much he should say. It was bound to come out … "She's seen some pretty horrifying things." Pete looked up, motioning Chad into the kitchen away from little ears. Rat followed.

"You see the base was attacked by something, something weird …" Chad's voice faded, trying to choose his words wisely.

"There was a whole swarm of them, heading east. We were so worried about you guys," Rat couldn't help himself. Chad glared, and he shut up abruptly.

Pete gestured to the kitchen table. "Tell me all about it. If we're going to take care of her, we need to know."

Chad briefly relayed of their visit to the camp. Pete sat pondering.

"How did you know what these things could do … there's more you're not telling me?" Rat glanced at Chad. It was not for him to say.

"One of them attacked some government officers in the old lodge …"

"You saw it?" Chad couldn't lie to Pete. He nodded.

"Me and Bart did."

"Bart? Is he that Hell's Angel you told me about?"

"Yeah. We came to check if they'd left. There were bodies, still alive, just like the camp. There was one of these things lurking in the bushes. It attacked us. Bullets were no use. I'd have been dead had Bart not drawn it off. He saved my life ..." his voice faltered for a moment. "It happened so fast. It went for Bart and this light appeared from nowhere and zapped it. Honest to God, that's what happened." Chad looked up expecting scepticism, but Pete's eyes remained steadfast as ever.

"What did it look like?" Pete pressed, not letting Chad off a full explanation.

"Like half man, half insect."

"It had an exoskeleton." Rat ventured.

"But with long hair?" Pete whispered.

Chad stared. "How did you ...?"

"And a tail like a scorpion?"

"Yes ..." Chad sat, jaw agape. Pete rose from the table.

"I'll be back in a minute," he whispered.

Rat and Chad exchanged glances. "How ...?" Chad breathed. Rat shook his head.

Pete returned, a large, leather bound book under his arm. Placing it on the table he thumbed through to near the end, tracing down the column with his finger.

"Here," he said turning the book towards them. Rat began to read.

"And the shapes of the locusts were like unto horses prepared to battle: and on their heads were as it were crowns like gold; and their faces were as the faces of men.

And they had hair as the hair of women and their teeth were as the teeth of lions." Rat paused to examine the cover of the book, but they already knew what it was.

"And they had breastplates as it were breastplates of iron," he continued. "and the sound of their wings was as the sound of chariots of many horses running to battle. And they had tails like unto scorpions, and there were stings in their tails ..." Rat fell silent.

"Bloody hell," Chad muttered.

"Exactly." Pete whispered. "No word of this around the children."

"Of course not."

There was silence for a moment.

"You don't seem worried Pete ..." Rat ventured glancing at Chad, but Chad was speechless.

"I'm not. You see this story has a happy ending."

"Don't see how that could be!" Rat replied.

"God intervenes," Pete replied, closing the book.

"If God was going to intervene, why the hell didn't he do it before? Before Ma and Sal died, before all those people died!" Chad pounded his fist down on the table rattling the dirty cups and dishes residing there.

"God has his times," Pete said softly.

"Well if there is a God, and I for one don't believe it, he must be a monster to stand by and let all this happen!" He raised his hand silencing Pete's reply. "Enough! I'm going outside, before I say something I'll be sorry for." The door slammed closed.

"I should ..." Rat went to rise, but Pete restrained him.

"Let him be a while. Chad's like a bear with a thorn in its foot. He'll never let you close enough to take it out ... but he's a good man." Rat nodded. He should go, but there were so many unanswered questions.

"Bart thinks the circle of light was an alien," he ventured.

Pete chuckled. "I can understand why he might think that."

"What do you think?" Pete smiled. Rat was pegging him down, as he had Chad.

"Well, I guess you could say they're aliens, definitely a different species, it's all in how you look at it."

"You think they're some kind of celestial beings?"

"Definitely, but you could call them aliens if you want." Pete set the dishes in the sink. Not to be put off, Rat grabbed a dish towel.

"And what about these insect things," he persisted. "Sofia calls them demons ...?"

"No good asking me that. I don't know the answer, only that it says just before the bit you read that they come out of the bottomless pit ... that a star or meteor opens it up ..."

"A bottomless pit? How can there be a bottomless pit?"

Pete smiled. "I thought you were the smart one – think a hole, a very deep hole, way down through the earth, think gravity ..." Pete plunged his hands into the soapy water. Rat stood pondering, cloth in hand. Suddenly it dawned.

"The earth's core. Theoretically speaking if something fell into a vast hole, say from the US to Australia, it'd end up falling upward and change direction, going back and forth, there'd be no bottom."

"Bingo!"

"You think these things are from the earth's core, a remnant of a past age, like the dinosaurs or something, and that last meteor released them?"

"Maybe, I don't know, or maybe Sofia is right, and they're demons that were bound down there. Who's to say?" Rat began to dry the dishes, lost in thought. His mind returned to his most pressing question.

"Why do you think they didn't attack Sofia?"

Pete turned to face him. "It says they can't touch those who God's sealed or claimed as his. You said she's a believer."

"Well, Bart's not, and one of those alien thingys intervened."

"Think about it Rat, I bet Chad was in his uniform. It probably mistook him for government, and what was Bart doing when it happened?"

"He was ... he was trying to save Chad ..." his voice faded as he realized what Pete was inferring.

"You mean it intervened because Bart risked his life to save Chad?" Pete nodded, placing another plate in the rack. "That's why you weren't worried when we told you, because ... because you think you guys have this God thing! That's crazy even for you Pete!"

Pete smiled. "Well, I'm a pretty crazy guy, but we're still here aren't we?" Rat continued drying, he didn't want to say more, even his fertile mind had too much to think about.

Dishes done, he strolled outside to join Chad. The air was crisp and fresh. He stood on the veranda, just breathing, watching the vapor dissipate in the air. Somehow, out here in nature, it made sense. There had to be some guiding force behind all this. He took in the shadowed firs, the stars gleaming in the heavens. Was Bart right, had some alien beings designed all this? Were they intervening on behalf of humanity? It was easier to swallow than Pete's belief in an all-powerful creator, who stood by while evil ruled. He thought of Sophia and all she'd been through, of Emmie, of all those bodies disintegrating beneath the snow. He couldn't accept Pete's simple faith, but he was beginning to think Bart might be on to something ... maybe that old Bible stuff had been left as messages for this time. Perhaps these beings, whoever they were, could time travel ...? His mind pondered, taking everything to pieces, analysing, theorizing, as he watched new flakes begin to fall, but reached no conclusion. Soon he saw Chad stalking through the snow, hands thrust in pockets.

"It's coming down harder," Rat said.

"Yes, hope it doesn't delay us tomorrow." Nothing more was said regarding demons, insect men or old prophecies, even when they had to stay an extra day due to the weather.

"Something eating you?" Rat asked. Chad was uncharacteristically quiet as they ambled home through the forest. Chad glared, then thought better of it. Rat was a good man, levelheaded, knew how to keep things to himself, and it was good someone else knew.

"Is it still about Pete? You know how Pete and Liz are ..."

"It's not Pete, well not really." Rat waited. He knew not to push.

"I listened on the radio last night ..." Rat looked enquiringly. "They're pulling out troops by the plane load. There's trouble in the Middle East."

"When was there not? I thought the last invasion settled that for good, totally destroyed the Israeli forces."

"He's had a major falling out with his Muslim cohorts."

"That's old news. It was bound to happen with that 'Man is God' speech. Nothing they can do, they can't take him on now, he's too strong."

"Not with conventional weapons perhaps, but it seems covert ops. have discovered a secret pact between Russia and the Muslim nations."

"That's an odd alliance?"

"Well, it seems Russia was expecting to use him as their puppet, and they found out he wasn't amenable."

"Sounds like what happened to his Jewish backers."

"Exactly!"

"I still don't get it. OK, Russia still has nukes, but I don't believe they'll use them so close to home, not after last time."

"No, I don't think their Middle East allies would go for that either. They don't need to. They only need one, released in the upper atmosphere ..." Rat reigned in to face Chad.

"An electromagnetic pulse!"

"You got it. Almost all government weaponry would be put out of action. It's put the whole regime into panic. Seems the Russians have been secretly assembling armies, millions of men all with non-tech weapons, old world war tanks and planes, some even on horseback, imagine ..."

"They'd be able to discriminate that way ..."

"Yes, and not only that. It seems the Chinese are joining forces. They have the manpower and they know how to fight with anything to hand. Martial arts have been part of the school curriculum for years. They are ready to make their grab at world power."

"The 'sleeping dragon' ... If only they'd all done this in the beginning, we wouldn't be where we are now."

"Perhaps not, but then one tyrant is as bad as another."

"Well, this one would take some beating!"

"Agreed."

They continued on, Rat digesting the news.

"Thanks for telling me, Chad," he broke the silence. "I appreciate your confiding this stuff."

"You're the only one who knows, so keep it to yourself."

"You're not going to tell Vince?"

"No, Vince can be a bit of a hot head sometimes."

"Like about the lodge."

"Yeah and shooting that guy at the camp."

"Why is he like that? I hate the troops as much as any, but at the end of the day they're people like us. I couldn't kill in cold blood like that."

"Sometimes you have to ... but Vince has his reasons for bitterness." Rat waited questioningly. "He was with me in special ops an' this one time they sent us to break up a student rally, anti-government stuff. Well, he was covering the back stairs, when these guys come hurtling down. He mowed down the first two, then he stopped ... It was his kid brother, barely fifteen years old."

"They got the kid of course. His partner blew his head off, but Vince had to go before a military tribunal, lost his stripes, position, everything. They delegated him to a desk job, said he didn't have what it took to be a soldier, he was mocked and vilified. It was Vince who forged the papers for our own 'special op'. That's how we got out of there, equipment and all. That raid was the final straw for me too. Some weren't much more than kids. There were four of us back then, but me and Vince are the only ones left. We took him out with us in the back of a truck, called to get Sal and Ma on the way ... it was a long time ago ..." Chad sighed.

"We've been through a lot together me and Vince. He saved my life once, but the hate is eating him up. You saw how it was about the lodge. You can't let your emotions get to you Rat, you need a clear head ... Oh, I know, I shouldn't be talking. I got all riled up at Pete. Wasn't his fault, everyone's free to believe what they want. That's something we're fighting to defend – free choice ..."

"Don't worry, Pete understands more than you think."

"Yeah?"

"Yes, he said you were like a bear with a thorn in your foot. That you wouldn't let anyone get close enough to pull it out." Chad laughed.

"That Pete! He's a sly one! Reckon he knows me better than I know myself ..."

12

Emmie stared at the bulge beneath her trousers, felt it move, wanted to tear it out of her, be free of its constant reminder. She'd sewn a few nightgowns to keep Dan happy. No use arguing, he didn't understand – she couldn't keep it! No one could expect that of her? The thought of it made her feel sick. Why hadn't it died like Greg's baby died? If only there were someone she could give it to. If Bessy had lived perhaps ... another woman would understand surely ...

A call from downstairs distracted her from the mirror. Dan was less active now, keeping mostly to his bed, getting weaker. Perhaps she should bring the bed into the main room where he could benefit from the fire. Cold had seeped into the house, damp spreading in the upper rooms. Perhaps she'd bring her mattress down too, hot water bottles and quilts no longer sufficed ...

Dan slouched in the armchair as she wrestled the bed frame through the door. Bedding lay piled on the sofa, the mattress slumped against it.

"I wish I could help you ... I feel so useless sitting here."

"You do help me Dan. You help just by being here, more than you ... know!" The last word exploded as the frame finally slid through.

Dan waved a hand. "Come and take a rest. You can set it up after. I want to talk with you about something."

Emmie plonked herself in the remaining sofa space, happy to catch her breath, but his tone had a serious tinge. She looked expectantly.

"It's about this," he held up his hand, the neat scar catching the gleam of the fire. "It wasn't mandatory for over 65s, but you couldn't get medical help without it." Emmie nodded. "Bessy didn't approve, but what else could we do, I needed the medicine?"

"There's nothing wrong in that Dan." Emmie leaned over enclosing his hand, a worn hand, only now losing its strength.

"Bessy never had hers done. One of us was enough back then, but I'm thinking I don't have so long ..."

"Don't say that!" Emmie's eyes filled with tears.

"Now, you know it's true Emmie. Let's make the most of our time we have left."

"You said you'd be there to help when the baby comes." He laughed.

"Don't think I'd be much help even now!"

"Just having you around helps."

"I'll stay just as long as I can Emmie, but there's something I have to talk about. Can you do something for me?"

"Sure Dan, anything!"

"I want you to take this blasted thing out of my hand."

"But ...?" Dan overrode her objection.

"Just listen, OK?" She nodded. "Like I said, Bessy didn't get hers done, didn't want me to either. She thought ... well ... she thought if you took it you'd be damned."

"But Dan that's non ..." Dan raised his eyebrows, silencing her.

"Nonsense or not, that's what she thought an' I don't want to be meeting her with this darn thing in my hand, like a badge of shame." Emmie opened her mouth, but he forestalled her. "I thought, you being a nurse an' all, maybe you could take it out?" His eyes were pleading.

"What if the soldiers come?"

"They ain't going to come now Emmie, you know that. It's coming to an end, all that stuff. But you, you and the child, you'll survive, I know you will." She bit back her reply, but he read it in her eyes. "I know you don't want it now, but when it's born you'll think differently. You're going to be lonesome when you're on your own again."

"Dan don't!" He held her hand, comfortingly. "Look we won't talk about it again. I know it upsets you, but I must ask. Will you do that for me?"

"OK, but not right now, not today."

"Tomorrow then?" She nodded teary eyed.

It wasn't as bad as she'd feared. His meds. blocked most of the pain and it slid out smoothly. She almost enjoyed smashing it under the heel of her boot.

"There Dan, you're one of us now." He smiled weakly, eyelids fluttering. The ordeal had worn him out. Gently she wiped the blood away, not much blood, not much of Dan left now. Outside the window snowdrops popped their heads through the blanket of snow and earth. First harbingers of a spring that would be long coming, would he be here to see it she wondered ...

ɣɣɣ

He was fading with every day that passed. Strumming the chords he'd taught her, she recalled a few of the old melodies ... she couldn't do the finger work yet ... The old eyes flickered as a smile traced his lips. He gestured her to sit beside him on the bed.

"You know where to put me don't you?" he whispered. "Right next to Bessy. The ground is getting softer now. I was thinking, you should start soon."

"Dan no!"

"I ain't dying yet, but you shouldn't do too much digging at a time in your condition. You might need to make it a long-term project, so by the time I go, it'll be there ready."

Emmie sleeved her eyes and tried to smile.

The ground was softer, winter frost losing its grip, for all that, it was hard work. Emmie pounded away with the pickaxe, shovelling the loosened earth aside. She didn't care if she lost the child. She wanted to lose the child, but what about Dan? A miscarriage was dangerous. She didn't care for herself, she'd long given up hope Greg would find her, even if he were alive. She cared about Dan though, wanted to be there for him till the end. Even if there were no complications, she'd be laid up for weeks ...

Sighing, she relinquished her task. Setting the tools aside she returned inside.

"You made a start then?" She nodded, stung by the weakness, remembering how he'd sung, played guitar ... Now it was hers, a heritage from him. Her eyes stung, as they often did these days.

"Come." A hand fluttered above the covers. She sat on the edge of the bed, endeavouring to hide her tears. He lay his hand on her enlarging belly, an intimate gesture of love for her and the child.

"I can feel it moving." He cracked a smile. She frowned. "There's life inside you Emmie. I know you hate the idea, but sometimes life comes from pain. It wasn't the child who did that to you. The child is a gift left in recompense; you'll see." She didn't see. She just wanted rid of it, he could perceive that.

"Oh, you stubborn thing!" He pulled her head down on his chest, ruffling her hair like a child. She heard breath flutter in his lungs. "It'll be alright Emmie, you'll see. You're stronger than you think. You'd never have made it this far if you weren't ..." The voice trembled to a whisper.

"You need to save your strength, Dan."

"What for? Bessy's waiting on me you know ..."

"No, Dan! Not yet! I don't have the hole dug. You promised you'd stay a while!" He stroked her hair, gentling her head back onto his chest.

"Yeah, I did ... Guess she'll have to wait a while longer, but she'll not wait forever." He fell quiet for a while. She was silent, unmoving, treasuring the closeness.

"We'll be watching over you, you know ... me and Bessy ... you won't really be alone ..."

"Dan, you know I don't believe that stuff ..."

93

"Doesn't matter, we'll be here whether you believe or not." He smiled, just a crack, then his eyes drifted, and the moment was gone.

She lay a while longer, listening to the thin trail of breath weaving in and out. Why did it have to end like this? Why did it always end like this? Everyone she loved died. Only the belligerent child within refused to succumb to fate. Only it remained, taunting her.

The hole yawned before her, awaiting the time. It wouldn't be long. Dan held on by sheer determination, the meds, no longer able to contain the pain. She had to let him go. It wasn't fair to keep him. Just one more thing …

His eyes flickered as she set the vase by his bed. He wasn't strong enough to go see them, but she could bring them to him. "Spring flowers Dan …" Her voice choked. He smiled, just a glimmer. She lay down beside him stroking the thin white hair. "It's OK Dan," she said, kissing his forehead. "You can go. Bessy's waited long enough." He smiled, one of his old smiles, as his eyes closed. That evening he was gone.

She couldn't bear to just drag him out and toss him in the hole. She headed back to Bessy's room. Seizing the hand sewn quilt, she bundled it downstairs. Jack stood guard beside the bed muzzling the old hand in hopes of a response. She leant over to rub his ears.

"He's gone now, Jack. It hurt too much to stay. You're my dog now." He waved his tail sadly as if in acknowledgement. Struggling, she managed to engulf Dan in the quilt.

"I'm wrapping you up with Bessy," she whispered, remembering a tiny body wrapped in a T-shirt. She understood now why ancient tribes wrapped their loved ones, burying them with familiar objects. Deftly she threaded her needle. Leaning into the lamplight she began to sew, each stitch a closure of the loving care they'd shown each other. Finally, she reached the face, his body encased in a giant cocoon of vibrant reds. She paused, kissing the withered old cheek. Then, resolute, she continued, heart pierced with every stitch, till nothing was left but the red sheath. Jack placed his nose on her lap, absently she rubbed his ears. Inviting him up on the chair beside her, she sobbed into his brindled coat.

Day broke to find her still curled on the armchair. Jack scratched at the door for his morning run. Outside was a beautiful spring morning. Dan would have loved to see this ... no she mustn't think that way ... The pain was over for Dan, either way he was at peace now ... It was fitting he should be buried on such a day.

Jack returned, as if aware of her need. Together they dragged the quilt across the ground bit by bit, Jack worrying the cover, as if reluctant to let Dan go.

"Jack, Jack, stop it!" she cried. "This is hard enough. We have to let him be." Jack whimpered backing off. Finally, with a whoosh, it slid into the hole. She looked down at the soiled red of the quilt. It seemed wrong to just shovel dirt on top.

"Goodbye Dan," she whispered. "I hope you are right. I hope you're safe with Bessy now, young and strong again. If there is a God somewhere in this God forsaken world, you'll surely find a home together with him. No one could deserve it more." Stifling her tears, she grabbed the shovel, piling on the earth till she ached with exhaustion. She felt weak, close to collapse.

"Stay Jack!" She stumbled back inside.

The sun was receding when she awoke. Jack remained as she left him, guarding his master. She tried to resume her task but had to stop. She'd do more tomorrow. Jack would watch over him, keep any scavengers away ...

❅❅❅

Reverently she lay the spring flowers atop the newly completed mound. Life seemed empty. The cottage seemed empty. Only she and Jack remained ... them and the monster growing within her ...

13

"Anything new on the radio?" Rat slid beside Chad, their breath twin clouds in silent air, the others were inside.

"Millions dead," he muttered. "Only skeleton troops left in the US. The Middle East and much of Europe is a blood bath and still it's not resolved." Rat shook his head.

"I had hoped ..."

"That they might topple him?"

"Yes ..."

Chad turned, clapped his shoulder and departed inside. Rat remained, gazing at the forest around. Perhaps they'd all wipe each other out. Only it wasn't only troops who were killed and injured, there was always "collateral damage" and now most weapons were back in operation ... It didn't bare thinking about. At least it wasn't happening here ... Winter had been blessedly quiet, no troops and no sign of the strange insect beasts, how long that would continue he didn't know ...

Snow patches still lay on the ground up here, his fingers numbed by the cold night air. Just a few more minutes ... He gazed at the stars, so far removed, at swaying branches weaving shadow patterns in the sky. If mankind destroyed itself, the stars would still be there, nature would go on. He remembered the decimated camp. It would be re-populated. Birds would nest in the eaves, foxes pillage, mice and rats invade. Something would continue, it always did, but would he be there to see it? Did he want to be there?

Restless, he wandered back in. Bart and Annie sat, hands playfully on her belly, Bart's face lighting up as he sensed movement. Rat looked on enviously. He'd once done the same ... It was tough to be happy for them when it wrenched his innards to see them together. He knew it did the same to Chad. Would they be the lucky ones? Would their child survive and grow? They'd need help when it came, food, a warm place for winter. That he could do, and the thought gave purpose to life.

ϗϗϗ

Rat raised his hand, restraining Bart. Someone had been tampering with the traps. He crept forward, silent. A smile lit his face as he returned to where Bart was hidden.

"What was it?"

"Come see."

"Someone's been stealing from our traps?"

"Yes, but look closely." Bart gazed on bewildered.

"City boy," Rat cuffed him playfully. "Look! That's no boot print. The native Americans are coming back."

"I thought they were wiped out?"

"Evidently they weren't, at least this one wasn't. They've probably been up in the mountains or Canada, but winter's drawn them back down south."

"And that's good?"

"You bet that's good. It means they figure it's safe."

"Hope that doesn't mean they'll be raiding our traps."

"I hope not ... probably just hungry. With no soldiers they'll be free to hunt again. I don't begrudge them a rabbit or two, we have our rifles. Maybe he had little ones to feed."

"I'm starting to realize how that is, and we don't even have one yet ... never thought I'd be a father."

"Bart, you'll do fine. We'll help all we can when the time comes."

"It must be hard for you and Chad though. I know you both ..."

"Yes, it is ... but more reason for us to stand with you and Annie. It helps – sort of." Bart put a chunky hand on his shoulder.

"Look Rat, it's for all of us. We'll share the kid, OK?"

"I don't think Annie would be OK with that. She'll be as protective as a wildcat!" Bart chuckled.

"Yeah, you're probably right about that."

Chad seemed unsurprised by the news of their new neighbours.

"So, they're coming back, are they?"

"You know about them?" Rat asked.

"Yeah, there were still a few around when we first came, kept away from us guys 'cos of the uniforms, but Sal and Ma got to know them. That's where a lot of Ma's medicines came from. They moved on when the raids started. Just kind of melted away."

"It's a good sign they're coming back don't you think?"

"Yeah, it is. Doubt we'll see much in the way of government units for a year or so."

"Heavy losses, huh?"

"Millions!" Bart looked puzzled.

"The radio," Rat explained, "there's been heavy fighting in the Middle East."

"But who would ...?"

"Russia, China and the Muslim nations," Chad said, with a glance at Rat to hold his tongue.

"My God!"

"Good news for us," Chad continued. "They've no men to waste searching out rebels in the wilderness." Bart nodded.

"No word of this to Annie, mind. Just tell her about them returning."

"Wouldn't it set her mind at rest?"

"Maybe, till she wanted to start listening in, you know how Annie is. Not all is good news. Those insect demons are still on the rampage, wiping out whole cities now the troops are not there to fight them off, and there's still no cure."

"Think they'll come this way?"

"They seem to be attacking large urban areas mostly."

"Government strongholds ..." Rat whispered under his breath, recalling Pete's words.

"Besides, Bart here is friends with the aliens!" Chad joked. "I'm sure they'd send a ship if he needed it." Bart didn't laugh, humour squelched by fears for the child.

ᵡᵡᵡ

Emmie noted tiny shoots peeping from Dan's grave, taking advantage of the loosened earth. Nature bringing life from death, colour and beauty from destruction. The great mound entombing the town was now clad in radiant wildflowers and grasses. Even some of the trees had sprouted, severed roots seeking hold in the earth and debris of their new habitat. Life was beginning again, even within her ...

She sat beside the graves, Jack's muzzle on her lap, as she'd once sat by Dan's bedside. It helped to talk to Dan, even if he couldn't hear her, wasn't even there.

"I made soup from the new nettles yesterday," she told him, "and the spring melt off from the mountains is making a pool by the pines. There's no fish, but it might attract frogs. Maybe I could try out my shooting if animals start to drink there. It's been so long since I had meat ..." She chatted on aimlessly. She liked to think of him and Bessy, holding hands beneath the earth, listening to her. She knew it was nonsense, but it was better than the overwhelming loneliness ...

ɤɤɤ

Spring was here in all its glory, defying tragedy, defying hate. Somehow deep in Rat's heart hope stirred. He pushed away memories of another spring, a spring wrenched from its promise, splattered in blood. No, He wouldn't think on that, this was a new spring. He gazed down the sights as something stirred in the thickets. A doe raised soulful eyes. He edged closer, careful to stay downwind. A fawn romped beside her. He lowered the rifle. He'd find other meat ...

The forest buzzed, birds fluttered, foraging for greedy offspring, bees hummed in search of nectar for the hive. He watched the mother nuzzle her young, a new generation, but not for him. His arms were empty, heart empty. Yet, through the pain hope rose. Life continued here, and with Annie, perhaps not for him, but for others. That was Chad's philosophy and it was a good one. He had a family of sorts, odd bunch though they were. Life was a spectator sport, his joys vicarious, but joys none the less.

99

There was a commotion as he re-entered the camp, something was wrong. Dropping his burden, he dashed forward. A shot rang out, then another.

"Don't shoot! You'll hit Chad!" A voice yelled. His pulses raced.

Bart lay in the dust, a red stain seeping. Two figures grappled among the foliage. Rat raised his rifle but there was no clear shot. Vince came dashing out of the cabin, leaping into the fray. A flash of steel and it was all over, blood spurted from a slit jugular. As the body collapsed, Rat recognized the officer they'd seen in the cabin. Vince and Chad stood over him as he slipped to the ground.

From nowhere a shot rang out.

"No!" Rat screamed. Raising his gun, he spotted the hidden figure. He had no hesitation. He fired again and again, emptying his rifle into the inert form.

"Stop! Stop!" Annie ran out, resisting all efforts to restrain her. Her cry brought Rat to his senses. Shouldering the rifle, he ran to Chad. One look was enough.

"Chad! Chad! No!" he wailed.

Chad turned his head. "So, you got ... the blighter ... Listen Rat ..." His voice was gasping, fighting for breath. "You and Vince ... you carry on ..." He looked up to Vince standing inert. "Vince, you got ... the military stuff ... but you need Rat ... you hear me Vince ...? He's a good man ... a thinker ... You'll need him." He grasped Rat's hand, spirit ebbing. "Promise me ... Rat ..." Rat nodded, brushing tears away. "Do it ... guys ... finish it ..." He tried to say more, but the blood welling from his lips drowned the words. His eyes rolled. He was gone.

Rat yelled his anger, fist pounding into fir bark. Strangely it was Annie who took charge, barking commands from where she knelt beside Bart.

"Get out here you cowards! Carry Bart and Chad inside. You two," at two emerging figures, "search the woods, make sure there's no one else – be careful!" Rising, she placed an arm around Rat's shoulders. He tried to shrug her off, but she wouldn't let him.

"Come on Rat, come inside ..." He looked up. Vince was staggering under the weight of his fallen comrade. One of the men rushed to help. "Come on Rat. Pull yourself together, they need you." He nodded, turning slowly towards the cabin.

"Bart?" he whispered.

"He's a bit messed up, but he'll be OK. Chad saved him." Her face was unmoved. They said she'd never cried, that her tears had been extinguished when her kids died ...

Stumbling inside he saw Bart on a sodden mattress, a sheet bunched up to staunch the flow from his shoulder.

"Chad?" Bart whispered. Rat shook his head.

"He came out of nowhere ... couldn't let him get near the cabin. I tried to stop him, but he had a pistol ... He was crazy, out of his mind. He wanted revenge for us leaving them there ..."

"Should have shot the bastards like I said," Vince butted in.

"Enough!" Annie commanded. "We're all angry, but that's not going to bring Chad back and we need to get that bullet out of Bart before it goes septic."

"I got some grog," Vince volunteered. "Medical purposes only." He rolled his eyes at Annie's look.

"I'd be mighty thankful," Bart croaked. "I remember last time and that was just the chip."

"Can someone give me a hand?" a man rushed in. "Alan's been hit pretty bad ... must have sneaked up on him. I can't carry him on my own." Rat seized the opportunity. He needed time alone. Alan had been on lookout, but they'd grown careless with the winter lull. That carelessness had cost Chad his life. If these men had recovered, the men from the camp might be reviving too, in what state? Bart's comments were far from reassuring. He had to pull himself together. He'd given Chad his word.

Looking down at the transmitter, he pressed the button, through the curtain he could hear Bart's yells and Annie admonishing him to "man up", as she dug out the slug. Rat had evaded holding him down, leaving that to Vince and one of the other big guys. He'd had enough blood for one day. He couldn't come to terms with his anger, the way he'd kept shooting ... Beside him Chad lay white and motionless, face oddly relaxed. Rat traced a finger across the lined forehead as he tuned in the radio.

"Rest in peace Chad," he whispered.

The curtain opened, Vince entered, hands blood stained.

"Anything?" Rat shook his head.

"Just the usual stuff out of Denver."

"Nothing from the camp?"

"No." Vince stood staring at Chad for a moment.

"How many were there in the lodge?" He'd been expecting the question.

"Two women and another officer."

"Right. Maybe we should do a little hunting tomorrow?" He had that disturbing look in his eyes, but he was right. They couldn't risk more attacks on the camp.

"What about Chad?"

"We bury him tonight. I set a couple of guys working on it before the light goes. They'll dig a hole for the other two also." Rat could see it was going to be tough working with this guy, there'd always been Chad between. While Vince had a better opinion of him than Bart (who'd just sunk considerably lower in his esteem), Rat knew Vince didn't respect him the way he had Chad. Still, Vince had gotten things rolling, and he agreed about checking out the lodge.

Finished with Bart, Annie joined them, bloodied sheet and Ma's sewing kit in her hands.

"Don't seem right to just shove him in a hole and this one's wrecked anyway," she said defensively.

Vince nodded, helping her lift Chad's stiffening body onto the sheet while Rat stowed away the radio. It was odd to see her, bent over her swelling tummy, needle and thread in hand. Her face was a mask, no tear welled, but Rat knew she was grieving, the hasty, angry stitches gave her away.

"Me and Vince will check the lodge tomorrow," Rat muttered. "Better safe than sorry."

"Yeah, and if there are any there, kill them, OK? If they'd done that Chad wouldn't ..."

Her voice broke for just a betraying moment. Vince nodded. She was satisfied. She knew he would follow through.

"Say something Rat," Annie hissed as they lowered Chad into the hole.

Rat glanced around; everyone was looking at him. He didn't know what to say. The usual jargon wouldn't fit ...

"What can I say, Chad?" he questioned, voice breaking through the silent dusk. "If it weren't for you, I wouldn't be here, probably none of us would ... there'd be no hope. You gave us that. You made us believe we were worth something, could do something. I'm only starting to understand the burden you carried. You could have gotten bitter ..." He glanced involuntarily at Vince. "Instead you tried to help, you always tried to help damn it ..." Rat broke for a moment then muttered. "I know you'd be mad at me for saying it, but I hope you're with Ma and Sal someway, somehow ..." his voice broke again. "And Chad we'll keep it going, best we can. This can't all die with you. I won't let it ... We won't let it." He strode off inside unable to take any more. He needed to get his emotions under control.

Bart looked up as he came in but said nothing. What could he say? He wasn't clever with words.

Rat felt an arm around his shoulder. He turned – Annie. She didn't say a word just held him close.

"Let it out Rat," she whispered. "I can't do that anymore, but you can. It was a good speech ..." He held her for a minute, struggling for control.

"No Annie, I have to bury it, like he did. People are looking to me and Vince. I need to keep it together." She nodded.

They set out before sunrise, Rat with his rifle and Vince in uniform with his automatic and a pistol in his belt. The place looked quiet. No smoke rose from the chimney, but then the weather was mild.

"I go first, you cover me, wait for my signal." Vince broke

103

cover, striding toward the cabin. A strange noise was coming from within. A man in a torn, filthy uniform appeared in the doorway, thrashing his arms about, stumbling onto the veranda as if fighting an unseen foe. Vince raised the automatic. The figure crumbled. Rat saw the tip of a rifle emerge from the window. He took the shot. There was a stifled cry. Vince raced forward. Another shot rang out inside.

"Another man and two women," a voice said in his head. He ran for the door, noting the blood-spattered figure laid out by the window. Vince held a finger to his lips as he pushed open the bedroom door. Hunched in a corner was a young girl, late teens, eyes wild, arms flailing.

"No, Vince, no!" He was too late. She dropped with barely a sound, blood oozing down the dirty white dress.

"You're too soft Rat." Vince glanced in his direction. "That's why Chad said for both of us to lead. Suppose she was to come at night, kill Annie, and Bart's kid."

"Maybe she was forced, did you ever think of that?" Rat glared angrily. Vince merely grabbed the fallen hand turning it to show the scar.

"She was one of them!"

"So were you once!"

"Maybe, but I got out. Whatever, we can't risk it. Sometimes life deals you a dirty card Rat, and you play it, Chad knew that. We can only do what we can do."

"But you don't have to enjoy it!"

"No, but it's easier if you do." Vince smiled disturbingly. "That's all of them. I finished off the one you got. Good shot that!" Rat felt nausea rising as they passed the form by the window. He'd shot a woman. She'd have killed Vince if he hadn't, but still his stomach churned. He understood why Emmie had nightmares about the officer she'd stabbed. Knowing it was necessary didn't make it easier. Rounding the corner of the cabin he spewed his guts up. Vince laughed, cuffing him round the head.

"Rookie!" He chuckled. "Still, you're a damned good shot with that rifle, glad I had you for back up. You saved my life back there."

Restless, Rat set aside his bowl and headed for the door. Faces kept drifting across his subconscious, bloody and accusing. He kicked out at the elm standing sentinel. Was it worth all the killing? Would he end up like Vince? An arm slipped around his waist.

"Stop beating yourself up, Rat." Annie must have followed him out, guessed his thoughts. "You guys did it to keep us and the baby safe. Vince is used to it, but you're not."

"But Annie ... I ...?"

"You did what you had to do. From what Vince said you saved his life, focus on that, not that you took life, but that you saved it." The arm slipped away, and she was gone, replaced by Vince.

"Was I interrupting something?"

"What do you mean?"

"I thought maybe Annie was going to show you her apprecia- tion. That's what they did in the old days when someone first got bloodied, found them a good whore!"

"Annie's not a whore!"

Vince laughed. "Could have fooled me!"

"Have you ...?"

"Only once, she was with Chad mostly."

"Well she's with Bart now."

"Think that would make a difference?"

"How's Alan doing?" Rat asked to change the subject. It was no use arguing with Vince.

"Still unconscious, but he's hanging in there. Annie's found herself a new role it seems 'angel of mercy'. He laughed bitterly as he returned inside. Rat remained, pondering what Annie had said. It was comforting.

14

Her belly was too big for this, Emmie told herself, squatting by the pile of weeds. Still, the tiny plants cheered her heart. She'd planted last year's seeds, in an old tray in the kitchen, now the transplanted lettuces were almost big enough to eat. Soon she'd have a variety of young vegetables.

She'd finished the cans when Dan was alive, and the sacks of carrots and potatoes had run out or sprouted, to be buried for new seedlings. Shooting had gone less well, she'd bagged an occasional rabbit, but she wasn't like Greg.

Setting aside the trowel, she strolled to where Dan and Bess lay under their green carpet, spring flowers replaced by early summer's abundance. The "mound", as she called it, sported a similar covering, one day there'd be no sign of the buried town.

Gently stroking the grassy curves, she told of her lettuce, of the dark green spinach leaves, of the ... She felt a vibration beneath her fingers. A swooshing sound alerted her to pebbles sliding down behind the house.

No! Not again! Stones began to fall, followed by rocks as the earth shook. She ran towards the door, slamming it behind her, she had no other refuge. Boulders were falling, smashing into the outcrop that had once all but devoured the dwelling, ricocheting off to land in the yard. The heavens darkened. Brilliant lights flashed in the sky. Hail began to fall, flaming balls careening through the atmosphere. No, not hail, meteors! Pain gripped her belly as terror engulfed her mind.

"Dan! Dan!" she called. She knew it was no use. Dan wasn't here, any more than Greg was here ... She was alone in the darkness.

※※※

Rat felt the ground tremble beneath his feet. The sky turned black. Glancing at Bart, he slung the rifle over his shoulder racing back towards the cabin. It was too late. Darkness over-took them as strange florescent orbs whizzed by, lights descending like a curtain of Neolithic fireworks.

"Shooting stars!" Bart breathed.

"No meteors!" Rat yelled.

"Oh God! Not here too!"

"We've got to find shelter!" Rat stared into blackness, groping forward. The sky burst into flaming light as a meteor struck in the valley. Lights whizzed above their heads.

"Look, that's what I saw Rat. See 'em, there! Aliens!"

Rat stood mystified, brain churning to make sense of things. They were in a meteor shower on a massive scale, that much was clear. Fire shot across the heavens, pounding the earth on the horizon. The ground shook beneath their feet bringing them to their knees. A noise, so loud they cowered, holding ears, flowed over them in pulsating rhythms, like a pebble hitting the water. With it came light, dazzling, all pervading, blinding. They cringed, hunched against the earth, shielding their heads. Then, it was over. A bird raised its voice to the heavens. A multitude of fowl took flight, swooping above, adding voice to the tumult.

They staggered up.

"What the hell ...?" Rat muttered. Bart looked blank.

"We'd better get back. Make sure the others are OK." Bart nodded.

Smoke belched through the thicket. The cabin was in flames. All was confusion as men dashed about trying to beat out the fire. A glance told Rat it was no use.

"Leave it!" He yelled. "The trees! Get the axes, cut down the trees or it'll spread. It's too late to save the cabin ... Is everyone OK?"

"Annie!" Bart yelled, gazing in panic at the blaze.

Vince appeared, restraining him, face blackened with soot. "She's out! I got them out, but all our stuff's in there."

"Too late, it's going to go up like a torch and there's ammo in there. All we can do is try to contain the fire. If it gets hold, it'll burn down the whole forest and us with it." Vince nodded sprinting to take over one of the axes.

"Bart, get the clothesline!"

"Clothesline?"

"Just get it!" Rat bellowed. "You, and you! Forget the cabin, use the blankets for those sparks, don't let it get hold anywhere else." He watched as a section of roof collapsed sending a welter of sparks into the closest tree.

"Get it down! Get it down!" He yelled, grabbing the line from Bart. The rope sped towards the kindling pine, then slipped away.

Rat swore as he gathered it to try again. This time it took hold. "Pull!" He yelled in Bart's face. The half-severed pine quivered in the air, then dove to the ground, narrowly missing them.

"Quick here!" Rat yelled at the blanket men. A second pine crashed down into the blaze sending up a new shower of sparks. Others were catching on, stamping or beating out embers before they could take hold. Frantic hands swung the axes. Rat cursed. They'd left the trees as camouflage. There were too many! When the ammo went up, they'd kindle. Vince was cussing, muscles straining as the axes pounded into the trees.

"Everyone get out!" Rat yelled. "Bart, get Annie and get out! Head for the river!" Suddenly they were not alone, other axes rose and fell. Trees tumbled.

"Stay! Keep at it!" Vince yelled over the noise. Rat grabbed a discarded blanket. There was a muffled explosion, flames leapt skyward but found no purchase. Boots and moccasins kicked and stamped the kindling timber. Women came with water, pouring it on the more established flames. At last it was under control. They stood exhausted, faces blackened by smoke, coughing, eyes streaming, but victorious.

Rat strode towards the leader of their strange compatriots. He wore a deerskin jacket and pants, obviously homemade. Greying black hair hung long down his back, blending perfectly with the forest. Rat reached out his hand. The man took it.

"It's our forest too!" He said by way of explanation. His voice was deep, holding a quiet dignity. "We knew you were here. You didn't trouble us; we didn't trouble you. We knew Ma ... is she still with you?"

Rat shook his head. "No, she's dead, Sally and Chad too."

"I'm sorry. They were good people, even if he did wear a uniform. I told my people he was a good man, not to shoot him." He cracked a smile.

"We're thankful for your help. We couldn't have stopped the blaze without you."

"We saw the stars come down. Thank the gods it was not dry season, or we'd all be dead, you for sure ..." He waved a hand at Rat's confederates. "What will you do now? No more cabin, no more things."

"I don't know. We'll need to decide."

"Maybe head down the valley, no more devil monsters there now. More game."

He turned, gesturing to his people. Gathering their things, they set off, melting into the trees.

Rat gazed at the solitary chimney rising from the smouldering ruins, nothing had survived the blaze. The men were slumped in exhaustion. Bart sat by Annie, a troubled expression on his face.

"Is she OK?" Rat asked.

"I'm alright, I tell you!" Annie flashed. One look convinced Rat otherwise.

"She was in the cabin when it hit, with Alan. He was getting those headaches again." Vince got them out, but it was a close thing. They got hit by some falling debris. She was pretty shaken."

"I'm alright! Leave me be!" Annie snapped, face contorted with pain.

"Annie!" Rat said sternly. "It's plain to see you're not alright. Where are you hurt?"

"Just a bit bruised, nothing much."

"Show me." She pulled away, but Rat persisted, gently moving the arm cradled across her lap. She yelped.

"Let me see."

"It's just bruised."

"I'll be the judge of that." Pulling back the sleeve he winced. The flesh was swollen and discoloured. He knew little about such things.

"I think she's having belly pains too," Bart interjected. Annie glared. Rat chewed his thumb nail, an unconscious gesture since Chad's passing.

Vince came over. "Is she OK?"

"She's hurt her arm, maybe broken. I can't tell."

"It's nothing, I tell you!"

"If it's nothing, then let me see." Vince glanced at the bruising. "Can you move the fingers?"

"A little." Grasping her forearm, he cautiously manoeuvred the hand. Annie winced.

"Don't think it's broken, but it'll be painful for a while," he muttered. "Put it in a sling and don't use it." Annie gasped, face contorted, other hand gripping her belly. Vince and Rat exchanged worried glances.

ƔƔƔ

Darkness thickened, a dense blanket, pervading the house, the atmosphere, her mind ... A cry escaped her lips as pain enveloped her. This was the end and she was alone! No ... not entirely alone. As she groped towards Dan's old room, she felt a wet muzzle against her hand. She gripped the bed post as the gripping ache intensified. Lights zoomed outside, punctuating the darkness. Fear gripped her. Jack ran barking for the door.

"It's no use, Jack. There's no one to bring. Come, stay with me Jack." She couldn't bear it alone. He returned, whining his frustration. The contractions came again, and she became oblivious to his presence. Through the window flashes exploded on the horizon. She closed her eyes against the vision of destruction, waiting for them to hit. Jack quieted. A sound began, the rumble of distant thunder, louder and louder till she couldn't stand it. Jack howled. Light followed, intense, all pervading, dazzling her eyes as another contraction invaded her body.

Then it was over, oddly silent. Jack began to bark fervently at the door. She couldn't open it. Birdsong broke forth, a strange, jubilant chorus. Jack was dancing in circles, barking and clawing at the door. For Emmie there was no such release, the pains continued, fear intensifying the contractions.

The sun still shone, the earth had survived another onslaught, and she was still here as Dan predicted. Her bag of delivery things sat serenely across the room. She must reach it ... The pains drew closer, more forceful as she collapsed back on the bed, clutching the bag. Jack returned as she gasped in agony, lips dry. She needed to keep control, couldn't let fear get out of hand. She knew little of birth, only loss. It could die for all she cared. It wasn't his child. She just needed to get it out, be rid of it forever! Jack nuzzled against her, then whined, turning in frustrated circles as her first screams rent the air. There was no one to hear, none but Jack and the strays haunting the mound ...

Some three hours later another sound pierced the air, the cry of a child newborn on the earth. Emmie lay exhausted in a mess of blood and mucus. The infant was balling, showing its aversion to the cold, bright world it had entered. She must cut the cord while her strength lasted. Finally, she'd be severed from the past, from the remnants of that day.

Summoning her flagging reserves, she propped herself on one elbow. Years in the wild had made her strong. She could do this.

Reaching down she picked up the babe, coated in white shiny vernix, reaching for the thread she'd prepared. Their eyes met. There was something about the child ... It looked like her, a tiny vessel stamped with her eyes and mouth. No matter the nose was unfamiliar, the skin more olive. She realized what had all this time evaded her. This was her child, made from her own body. It wasn't Greg's, but it was hers, part of her. Frightened eyes confronted her own, the button mouth cried in fear and wonder at the strange world that surrounded it.

Impulsively she pressed it to her chest. The crying ceased, the tiny mouth quivered, in search of something. Was it hungry?

She pressed her nipple against its lips. It tried to grasp, gulping air, searching. It took a few minutes before success, by then, gazing at the tiny infant, so utterly dependent, she knew she couldn't abandon it. It was part of her. She once more had someone to love.

15

It was decided. Rat would take Bart and Annie to Pete's while Vince took the others down to the lodge. The pains had stopped, but she'd be better off under Liz's care. He and Brad took turns to lead her horse while the other rode. They were taking it slow, very slow, afraid to bring on the baby. Annie sat, pale, arm bound across her chest, but mouth resolute.

Night was falling as they wound towards the cottage, relieved as it appeared, serene, untouched by fire or stone.

"Pete! Pete!" Rat called, pulling the weary beast behind him. After a moment a face emerged.

"Pete's not here ... None of them are ... just me and Lenny."

"What ... what happened!"

"Dunno. It got dark. There was stuff falling, explosions ... I was out in the plots. When I finally managed to get back, they were gone."

Bart helped Annie down from the horse. "Can we go inside, she's exhausted?" Bill looked up, noticing them for the first time.

"Of course! Lenny, come help them get settled." Lenny had grown long and lanky, spiraling dirty blond curls framing a grin of welcome – still using the stick Rat noticed.

"I'll get the horses settled," Bill said. Rat went with him.

"They can't just have disappeared," Rat hissed. "Did you search for them ... maybe they ..."

"I looked everywhere ... Not a sight nor sound of them, not so much as a track."

"The horses ... were they ...?"

"Still in the stable, they all were ... all the animals, just as we

112

left them, even the dogs ..."

"You could have ..."

"Look Rat," Bill turned to face him over the harness. "I scoured the woods for miles. Lenny can't walk far, but ..." Rat sensed his anguish.

"I know you did all you could, Bill." He placed a hand on his shoulder. "Look, tomorrow I'll search, perhaps I can find some tracks, some clue. Maybe the natives took them?"

"Why should they? Besides there's been none in years."

"Well, they're back now." Bill slid off the bridle, turning to hang it on the peg.

"I don't know, Rat. You can try, but Lenny was working with Liz in the kitchen. The kids were playing in the yard. He could see them through the window. Then it went dark, and there were lights falling from the sky ..."

"The meteor showers," Rat interjected.

"Was that what it was? Scared the pants off me."

"So anyway ... He said Liz was rushing to get to the kids when it went pitch black. He could hear them yelling and Liz calling to stay still, that she was coming. Then there was this noise, he couldn't hear anything, and a rush of light." Rat nodded.

"Anyway, when he could see again, the door was open, but there was no sign of any of them, just this disk of light that hovered for a moment then zoomed off at incredible speed. He swears it's true, an' he wouldn't lie about something like that." Rat nodded slowly, brain on overdrive, remembering the globes of light he'd seen then. Was Bart right about the aliens? If so, why would they take Liz and the kids ...?

"What about Pete?"

"Pete was out working like me. I never saw him since breakfast that day. I searched all the plots!" Rat reached an arm around Bill's shoulder.

"I'm sure you did everything you could, Bill. Come on, let's see how Annie's doing. I was hoping Liz could help her. She has an injured arm and was getting belly pains yesterday ..."

"Lenny might know something to put on the arm, he's been

helping Liz, but for sure he won't know about babies."

Emmie looked down at the tiny form dozing in its blanketed draw. She'd thought to call it Greg, but that was too painful a reminder of another child, so she'd settled on Daniel. It seemed fitting somehow. Dan had cared about the baby, insisting she could not abandon it. Had he lived he'd have made a great grandpa. She could picture him with little Danny on his lap. How would Greg feel, his baby supplanted by the child of her rapist? How could he understand? What did it matter? Greg wasn't coming back, she had to face that. At least she wouldn't be alone. Somehow, they'd make it through, as Dan said.

✗✗✗

Rat's investigations came to nothing, the mystery remained. Bart elected to stay, help Bill run the farm and take care of Annie. Rat couldn't imagine Bart fulfilling either role, but what choice was there? Annie was better off here than in the lodge.

Rat rode home, leading the other horse. He was going to miss Bart's inane humour, and yes, he'd miss Annie's motherly concern, even her waspish temper. What would life hold now he wondered? He had no close bond with Vince, could barely stand the guy. The weight of responsibility rode heavy on his shoulders ...

Down at the lodge order reigned. Lookouts were posted, the door repaired. Vince emerged to meet him, motioning Rat aside.

"There's something I need to show you," he hissed. Venturing into the surrounding trees, he rummaged with his boot among a pile of leaves revealing soiled army fatigues. Rat's stomach churned – not again.

"Came staggering towards the hut yesterday ... the lookout spotted him before he spotted us.

"From the camp?" Rat queried.

"Reckon so. Must have known about the lodge ... but look at this." Vince prodded the head. A face emerged, distorted by gaping sores and puss.

"Ugh!" Rat grimaced. "An after effect of the venom?"

"Maybe, but the other guys didn't have it. I'm worried it could be contagious, that's why I kept him out here ... wanted you to see it though."

"I don't know Vince. Your guess is as good as mine. Better safe than sorry. Think we could burn the body?"

"Sure, away from the trees though, don't want another place going up in smoke!" They knew they were taking a chance, the smoke could draw others, but if it were contagious ... The camp was a good distance away and surely the troopers would head south or east towards other bases ...

Emmie was dancing in the woods. They were all there ... Rat relaxed; his mind engulfed in transitory illusion. Bill was playing his mouth organ. He took her hand, joining the circle. Laughter suffused the air, his lips creeping upward. Darkness appeared, eclipsing the scattered sunshine, the dancers sped in different directions. She vanished, and he was left alone to face the night ...

The crack of a rifle permeated the darkness. Someone was shaking him.

"Rat, wake up! Wake up! There's a bunch of them out there!" He glimpsed Vince in vest and shorts, yelling orders. Grabbing his rifle, he joined him at the window. Both lookouts were inside.

"They're coming up the rise," one explained.

"How many?"

"Hard to see ... ten? Maybe more ... they veered off back into the trees when Phil winged one of them."

"Cover all the windows!" Vince ordered. "They'll most likely circle round but save your ammo. Have rifles front and back to pick them off, keep the automatics in case they try to rush us ... I never thought I'd say it," he glanced at Rat, "but I wish Bart was here, we could use him right now!" Rat kept silent; this was Vince's domain. He was glad Bart wasn't here though, that he and Annie were safe ... well, as safe as anyone could be ...

"Don't want to come to grips if they're infected," Vince muttered. Rat saw movement in the trees. He hesitated just a moment before squeezing the trigger. A cry went up.

"Got him!" Vince grinned.

"Why don't they just leave us alone ..." Rat muttered. He'd had enough killing.

"Probably off their rockers!" Vice smirked.

Seconds later firing burst out at the back of the house.

"Keep watch here, Rat I'm going to help out back." From the rapid firing, Rat figured they'd tried to make a rush attack and failed. Firing stopped, and Vince returned.

"There's a slew of them out there! What the hell they're doing here, I can't imagine!"

"Maybe they're deserters." Rat queried. "Maybe they've had enough!"

"Maybe, but we can't chance it."

"Couldn't we at least give them the chance to surrender?"

"Surrender! Are you nuts Rat?!" Vince glared at him. "They can walk away any time they want. You're too soft Rat. You gotta toughen up and fast! Just watch that window and if you see anything kill it! Understood!" Rat nodded. Vince was right, but it didn't make it any easier.

Nothing happened for a while.

"Reckon they've given up?" Rat asked, peering into the darkness.

"They're out there alright. They'll be up to something."

A hail of bullets made them take shelter. Vince scrutinized the gloom from the cover of the wall.

"Can't see nothing." Rat peered warily from the other side.

"That bush there before, Vince?"

"Nope, it wasn't!" Vince stood for a moment. One short blast and the "bush" collapsed amidst groans and screams.

There were no further attacks. Daybreak came to find them red eyed and listless.

"The waiting game," Vince commented. We're pretty well stocked 'cept for water. The barrel is full, but I don't relish going out there to get it. Rat nodded.

ⱷⱷⱷ

Emmie watched minuscule fingers grasping her thumb, native tenacity in one so vulnerable to a hostile world. She wished Dan had lived to see it, to note the beginnings of a triangular smile. He'd been right about the child, right about a lot of things.

"One day, all this will be yours, Daniel," she whispered.

They'd seen no sign of troops, no sign of anyone apart from Dan since that fateful day it all began. The radio told of catastrophic wars, of strange new diseases and, weirdest of all, alien invasions. The world had gone crazy, but here, in their little refuge, all was calm and quiet.

She treasured these days with little Daniel, venturing only to the vegetable plot. She was recovering fast. She'd heard pioneer women gave birth and were back next day in the fields or caring for their young ones. It must have been the lifestyle that made them strong.

Jack wriggled his nose onto her lap, sniffing at the baby, before turning in whining circles, heading for the door. Probably hungry she thought, letting him out. Dog food was long exhausted and there wasn't much in the way of scraps. The cellar bags gaped empty, only lentils remained (not the best when nursing a child). They needed meat and she needed to do some foraging if only for the ever-abundant nettles ...

Daniel tied securely in one of Bessy's shawls, she set out, rifle on her shoulder, for the pond. Jack bounded beside her. He'd caught a rabbit while she'd been laid up, leaving the grisly remains on the doorstep in token of his new prowess. She wasn't sure if his presence would help or hinder but felt safer having him along, remembering the footprints.

Shadows grew long, a time animals came to drink. This evening was different. Towering beside the pool stood an elk, antlers lowered as it drank. She'd only glimpsed them before, or seen one dragged in by the hunters. Did she dare to take a shot? If she missed, she and Daniel could be in danger.

Jack barked. Antlers raised, water streaming from its muzzle, the eyes gleamed angrily. Spines lowered as Jack dashed in, grabbing at a foreleg. She grabbed the rifle. The first shot went wide as it tossed Jack in the air to land with a howl. She took aim again, squeezing the trigger. The head turned, a stream of red flowing from the shoulder. She fired again, and again, stopping only when the cartridges were exhausted. It fell to its knees, glorious antlers surrendered to dust.

Jack lay squirming, a red gash in his side. She ran to examine him. He snarled, pain and confusion making him vicious. She spoke softly.

"It's me Jack. It's OK, I'm just going to look at it." He calmed, reassured by the familiar voice. It was nasty, but not deadly. Shouldering the rifle, she looked around for a means of carrying him. Branches lay in abundance, but she needed something to tie them, a blanket and string perhaps? She had to deal with the elk, but Jack was more important. He'd been her solace. Jack was Dan's dog.

"Wait here Jack," she whispered. "I'll be right back."

Light was dimming as she returned. Jack whimpered at her approach. Hastily assembling a stretcher, she dragged it back towards the house. Thankfully he was no great weight. Once there she cleaned and bound the wound. It needed stitching, but that would have to wait. She needed to get meat.

Lighting an oil lamp, she set out, Dan's swathed kitchen knife in a plastic bag. Already scavengers had started. She chased them away, small wary creatures with glowing eyes. She got to work. The elk was bigger than she'd helped with before, but the principle was the same, cut it to manageable portions. She hacked away at the rump. Daniel began to cry ...

Outpaced by darkness she dragged her grisly burden over the rubble filled terrain. It wasn't far, but this load was heavier than Jack had been. She'd taken as much as she could manage. Who knew how much there'd be left by morning. Perhaps it was just as well. With no smoke house how could she store it? Let the creatures have their share.

Collapsing on the kitchen chair she glanced over at Jack, tail wagging weakly. How on earth was she going to stitch him?

16

Thirst ached as Rat woke, shaken from depths of exhaustion.

"Your watch."

"Anything happening out there?"

"Not that I can tell."

Rat took his place by the window. Outside, shadows were lengthening. He glanced at Vince sprawled on the floor.

"Said to wake him when it's dark," his companion explained. Rat raised a questioning eyebrow. "Figures there's more chance of getting water under cover of darkness."

"Maybe, maybe not. It'll also be harder to spot snipers." *Guess Vince knows what he's doing,* he thought. Night drew a blanket over the surrounding clearing. Still no sign of movement. Vince was awakened. Rummaging in his old kit bag, he came over to Rat thrusting something in his hands.

"Night goggles. Reckon you're the best shot."

"What are you planning?"

"We open this window, wait an hour or so, then I slip over the ledge with a man stationed at the door to help bring in the barrel."

"Risky!"

"Yeah, but I don't see another option."

"We could pull straws for who goes out."

"Sure, and have some bungling imbecile wreck our chances. You know I'm the best for the job."

"But what if you're hit? We need you."

"If I'm hit, you better toughen up and fast. Hopefully I won't be. The trick will be to get between the barrel and the door before they see what's going on."

"Maybe they've gone ..." Rat said lamely.

"Unlikely. We'll find out."

The hour dragged by. Vince woke the others, stationing two automatics at each window.

"They won't be able to spot them. I'm relying on you for that. They'll follow your lead." Rat nodded. Heart in mouth, he couldn't speak. Vince slid smoothly over the sill, edging along the base of the wall, towards the barrel. Perhaps they've gone, perhaps they've gone, Rat recited, scanning the surrounding forest.

It was only when the barrel began to move a shot rang out. Even with the glasses Rat could see nothing but fired at the area it came from. A hail of bullets rent the undergrowth. A scream rang out followed by returning fire. Seeing a target Rat fired, and again ...

The barrel was dragged through the doorway amid a hail of gunfire. Vince was dragged in with it. Firing continued as the door slammed, petering out after a few minutes.

"How bad is it?" Rat hissed at the men gathered round the entrance.

"Can't see." A torch was produced. "Nasty bang on the head, but the bullet is in the shin."

"Thank God for that. Anyone else hurt?"

"A couple of flesh wounds, nothing major. The barrel is a bit shot up though."

"Stop the holes as best you can and fill the buckets."

Rat waited a few minutes, before passing on the goggles to appraise the situation. Most of the water was salvaged. Vince, regaining consciousness, was moved to one of the beds.

"Rat, Rat, stay on guard! You hear me!" he hissed. Rat nodded, briefly clasping his shoulder.

"You did it Vince. We got the water. Don't worry, I'll keep watch."

"You do that! Damn bullet ricocheted off the post, caught me off guard. You'll need to get it out, but not now. No lights, it can wait till morning."

"OK, Vince. Get some rest."

"Set watches, two on the front, two on the back, like before."

"OK, I got it."

"Keep the automatics to hand and make sure there's ammo. They may try and rush us again."

"OK, I will."

Morning dawned. Vince was wrong for once, there'd been no rush, all was quiet save for some flashing lights. He knew what they were, they all did, but said nothing.

The lookouts changed, relinquishing their posts to eyes marginally less red. Danger lessened with the dawn ... but, in his heart, he knew they were no longer there. Maybe now he could sleep. There was one thing more first ...

Rat felt nauseous. He wiped the knife on a rag, gazing at the blood staining his hands. Thankfully, the bullet lost most of its impact prior to burying itself in Vince's leg. There was muscle damage, but the bone was intact. Vince had insisted he dig it out, though others had offered. "It'll toughen you up," he'd said, but Rat suspected Vince simply thought him more competent. Vince had endured stoically, insisting the remaining alcohol be reserved for cleaning the wound.

While Rat admired his courage and resilience, he had no wish to "toughen up". What use "survival at any cost" if we become little more than animals, he reasoned. Exhausted, sleep came like falling off a cliff.

Shadows were lengthening when he awoke. Vince, despite his injury, had taken charge.

"Sorry, didn't mean to sleep so long," Rat muttered.

"I told them to let you be. It's been quiet, no movement, nothing."

"Think they've given up?"

"Hard to say."

"How long should we wait before someone tries going out?"

"Tomorrow, next day, maybe. We can last till then. No sense putting anyone in danger unless we have to." Rat agreed.

ႱႱႱ

Jack was recovering well. Her gamble feeding him a morsel from Dan's old capsules had paid off. She'd been so afraid to get the dose wrong but couldn't face the alternative. She rubbed his ears affectionately as little Daniel greedily imbibed his milk, moose meat suiting better than lentils. The muzzle shifted, nose twitching. He grew restless, growling softly. Setting Daniel down, she reached for the gun. Jack moved towards the door barking loudly. She raised the rifle. Footsteps receded down the side wall. Silence! Jack hobbled to and thro, nose twitching – on guard. Face tight to the wall she peered through the window – nothing. Jack continued his low growl. Suddenly a face peered in, a face distorted by open sores, pus and a terrible leering expression. He'd seen her!

A bullet exploded the glass, shattering the face. She hadn't meant to pull the trigger, it just happened.

"Oh my God! Oh my God!" she sobbed. Jack barked, then subsided into a low growl once more. Were there others she wondered? She stood frozen, gun raised. Brilliant light swept by at incredible speed, dazzling her eyes. A cry rang out, then silence. She'd seen a light like that when Daniel was born. Could it be? Could it be Dan? She chastised herself. Stupid! Stupid! The world had gone crazy, was she going crazy also, alone like this? Unless ... unless the reports of alien craft were true? She stopped, slowing her breathing to get control. Whatever the lights were they'd not hurt her before, they wouldn't this time, she told herself. As to Dan, he'd left her a precious gift. She fondled Jack's nose. Thank goodness she hadn't lost him. Without him she'd not have been ready. She slumped into the old armchair. Gun propped on the arm, she reached for the bawling Daniel.

Night came and went uneventfully, Jack curled on the end the bed, little Daniel snuggled beside her. She'd wedged some old boards across the shattered glass, but she knew it was safe again now. She trusted her furry sentinel.

Morning dawned to peaceful sunshine. She must do something about the bloody mess outside her window. There'd been talk of a sickness ... might this man have been infected? Could he have been seeking help? Had she shot an innocent man? The vision rose once more, the face demented, crazy. She'd been protecting her child, she reasoned. Besides, she'd not meant to pull the trigger, it was just the shock, the horror that jolted her finger. What's done is done, she told herself. No point thinking about it. The question was what to do with the body, even were it not infectious a dead body would decompose quickly in this heat.

Jack limping at her side, scarf across her nose, she grasped the blanket. It seemed the best plan. She noted the uniform. She'd been right to kill him. Spreading the blanket, she kicked and levered him with the broom handle. Calling Jack to keep watch, she dragged her burden to the edge of the wrecked barn. Dropping the blanket, she edged up the pile sending a scurry of bricks and debris in her wake. Wrenching out a supporting beam she jumped aside as a landslide hurtled down covering the gruesome bundle below. A little more ... Jack whined, coming closer.

"No Jack! Stay away!" she yelled. He looked up with doleful eyes. Perhaps she should leave it at that ...? Relenting, she instead shovelled earth over the pile. Jack looked on approvingly. Daniel began to wail from the house.

ɣɣɣ

The teams returned, reporting the area clear. Deciding against the mammoth blaze needed for that number of corpses they'd elected to dig a mass grave some distance from the lodge. Men were taking turns with the only available spade; others dragged the decomposing bodies to the area. Rat imposed all precautions he could, but suppose it were airborne? Might they all suffer the same fate, or was it the effects of the venom? They'd find out. Meanwhile the water needed replenishing and they needed food.

ɣɣɣ

All had been peaceful, no sign of life other than the birds, bugs and small creatures that came to steal the vegetables. She watched the soil guzzle the water beneath its protective chicken wire tunnels. The sun had been down for hours, yet it was still stiflingly hot, more like Texas than Wyoming. Feeling weak and dizzy she replenished the pail and headed inside.

Daniel was fussy. She didn't blame him, the house felt like an oven. She remembered the chill darkness of the cellar. Wasn't that a little extreme? At least she could cool off, they both could. Picking him up she undid the basement door, cold, relieving air enveloped her. Leaving the door ajar she sat on the steps to nurse him. He guzzled greedily. I must drink more water she told herself.

४४४

Rat was likewise feeling the heat. More worrying, the well that supplemented the water barrel, had not only shown signs of drying up, but gained a putrid red tinge. He'd ordered the repaired barrel filled and every bucket and container they could find. Already it tasted bitter and several men had complained of belly aches. After that, Rat had ordered their drinking water boiled and imposed drastic conservation measures. The cabin stank with unwashed masculine bodies. The heat wave was unending. He'd never seen weather like this before, especially this far north. Teams went to the river, a two-mile hike, to bathe and look for game. It gave no relief, within minutes clothes were dry, the waters more a tepid bath than an icy mountain flow. They stayed inside for the most part covering their skin if they had to go out. Though not yet able to walk, Vince made his presence felt.

"Team back yet?" he asked. Rat shook his head. They'd gone at first light sporting automatics – just in case. "Sun's well up," Vince continued. "Should be back if they know what's good for them." Rat agreed, sunstroke was a definite possibility. He peered towards the forest. He'd not long to wait.

The men came staggering, gasping for water.

"The river ..." one stammered between drafts. "It's red, totally

124

red! ... We couldn't drink it ... there was a deer ... floating on the water ... dead ... frogs an' fish all belly up ..."

"What the hell?" Vince began, Rat cut him off.

"The red tide! Remember what Bart said, and the radio ... only this time it's not just the sea ..." There was silence for a moment.

"But the well. Surely the well water will be OK?"

"Who's to say?" Rat scraped his hand through sweat sodden hair, now cropped short against the heat. "Look the water we stored, seems OK. We use it only for drinking, anything else we draw from the well, agreed." Heads nodded.

४४४

She felt uneasy in the cellar with only Daniel and the oil lamp for company. Jack had chosen to remain above ground panting fit to burst. For the hundredth time she checked for the torch and matches beside their mattress ...

She awoke to Daniel's bleating. The lamp was still burning. She checked her watch 4:30 a.m. Having fed and cozied him down to sleep she took the torch and ventured above. She was hungry but there was nothing to eat besides dried elk. She couldn't stand to cook in this heat even at night. What she wouldn't give for a bowl of ice cream. "Ice cream!" She chuckled, even a crust of bread.

Jack awoke, tail wagging weakly. She refilled his water bowl and shared her dried meat. Perhaps some of the veggies were still alive. She'd watered them the night before. Better fill the pails too she thought. Life had turned nocturnal, cowering in the cellar by day and doing chores by night. The lettuce was unusable, but some spinach remained, limp and tasteless. She broke off a few stems wishing the carrots, with their wilted tops, were bigger. She mustn't pick them yet, nor the potatoes and parsnips. They'd survive down beneath the earth, like her.

४४४

The heat was extreme, water running low. Rat shone the torch into the well. He could see nothing. He gestured to his compan-

125

ion to lower the bucket. It came up red, putrid and smelly. That was it. His throat was dry, tongue swollen from short rations. At Vince's advice he'd set a guard over the remaining water, a mere half bucket. Was it to end this way, after all they'd been through? He thought about Bart, Annie and the child, please God let it have not affected them … a thought occurred to him … desperate times call for desperate measures. If they stayed here, they'd die anyway. Perhaps … just perhaps, on the other side of the valley there might be fresh water. If nothing else, he could see the place one more time before he died. Pouring the polluted water on dusty soil he went to talk to Vince.

"You're right Rat. At least there's a chance. Divide the water up between the men and leave me a canteen."

"But you're coming with us Vince."

"With this?" He gestured to the injured calf.

"You can use one of the horses."

Vince laughed bitterly. "If they're not already dead, they're in no state to carry a man my size. It would only slow you down."

"We're not leaving you Vince." There was a finality to Rat's voice, as he turned away, Vince hadn't heard before. He peered at the pussy mess beneath the pad encompassing his leg. He'd hoped they'd leave him without knowing. Now he had no alternative …

Rat looked over the horses. Vince was right. With no water to spare they'd been using the less contaminated well water. That, and the heat in the lean to under which they'd been tethered, had reduced them to near exhaustion.

"Come on. Come on, stand boy." He pulled at the halter. After a few minutes fruitless pulling the horse staggered to his feet, legs shaking. "We're gonna go find us some clean water," Rat whispered. "If you stay here, you'll die."

He had more success with the mare. She rose swiftly, gazing wistfully at the empty feed box and water pail. The mare, Rat decided. The men were streaming out into the darkness, travelling light. If successful they could return for stuff. Guns and water were the essential items. Waving a couple of guys over he proceeded to get Vince.

"Look, Rat, I didn't want to tell you, but the leg ... I have gangrene. Leave me here to die in peace will you. Better still put a bullet through my head and make it quick, or are you not man enough for that?" He was taunting him, trying to make him mad enough to go.

"We die together Vince. I'm not leaving you behind. We're probably all gonna die anyway, one way or another, what difference!"

"Because some of you might just make it!"

"What happened to the old 'no man left behind'?"

"That was bullshit, bullshit."

"OK Vince, are you going to make this hard or easy? Do you want to further deplete our strength wrestling with you?"

"Have it your own way Rat, you always did, but I think you're making a mistake."

"It's my decision."

"Says who? Chad left us both in charge."

"Let's see who the men listen to, shall we?" Vince sighed, acknowledging defeat.

"Bunch of pussys!" He scowled, levering himself up on Rat's arm. "Get me a stick or something, will you?" Rat thought he glimpsed a hint of a smile, not the leer, something different.

The mare was stumbling, exhausted. Light glimmered among the trees heralding dawn. Stumbling through darkness, even with oil lamps, progress was agonizingly slow.

"Let's take a rest, sun's coming up anyway."

"No!" Vince contradicted. "You need to keep going, you'll go faster with a little light."

"The mare's had it, Vince."

"So, leave me! I said this would happen."

"Stop playing the hero, the men are exhausted too." They were already collapsing where they stood. Vince edged down from the horse assisted by Rat. His face crumpled.

"Painful?" Rat asked.

"Not as damn painful as it should be, that's what worries me."

"Look, if we can get help … Maybe they'll have antibiotics at the farm."

"And pigs might fly!"

Rat knew what was eating him, even with modern medicine, gangrene could lead to amputation, and they had nothing, not even clean water. Hell, that he couldn't do! No way! Besides Vince was not the type of man to relish being a cripple. Perhaps he should have left him. Maybe Vince was right. Well, they'd die anyway, better together. He thought of Emmie and the child peacefully sleeping under the half-submerged forest, maybe death was the better option … I'm coming soon Emmie he whispered …

Ɛ⅄Ɛ

The ground trembled. Jack began to bark frantically. Grabbing Daniel, she dashed up the cellar steps. Sunrise dawned innocently through the window, flooding the landscape with dazzling light. Her rush outside was curtailed as rocks hurtled from the slopes above, narrowly missing her. Better to stay put she told herself. The earth shook. Through the back window she could see the mountains convulsing, rising, then, with a thunderous roar collapsing in on themselves. Above black thunder clouds rolled in …

Ɛ⅄Ɛ

Rat was dreaming. He felt the tremble of the oncoming train. He'd been waiting so long, lying here on the platform. The train to take him to Emmie had come at last. The vibrations increased as it drew alongside the station. The platform beneath him began to break up, cracks appearing between jagged concrete slabs. Like the death spasms of a long-forgotten beast, it twisted in agony. He was awake!

"Earthquake!" he screamed. Around him others were stumbling to gain footing as earth slipped from beneath their feet. Storm clouds exploded overhead spilling a deluge of heavy rain. Lightening flashed as the ground heaved and convulsed, lifting the trees, lifting the ground, like a gigantic wave. Lights flashed and zoomed around them. They were falling, down, down, then rushing up. Rat heaved, emptying his stomach into the surrounding air. Trees crashed around him. All was confusion.

☙❦❧

She watched quivering through the window, unable to look away. Jack whined and barked, circling her legs in a futile quest for reassurance. This is it, she reasoned ... the end of all things ... Rain thundered from the heavens breaking the heat. Lightning flashed, and noise erupted all around her. Sinking to her knees she hugged Jack and Daniel to her. She was not alone ...

How long she cowered there she didn't know, eyes squinted, waiting for the end ... The rain eased. Silence gripped her, broken only by the sound of a bird, then another, a strange chorus filling the heavens. Jack wriggled. Pulling free, he barked, turning in frenzied circles. They were alive! Once more they were still alive! Tentatively she rose to her feet, eyes seeking the chorus. There they were, thousands of birds circling the heavens, spinning, swooping, tiny voices raised in triumph.

But it was not the birds that claimed her vision. It was the sky, a vacuum of cloud filling the void where once mountains had stood.

☙❦❧

Motion ceased. He squinted through earth splattered eyes into the deluge of falling rain, opening parched lips to the life-giving flow. Where was he? Where were the others? The earth was still, motionless – quiet, save for the overwhelming torrent depleting his vision. What he could see was unrecognisable. Perhaps he was dead? What else could explain it?

Someone raised a filthy arm, surrounded by broken branches, rocks and tree roots. Rat examined his limbs. He appeared

129

uninjured, other than minor bruising and scrapes. He glanced to his companion, now trying to gain his feet.

"What the hell happened?" The mud caked apparition spoke, dispelling the strange peace that had descended.

"Damned if I know. Should all be dead."

As overwhelming rain eased to a steady downpour, a profound silence gripped them. Nature held its breath. Other shapes appeared amidst the debris, filthy, begrimed, clothes in tatters, but alive. No one spoke. A ray of sunshine penetrated the gloom, clouds began to disperse. Birds heralded the light, and nature sprang to life in a crescendo of song and humming incest life. Strange cries rent the air as the creatures of the earth sang forth their joy of life. The men stood rooted, watching, listening, what did it mean?

An intense oval of light appeared, slowly descending towards them, silent, awe inspiring. The men scattered in terror, but Rat stood firm. He'd known all along, just couldn't accept it till now. The sphere descended, a few feet away. His heart pounded.

A form appeared, a wavering shadow against the dazzling orb. Rat swallowed his fear. Whatever they were, they'd intervened to save them more than once. He'd glimpsed them as the ground fell away, as the trees crashed. He knew they were friends. The form took shape and stepped forth. No, it couldn't be ... how could he ...? Rat stood open mouthed as Vince walked towards him.

17

Rain continued for some time, gradually growing lighter. She sat, Daniel on her lap, Jack gone to explore the strange new world outside. Joy and relief had dimmed. Was this another brief prelude to further destruction? When would it end, would it ever end? She remembered the joyful chorus after Daniel's birth. Then the face in the window, the horror, and now this catastrophic quake. Was she the only one left alive? The thought chilled her.

No, there would be others ... there must be others ... She seized the radio – static. Feverishly she turned the dials, nothing, nothing! It doesn't mean I'm the only one ... it doesn't mean I'm the only one, she told herself. Seeking to harness flooding emotions, she breathed deeply. The antenna would be down ... broadcasting stations destroyed ... she told herself. Anyway, she wasn't seeking government forces. Surely, somewhere, someone like her had survived? Images remained to taunt her. The devastation of the mountains, no one could survive that! But perhaps other places ...? A thread of hope flickered in the darkness. When Daniel was older, she'd go search!

Jack returned, tail wagging, depositing an offering on the kitchen floor, warm nose prodding. Jack was a comfort, but she needed her own kind. Tears fell freely as she petted his ears, it didn't matter, there was no one to see.

The vegetable plot lay under a pile of rocks and snapped branches, thankfully nothing too heavy. The carrots and root veg might survive, but the rest were destroyed. Only around the pump was there life, dandelions and a few sprouting nettles. She sighed. At least there was Jack's squirrel tonight, a welcome change from dried elk meat. Tonight, it was cool, she'd sleep in her own bed. Her heart lifted a little at the thought.

☙☙☙

Vince stepped forward.

"Don't be scared Rat, it's only me ... You look about to pee your pants!" Vince laughed sarcastically. He was walking! Was this Vince or some illusion? Was it a trick?

"You're learning to man up, finally growing some balls," he chaffed. This had to be Vince. Throwing caution to the wind, Rat ran to embrace him.

"Hey! Don't get soft on me." Vince pushed him away, but not before Rat glimpsed the tear gleaming. Even Vince could be moved it seemed. The sphere pulsed and careened skyward.

"Come on, it's gone now, you yellow livered chickens!" Vince's

131

voice boomed out. It took a while before the others were convinced. Rat gazed at Vince's leg, no bandage, no gangrene, just sound healthy flesh.

"Your leg ..." Rat muttered. "What happened to your leg?"

"Didn't much like the idea of you trying to cut it off. healed up in an instant ... He just touched it ..." Vince's voice trailed off. "Look, I don't get it myself. One minute I'm being swallowed up in the earth and the next I'm in this globe of light with this being ... I can't explain it. But, he said no guns, OK? No more killing, not even the animals. The government forces are gone. We're free, man!" Vince broke into a grin, clapping Rat on the shoulder. "You hear that guys? We're free!"

Figures emerged, hesitant at first, then more confident. Smiles burst forth, then laughter, sheer all enveloping laughter, till tears flowed and they jumped and yelled and clasped each other in jubilant embrace.

The sun was setting as they settled for the night, heady rejoicing reverting to the need to cover ground. There'd been no sign of the horses, they'd brought little in the way of food and, minus the guns (buried where they should have been entombed) hunting was not an option. They'd seen no sign of animals, their numbers decimated by draught, contaminated water and now the quake. Their hopes lay in the farm, if they could find it in this changed environment. The mountains were vanquished, replaced by hill size mounds of debris. No paths remained, they had no idea where they were, only the general direction of the sun. What they'd find, even if they got there, they didn't know. Only trees and bushes, with their deep rooting systems, seemed to have survived the intense heat.

Water now lurked in every gully, slowly sinking into the hard ground. In some places shallow, lifeless, lakes had appeared out of nowhere. It was a strange new world they'd inherited.

Vince sat to one side seeking solitude. Rat hesitated, then flopped down beside him. Vince had not been forthcoming about his experience, resisting all enquiries. He raised irritated eyebrows at the intruder.

"Can't a man get some peace, damn it!" he flared.

"Not till you tell me what happened," Rat said determinedly.

"I told you already."

"Not enough."

"What do you want from me!"

"The truth – details. The alien, what did it look like?"

"It weren't no alien. Who'd you think I am? Bart?"

"Then what? What else could heal your leg like that? And that thing we saw, was it a spaceship or its body?"

"Damned if I know! All I can tell you was, it didn't have tentacles, or big green eyes."

"It looked like a man?"

Vince nodded, turning his back as he lay down to sleep. That was all he'd get for the moment Rat figured.

Dawn broke, sunrise rung in by flocks of birds once more circling the heavens. They'd survived better than their earth bound cousins. Rat noticed a dark green blot towards the horizon. Most trees had lost their leaves in the drought, the remainder shrivelled and yellowed. This area alone retained its vibrant hue. It had to be the redwoods, giant sentinels of time whose roots dug deep, deep down in the earth. Redwoods sheltering the farm ... yes, that was it, that had to be it!

Stomachs growling, they trudged on, enjoying blue skies and a refreshing breeze. The weather seemed back to normal, better than normal. The intense heat was vanquished, and heavy rains brought life back to the parched earth.

Mid-morning, they came across an old riverbed. Receding watermarks, tinged with crimson flushes, edged its side. Decomposing bodies of fish and small rodents lined its inner recesses. Saddened, Rat recalled the pretty, bubbling waterway they'd crossed on his last visit.

"It's all gonna come back." The voice startled him, an odd statement from Vince?

"He said it would ..." Vince mumbled picking up the pace. Rat looked up, chasing after.

"There's more, isn't there? What else did it say?"

"Not it, he! I keep telling you it weren't no alien!"

"What did <u>he</u> say?"

"He said it'd all be OK! Alright! I say one thing and you all start pestering me." Vince stomped off. Clearly there was more to the story. Rat would have to wheedle it out bit by bit. What was Vince hiding?

� ϒϒϒ

The sun was well up. Only Jack's scratching at the door had woken her. Even Daniel had slept through. She watched him nuzzle his pillow before picking him up to nurse. Jack barked, heading off for his morning exploration. She gazed out of the window as Daniel devoured his breakfast. Perhaps she'd take a walk? Her stomach growled, but she was sick of elk. The stewed squirrel had been delicious with its nettle and dandelion garnish. Perhaps there were things growing by the lake? In her heart she knew it was not just the thought of forage. It was that perhaps, just perhaps, there might be someone ... someone alone like her.

Carrion birds took flight as she neared her destination. Debris was everywhere, a landslide having devoured most of the area. The "lake" was discernable only by the smell of dead and rotting carcasses. Puddles remained, red and putrid, slime coating their edges. No frogs jumped; no animals flitted away, only buzzards feasted on grim remains. She turned away from the stench. It must have happened before the earthquake; these creatures were decomposing. Thank God for Dan's pump. She imagined being without it in the heat. These animals must have died a slow and agonizing death.

Calling Jack away from the decomposing meat, she returned to the house. Desperate for some sign of life she soon set off again. "The mound" no longer sported its luxuriant growth of flowers and foliage but had fared better than the lake. She remembered the leaky garden tap. Clusters of dock and nettle still waved shrivelled heads around it. She cut them carefully, hands wrapped in her T-shirt. They'd grow back if she left the roots. She turned the tap a little more to encourage surviving plants. Jack was sniffing eagerly at a hole. Rabbits perhaps? She'd not brought the rifle ... Jack leapt back howling, blood smearing his nose as a rat emerged. She jumped aside, watching it scamper off. Where there were rats there was food. Stowing her forage in the backpack, she loosened the earth. Jack watched her efforts.

The search was rewarded with a half-decomposed shopping bag. The staples were no longer edible, but the cans remained intact – beans and corned beef. She laughed with pleasure. She'd feast tonight! She scoured the mound for other rat holes but was disappointed.

☙☙☙

Shadows lengthened as they approached the farm. The heat had taken less toll here, perhaps the shading trees? All was as he remembered it, a little drier, a little paler, but much the same. The door was open. He heard laughter. Annie appeared, tummy huge and rotund, a basket and peg bag cradled under her arm. She rushed to greet them; enthusiastic hugs curtailed as she caught close sight of them.

"What the hell happened? God, you stink!"

"What kind of a greeting is that Annie?" Rat countered.

"If you knew what we've been through you'd be glad we're still alive!" one of the men yelled.

"I am glad, I am! But boy you smell! Go use the pump and I'll see if I can find any decent clothes for you, you look like you've been through a war!"

"We have," Vince confirmed.

"Not to mention an earthquake," someone added. Bart issued forth.

"What the hell?" Bart's smile extended to a huge grin as, less picky than Annie, he opened his arms to envelope them in one of his renowned bear hugs.

"Don't you dare Bart!" Annie flashed. "Can't you see they're filthy! You think I got nothing better to do than wash clothes!" Bart lowered his arms. It was clear to see who ruled the roost.

"Come on guys, let's hit the pump," Rat intervened. Bart walked along with them while Annie proceeded to recover the laundry, muttering about men and dirty clothes.

"What happened to you guys after we left?" Bart asked. "We've been worried about you."

"Annie didn't seem too anxious," Rat parried.

"That's just her way, you know how she is. We saw the quake. Never seen anything like that in my life ... It was like when California got it, but different. Figured if you were at the lodge there was no way ..." he trailed off.

"We'd already left, though we were still caught up in it."

"Then how?"

"Blowed if I know. It's a long story. Do you guys have any food? We haven't eaten properly in days."

"Food? Sure, plenty and more in the fields."

"I noticed you guys have fresh water."

"Yeah, it dried up a bit in the hot spell, but it's all filled up now. Never saw weather like that this far north or anywhere for that matter."

"Me neither."

"Look I'll go rustle up some food while you clean up. Bacon and eggs alright?"

"You bet, but we can't kill animals anymore." Bart looked quizzical. "It's a long story."

"Well this one's been dead a good while," Bart laughed. "I'll go get started."

Stomachs full, they sat around the table clad in blankets, Bill and Lenny joining them, from the fields. Annie had relented and added fried potatoes and veg to the spread along with fresh bread.

"You've become quite the cook, Annie," Rat complimented.

"Well not much else I can do ... Baby's so big now." Bart

grabbed her hand in passing, pulling her towards him affectionately. "Now you leave off, you big bear!" she hissed. "This is all
your fault!" she gestured to her expanded girth.

"You weren't quibbling at the time as I remember!" Bart retaliated with a wink. She flicked the dish towel at him, but Rat
noted the tender look in her eye. His thoughts turned to Emmie ...

"Penny for them?" Bill asked.

Rat chuckled. "You'd need more than a penny!"

"So, you guys gonna fill us in on what happened? I've been
hearing all kinds of stuff but can't make head nor tail of it."

"A lot of it we don't understand ourselves. We've more questions than answers." Rat began ...

"See, I told you there was aliens," Bart burst in with a gleeful
look at Annie.

"It weren't no bloody alien!" Vince cut him off.

"Why shouldn't aliens look like us? Why'd they need to have
big green heads or something?"

"Oh, have it your own way!" Vince swore, loud and colourful.
Tossing the chair aside he pushed from the table slamming the
door behind him.

"Now look what you've done Bart!" Rat exploded. Bart looked
sheepish.

"Didn't mean no hurt ..." he mumbled. "How was I to know ..."

"I'd better go after him. He's been weird ever since the quake."

Vince hadn't gone far, just to the corner of the barn. He appeared to have collapsed. Rat ran forward, then stopped, just in
time. Vince was weeping. Heaving such heartrending sobs, it
pained Rat to hear him. Hesitant, Rat edged forward, sensing
the fragility of the situation. Vince could be dangerous.

"Vince ..." Rat whispered.

"Go the hell away!" Vince snarled. Rat recalled his one and
only encounter with a mountain lion, only then he'd had his
gun ... He should retreat. He remembered what Pete said of
Chad ... the bear with a thorn he won't let you draw. Vince was

in pain alright, but did he dare?

"Talk to me Vince. It's gonna tear you up inside if you don't let it out."

"Why should you care?"

"I don't know. I just do. I didn't leave you at the lodge and I'm not leaving now."

"I'm warning you!" Vince turned, tears negating the savage glare.

"What you gonna do Vince, kill me too?" A strange half grin appeared.

"I ain't got a gun." Something snapped. Seizing the opportunity Rat sat down, resting a tentative arm on his shoulder. Vince shoved it away.

"Don't push your luck man," but again the glimpse of a smile. "I'm OK, now." Vince went to get up. Rat restrained him.

"Not till you tell me what's eating you." Vince looked reprehensively at the hand on his arm and for a moment all hung in the balance. Rat swallowed hard. Vince had always scared him.

"Tell me Vince."

"You gonna spread it around?" Rat heaved a sigh of relief.

"Just between us man. I swear on Emmie's body, just us." Vince patted his hand.

"You can't swear no better than that Rat."

"So, it has something to do with the aliens, right?" Rat bit his tongue. Stupid, stupid idiot, he berated himself, but Vince stayed calm.

"Told you it wasn't an alien." Rat bit his lip, feeling silence the best option.

"So ..." he ventured after a while.

"So, I wasn't meant to be rescued along with you guys."

"Then they did save us!" It burst forth.

"Of course they did! How the hell you think you got out of that alive!" Rat pressed his mouth closed.

"But it was different for me ..." silence reigned, followed by the faintest whisper, "They weren't meant to save me."

"But?" with an effort Rat restrained himself.

"It was Chad, Chad damn well pleaded for me ..." Vince's voice broke and the tears rushed down again.

"Chad ..." Rat breathed, "but Chad's ..."

"Yeah, I know, Chad's damned well dead! ... But he ain't dead I tell you ... I saw him. He was there, begging them ... said it wasn't my fault, asked them to give me a chance ... That's when he touched my leg ..."

"Chad?" This was getting weirder.

"No, not Chad, you imbecile!"

"Then who?"

"Some kind of ... like a ... like a celestial warrior."

Rat's expression changed to incredulity. "You were hallucinating."

Vince pointed to his leg. "Is this a hallucination?"

"What makes you think it wasn't an alien. I mean did it have wings or a halo or something?" Rat's smirk vanished as Vince grabbed his throat.

"You mocking me?"

"No way Vince," Rat felt the blood drain from his face.

"That's why I didn't want to tell no one." Vince loosened his grip tossing Rat to one side.

"I'm sorry, Vince." Rat regarded him warily. "It's just ... Why would you think that?"

"D'know, I just knew it somehow. Weren't nothing like in pictures. This guy was pure power. Almost shit myself!" Vince nudged Rat's shoulder in reference to Rat's encounter.

"So, you think these things are ...?" Rat was being careful. Handling Vince was like holding a stick of dynamite in your hand.

"I don't think, I know it. And if it hadn't been for Chad, I'd ..." emotions rolled in again. "But they gave me the chance and I took it. Boy, did I take it! That was when he said no more guns. I was shaking in my boots ... don't know what was worse, being sucked in by the quake or that guy. I felt like an ant."

"Was it big?"

"He," Vince emphasized the word, "wasn't that much bigger

than me but the power that came off him!" Rat recalled the bolt that incinerated the beast.

"So listen, you swore, right?"

"Yes, I swore. I won't tell anyone." Vince extended a shaky arm over Rat's shoulder in a rare gesture of comradery.

"I know, I know."

Rat refrained from adding, even had he not sworn, no way was he going to recount this story to anyone. He needed to figure things out. Vince must be mistaken, but what about Chad? Vince would never make that up, he and Chad had been too close ...

18

Rat looked up from tending the plot. A man was approaching. His first reaction was to grab his rifle, but the guns were gone. Then he remembered, Bill had told him of an elderly friend of Pete's who lived in these parts. This had to be him, he too must have survived. Besides, the alien, or whatever it was, said it was safe now, no more troops. He stood up warily, surveying the bent figure in drab clothes and old straw hat.

"Don't worry, it's only me – Tom," the figure said, as if Rat would know him.

"Are you Pete's friend?"

"Sure am! How's it going? See your crops survived alright."

"Pretty much. You should see the state of most of the land."

"Bound to be, but it'll grow back, you know how nature is. We've most of the summer ahead. That rain will sprout the seeds ... There's always seeds you know." The man strolled closer. Taking a seat on a nearby rock he motioned Rat to join him. "I got some good stuff," he patted his flask.

"I don't ..."

"It's not alcohol," he smirked.

"So, what about you Rat, how are you doing?" Rat was startled. How come he knew his name? Picking up on his expression he continued. "Pete talked a lot about you ... Said you'd been through some pretty bad stuff?" Rat nodded, so that was it. It was comforting to know Pete had thought of him.

"Yeah, I wish he was here, it would be great to talk with him just now. No one could figure what happened to them ... they just vanished!" Rat looked away, couldn't release the floodgates. It was too much for him sometimes. All he'd ever wanted was to settle in the woods with Emmie and see his child safely into the world ...

"It hangs heavy on you, don't it?" Rat said nothing. "I'm not Pete, but you can talk to me if you want."

"You wouldn't understand."

"Try me. I ain't such an old codger as I look." Rat was reminded of Vince. Was he being the same? It all came bursting out, the pain, the confusion, the broken, aching, heart.

"I don't want to live anymore," he finished. "I want to die and be with Emmie, but I can't, the guys depend on me. I'm trapped, don't you see, I'm trapped!" The old man draped an arm around his shoulder.

"You've had to carry so much, but the worst is over. Things will get better. I promise you they will. He held Rat at arm's length. The arms, the eyes, were a comfort, immensely soothing. Rat recalled his grandfather, his strength, good humour and integrity. He was part of the reason Rat was who he was today.

"You have hidden strength, Rat. What do you think has seen you through all this time? One day the joy will come back, just like the seeds. It'll start to grow, slowly at first, then as the sun and rain tend it, over time it will grow high and strong. See the redwoods? It'll grow like them, tall and resilient, sheltering all beneath. You're like those trees Rat, you shelter, you bring hope and life. You see your weakness, others see your strength. I need to go now, but remember what I said. Keep looking at those redwoods, OK?" Rat nodded, comforted. The old man stood up, walked a few steps then turned.

"And don't worry about Pete and the others, they're all fine." He winked as an odd glow suffused him. As Rat staggered back in confusion, it erupted to a sphere of glowing particles encircling and transforming. He glimpsed a being so magnificent, so potent he fell to his knees in terror as it zoomed into the heavens.

Rat crouched shaking. What the hell just happened? Was he going crazy? No, it was real. He remembered the feel of the arms, the timeless eyes. What the hell was that? Friend or not, for sure it was no man!

"You OK, Rat? You look a bit shaken?" Annie asked as he came in for the evening meal.

"I'm fine Annie, just need to rest up a bit."

"Not used to working the fields?" Bart joked.

"Guess not," Rat replied, keeping it light. Vince looked up, not so easily fooled.

"Hope you're not coming down with something," Annie continued, spooning a ladle of food on his plate.

"No, I'll be fine Annie. "I just need some chill time."

"You and me both!" Bart quipped. Attention diverted as Annie bashed him with the label, dripping gravy down his cheek. He retaliated, grabbing her onto his lap and placing a stew flavoured kiss on her mouth. She shrieked with laughter, pushing him away. It was strange to Rat, this laughter. It brought too many memories. He slid from the table.

"I need some air ..." he excused himself. Outside he took deep breaths of cool evening mist. He was happy for Annie, glad she'd found someone to make her laugh, but it was too painful to watch sometimes ...

"Hypocrite!" A voice came from behind. He turned to see Vince propped against the porch rail. "Too proud to take your own medicine, I see."

"It's no secret, Vince, I find it hard, that's all ..."

"Bart and Annie?"

"Yeah."

"But there was something before that, and don't go telling me you're tired, because I won't believe you. You may be skinny as a rail, but you've always been able to keep up with the best of us."

"I don't want to talk about it."

"'Fraid I'll laugh at you?"

Rat smirked. That hit close to home. "OK ... I met Tom, that old friend of Pete's Bill told us about."

Vince nodded. "And?"

Rat's voice quivered, "Well, he was no friend of Pete's, least ways he wasn't human ..." Vince let out his breath in a long low whistle.

"Was he ..."

"Look, I don't know what it was. He looked like an old farmer. We were talking a long time. He said ... some stuff. Then he said he had to go, an' he started to glow. These lights started spinning all around him and he was gone, like a rocket!"

"One of Bart's aliens?" The tone was caustic.

"No ... I don't know what it was ... I just caught a glimpse before it took off. It sure wasn't an old man."

Vince laughed. "No way, not if you saw what I saw." He propped an arm round Rat's shoulders, caught himself and withdrew.

"Look Rat, I won't tell no one, but maybe you should. What did he say anyway? Bet he didn't say, you deserve to be dead, but we're giving you one last chance?" Rat shook his head. "No, thought not. So, come on, out with it."

"It was personal stuff, between me and him."

"Couldn't get more personal than what I told you."

Rat smiled. "No, guess not, but look, this I'll tell you. He said Pete, Liz, and all, they're fine, and he said it's all going to be OK. He talked a lot about seeds and how it will all come back ... and ... and ... he said one day I'd laugh again ... like Bart and Annie," he added sheepishly.

"Sure you will man, sure you will, I believe it."

"But not without Emmie ... how can I be happy without Emmie?" Vince sobered.

"Look don't go getting any crazy ideas. Just 'cos I saw Chad doesn't mean Emmie's around too. Don't do anything stupid. We need you, Rat. Somehow it'll all work out, sooner or later, like it did for Annie."

Rat stared at the bookshelf. Finally, he took it down, and, stuffing it under his arm, walked up to sit beneath the redwoods. He gazed down at the old book remembering … Perhaps there were other clues, things that would help him understand what was going on. He searched for the passage Pete had shown him. He knew it was at the very end somewhere, but where? He was about to give up, idly flipping pages when something caught his eye, "and the third part of the sea became blood." Blood? His mind flashed to the red rimmed creak, the pink tinge of the well water, not blood, but sure looked like it. He read on, read of a star, of poisoned waters, of darkness and, there it was, the passage …

Somehow, hidden in the book, was a map for his time. Its source he didn't know or care, he just wanted to know what would happen. Pete had talked of a happy ending …

Much of the next passages he couldn't understand, but one part was clear – an army of two hundred, thousand, thousand! 200 million? He did it over in his head. War on a huge scale, war with horsemen involved – a war that decimated half the world's population? He didn't have the figures, but from what they'd heard via the radio it fitted … He delved into the next chapters, but nothing made sense, only that the word "messenger" was used again and again. "Messengers" and the "spacemen" they'd encountered must be one the same. He remembered Pete's words, "Well I guess you could call them aliens, makes no difference."

A voice rang out close at hand. "There you are, Rat, been looking for you everywhere. Annie was worried you'd come down sick or something."

"I'm fine, just fine, Bill. She's probably worried because of last night."

"Well, you been acting strange of late." Bill glanced down at the book. "Didn't have you down as a Bible man!" He chuckled.

"I'm not. Just looking for answers."

"Pete was always studying it of an evening. Tried to get me to join in, but you know me."

"He showed me and Chad a passage once about these weird insect things that were attacking the soldiers," Rat explained.

"Insect things?" Clearly Bill had heard nothing of their story.

"You missed a lot of stuff tucked away here. You can be glad you did. It's not important now ... Tell me, did you ever meet Pete's friend, the one up in the woods?"

"I met him once. It was him who told me how to make mulch for the crops. Said there'd be a drought and sure enough he was right. Amazing these old farmers, how the hell do they know this stuff?" Rat was about to blurt out the truth but thought better of it.

"What about Pete?"

"Oh, Pete saw him quite often. They used to hang out together sometimes, a 'fellow believer' and all that. He was always talking about stuff he'd said. Apparently, Tom and Pete's father were friends. Went back years, those guys. Sofia was friends with him too, but I only ever met him the once."

"I'd forgotten about Sofia. Did she ever recover?"

"Pretty much, except for the angel thing ... She said Pete's friend was her angel. That she'd go talk with him down by the redwoods. Can you imagine that? Her angel?" He laughed. "It seemed to calm her, so Pete said to let it be, there are worse things."

"So, Pete didn't think he was an angel?" Bill glared at Rat.

"Look Pete was a bit weird; I'll give you that, but he wasn't crazy! What put that idea in your head?"

"Nothing? I just wondered." Bill gave Rat an odd glance.

"We'd better get back or Annie will have my guts for garters!" Bill moved away eager to end the conversation.

"Look Vince, I never told you this," Rat ventured. "You remember when Chad and I brought that woman up here, the one from the camp?"

"The crazy bitch?" Rat nodded.

145

"Well, we got talking with Pete and ..." Rat paused scuffing dirt with his boot.

"And ..."

"Well, he didn't seem surprised about those insect-man thingies." Vince looked up. "He read us this passage about them," Rat continued.

"Seriously? How?"

"Don't ask me."

Vince peered sideways. "There's more right?"

"You bet. I checked it out and there's tons of stuff – the red tide, the war, poisoned water ... probably more, I haven't got it all figured out yet."

"Where?"

"Here ..." Hesitantly Rat pulled the book out of his pack. Vince began to laugh, loud and long.

"OK, OK, Vince, maybe I shouldn't have told you, but look for yourself, it's all there."

"Oh, I believe you," Vince chuckled. "I wasn't laughing 'cos of that. I was laughing because it took you so long to catch on. I told you that guy was some kind of angel."

"Angel, messenger, spaceman, what does it matter? They probably just called them that back then." Vince shook his head still chuckling.

"Rat, you think too much, you know that."

"So, you think there's a God of some sort? That all this is true?" He pounded his forefinger on the book.

"I don't know Rat. I don't know anything anymore. I just know I got a second chance and I'm gonna go with that. Celestial beings, aliens, or whatever, the important thing is they're benign. They ain't going to wipe us out or anything. Hey man, we got the whole earth to ourselves!"

"I don't think so, there have to be others. Hell, we're going to have a hard time repopulating with just Annie!" Vince erupted into laughter.

"I sure as hell don't fancy that one! ... Look Rat, just take it one day at a time, OK? I wouldn't mind a look at that book though.

Where did it say about those weird insect things?"

"Here, right near the back." Rat showed him the dog-eared page. "There's a small one on the bookcase you could take if you want, I need to figure this one out."

"I'll do that, but don't go figuring too much!"

"I just want to know who they are ... and ..."

"And?"

"And if maybe they know about Emmie ..." Rat whispered. Vince set an awkward arm round his shoulders, unused to the role of comforter.

"Maybe you should ask ... if we see any of them again that is. Meanwhile, don't think of doing anything stupid, there's few enough of us as is, an' you got talents. We're going to need a lot building, especially with this repopulation stuff." Vince grinned. He was beginning to change, Rat realized, slowly, slowly, the hate and bitterness was starting to drain away.

19

Rat paused his digging. They were hoping for a second, late autumn, crop. Several bouts of rain had loosened the soil, the weather was good, crops growing fast. Some had a hard time adapting to the slow pace of working the land, but for Rat it was balm to an aching soul. He loved to work the soil, to watch things spring back to life.

He wiped the sweat from his brow, taking in the quiet ease of nature. He was needed less and less these days. Life had ceased to be a day to day struggle for survival. With many hands the work was becoming easier, Bill slowly educating the men in the art of farming. A cooling breeze spread across the land bringing with it the sound of singing. It couldn't be, but no bird sounded that way? Plunging his shovel into the earth, he made towards the voices.

As he approached it drew clearer, male voices raised in some form of hymns or joyful praises. Through the trees, he glimpsed a strange procession, a group of men in their teens or early twenties leading pack ponies, a young woman on the arm of the leading man. Pushing through sprouting undergrowth, he came out onto an old Indian pathway.

"Hello there stranger!" The leader called out. "Didn't know there was anyone around these parts."

"Who, who are you guys?" Rat stuttered amazed.

"Name's John." He held out his hand. "And this is my wife Ellen."

"Er ... Pleased to meet you," Rat stammered, taken aback by the formal greeting, neat clothes and general scrubbed demeanour, like something out of a time capsule.

"But I mean, where did you come from? Who are you?"

"We've been holding up a while, quite a while ..." He grinned. "Let's just say we didn't much care for what was happening in the world, and we'd had a place prepared for years ...?" He looked teasingly at Rat.

"Mormons ... you're Mormons?"

"You're close," John chuckled. "We're a split off group, but we picked up on their survival refuge doctrines and, from the state of things, I'm glad of that. Must have been bad out here?"

"You can say that again!"

"So, are you the only one, or are there others? You can come with us if you want, we're heading west."

"Not much left out west, if I'm not mistaken."

John laughed. "Oh, but we're heading very far west." There were chuckles behind him. "Right across the Pacific in fact, if we can find a suitable vessel."

"But why?"

John smiled. "We got a commission you might say." One of the younger men chuckled, silenced by a stern look from John, Rat looked questioningly.

"You see, we were visited by a messenger," John continued. "You don't seem surprised?"

"Nothing surprises me these days. So, what did it say?"

"He told us about the far east, China in particular. There are

148

whole regions decimated out there. The cities are gone, but many villages remain almost intact. The men went off to war and never returned."

"Whole villages without a guy over the age of ten!" the youngster interrupted.

"So we're going to help," John cut in quickly.

Rat smiled, "So let me guess, you guys are single, right?"

"Except for me." Rat's smile turned to a grin.

"Well that sure beats working the land."

"Oh, don't get us wrong, we're going to work, probably work hard. There'll be children, kids who need a father, women who need help to plant and sow, old folk who need taking care of, it won't be all fun and games."

"So are you like the leader, or are you ..."

"If John wants to take another wife he can," Ellen looked up adoringly. "He's a good man. It would be selfish to keep him to myself if others are in need. It talks about it in the Old Testament, how many women will share one man."

"W ... Wow!" Rat stammered, taking mental note. He could understand the motivation for the young guys, but this lady ...

"So," John said, "what do you think? Want to join us? ... You don't have to share our beliefs," he chuckled.

"Not me, I'm staying here, but you could ask the others. We've got more hands than we need and some of the guys are kind of restless."

That evening was a celebration of life, of new beginnings. It had been a long, long time since they had interacted with anyone outside their group and these young folks, full of life and expectations, were like a breath of fresh air. They sat round a campfire enjoying the warm summer evening, chatting and playing guitar. They had entered their underground refuge back when the camps first began, being prime candidates for internment, remaining till "the visitation" announced it was time to go "replenish the earth". The young men's commission was part of that, but most were simply setting out in small groups to reclaim the land.

"Any around here?" Rat asked.

"No, not close. Don't think you'll have neighbours anytime soon." Pity Rat thought. How good it felt to be together with others, and he liked these well-mannered young men with their humour and free open spirits. He said little of the things they'd been through (though some did) not wishing to dampen their outlook.

"So, you sure you don't want to come Rat?" John asked as the evening came to a close. "You fit well with us."

"No, not me, I like you guys, but I belong here."

"Did you lose someone?" Rat nodded. "Your wife?"

"We weren't married, but I loved her ... still do. We were having a child ..." John clasped his arm.

"That's hard, very hard. Perhaps if you find someone who lost a loved one too, you could console each other?"

"I tried, but it doesn't work."

"Perhaps it's too early, these things take time."

"So everyone tells me."

"Well, if you change your mind come join us."

Rat laughed. "Like I'd be able to find you in the middle of China!"

"The messengers would guide you. You've seen them, haven't you?" Rat nodded.

"Talked to one once, though I didn't know what he was at the time."

"What did he tell you?"

"That it would be OK. That I'd find joy again ..."

"Then you will. God has his times."

The group stayed a couple of days, so the men could have time to decide. Several opted to join them. "Getting boring around here," they said. Rat wasn't sure if it was the thought of adventure or women that stirred them to go. It had been a long time for them all ...

The last evening Vince came to sit beside him as he watched

the dwindling fire.

"Been wanting to talk with you." Rat looked up. "Don't tell me you want to join up with those guys!" Rat joked. Vince smiled, but his tone was serious.

"Matter of fact I do." Rat was incredulous. "Now hear me out Rat. You know I ain't no farmer, and these guys are still wet behind the ears. What'll they do when supplies run low, if they can't find a boat, or someone to sail it. I know they say, 'God will supply'. Maybe he will, but they could use someone a bit more practical."

"Seemed pretty practical to me."

"They ain't seen nothing yet, wait till they get a whiff of the carnage, till they see what's out there ... whatever is out there. Besides," he joked, "I've always had a thing for Orientals. Maybe I'll find one to help me settle, raise some kids." Rat laughed.

"Can't quite see you in that role, Vince."

"Maybe not, but it might happen. If not, maybe I'll find one of those villages with no men and make the rounds, help repopulate the earth!"

"Now that I could see!" They laughed together, voices carrying on the night breeze.

"If that's what you want, go for it Vince. Maybe you're right. You could make a new start, a new life."

"That's what I was thinking, an' I think being with them might keep me in line."

"That or drive you crazy!"

"Well, maybe I should learn about that stuff. I'm on probation, right? And they don't seem too holier than thou to me." Rat had to admit they didn't. Perhaps Vince was right.

"What about you Rat, you staying here?"

"Yeah, I guess."

"You don't have to. The guys will be fine on their own now."

"I know. I just feel bound to this place, at least for a while, until I can get some answers."

"Don't wait too long Rat, life can pass you by."

"I'll try not to, but it's hard to let her go."

"Some folks are like that. It was like that for Chad."

"Yes, I wonder if they're together now."

"I hope they are Rat, maybe you will be someday too, but meanwhile life goes on."

"Yes, I know Vince."

It was a sad parting. Their lives had been welded together through danger and hardship. They were all more than brothers. Rat clasped each one in turn, finding it hard to let go. Strangely Vince was the toughest. Rat's prior enmity had melted into a hard-knit comradery. He watched as they headed off west, a song picking up on the breeze. It was as if they'd never been, yet the gaps in their fellowship showed like pulled teeth in a gaping jaw.

ꙮꙮꙮ

Morning sun and misty evening rains had resurrected the garden plot. Leafy lettuce and spinach grew from new seed and the first of the carrots and onions lent their taste to elk stew. Pausing to wipe the sweat from her eyes, she squinted into the sunlight. She froze – sure she saw something in the trees. Yes, there it was – a man, bare-chested, black hair long and braided. For a moment their eyes locked, before he sank into the shadows.

"Wait, wait!" she called, but he was gone. Fool! She thought, he could be dangerous, but he hadn't looked dangerous, just inquisitive. Perhaps he was alone like her ...

Days passed, Daniel learnt to roll over, could sit propped up on cushions. The food was growing well, yet she worried about winter. There'd be a little to store, but not like before. The apple trees were crushed, and Dan's crop fields lay untended, half covered in debris. There were blackcurrant and raspberry canes growing on the "the mound" as she called it, but it wouldn't be like last autumn and she'd seen barely a sign of animal life. Even squirrels and rabbits seemed in short supply. She set the thought aside. Today the sun was shining, a breeze rustled the leaves, and everything felt possible.

Bringing in freshly washed sheets, she absorbed the smell of sunshine bathed in the cotton. Bored of coaxing food from the earth and meeting baby Daniel's needs, she'd decided on a little spring cleaning.

Daniel gurgled happily in his nest of pillows as she set to making the bed. She'd moved back to the son's room, making it her own – too many memories downstairs. Daniel was her life now, her sole companion aside from Jack. Occasionally she'd glimpsed the stranger. Whether it was the same man, she couldn't tell, only that she was not entirely alone.

20

Annie's time was growing near. Rat was concerned. He'd learned all he could before, from the women in the camp, but he'd thought they'd be there when the time came. Instead, like Emmie, they lay where the roots of the mountains had eased their gentle slopes, somewhere beneath the debris. No one else had any idea, apart from Annie herself. He knew she was scared. Things could go wrong ... He was mulling over an idea. Chad said Ma learned herbal medicines from the Native Americans. Perhaps they could help ... if they were still alive? He put the idea to Bart who was not keen on Rat going.

"It's not like before Bart. No more troopers – remember?"

"Maybe, but that doesn't mean no more bad stuff out there. At least take someone with you."

"I'll go faster and safer alone."

"The woodsman, huh?"

"Yeah."

Annie was keen on the idea, another woman, if there were one, with knowledge of these things, would be a God send.

"Let him go Bart," she blustered. "I sure as hell don't want you lumbering around trying to deliver this baby, nor any of the other guys for that matter!"

"Not even ..."

"Rat if it comes to it, but let's hope it don't come to that. Nothing personal Rat."

"Don't worry Annie. I'm no keener on the idea than you."

"What if it comes while you're gone?" Bart voiced his secret fear.

"Let's hope it doesn't. I'll only be gone a day or two. And I think we have a bit of time, right Annie?"

"Yeah well, don't count on it, stick with two days max."

Water would be the best place, Rat reasoned. He was right. Spotting imprints further upstream he tracked through the reviving bracken coming upon signs of foraging. Bending to examine the stems, he caught a swish of leaves behind him. Instinctively he reached for the rifle that was no longer there. Spinning round, he faced a young man, olive skin darkened by the sun, long hair bound back, limbs lithe and lean.

"Good tracking for a white man." He grinned, choosing to ignore Rat's previous threatening gesture.

"I'm sorry, you startled me ..." Rat apologized. The man laughed.

"A bit jumpy? No need. There are no more soldiers. But why are you tracking us. We took nothing from you."

"No, no," Rat answered quickly. "We need your help ... I thought maybe ..." he trailed off. This wasn't going well.

"What kind of help?"

"It's Annie, she's going to have a baby any day and there's only us men ..."

"Only one woman?" he raised an eyebrow. "What happened to the women? A man should take care of his women."

"There were only Ma and Chad's wife and they both died of sickness."

"So, you want one of our women to come and help when the baby is born?"

"Yes."

"Just when the baby is born! We take care of our women!" There was a warning edge to the voice.

154

"Of course."

"OK, we'll send a woman, an <u>old</u> woman."

"Someone who knows about babies. You can come with her ... we have food."

"You have food?" The dark eyes brightened.

"Yes, we'll pay her in food."

"Food is good. So many animals have died, the hunting's no good anymore. If I bring a woman to help, you'll give us food?"

"Yes."

The young man paused with a knowing look.

"If you want a woman, there's one east of here, one of your kind, pretty. We've seen her many times. She has a child. She'd be glad of a man to hunt for her. I'd take her myself, but we have barely enough to feed our own."

A child! A flicker of hope dawned.

"How old is the child?"

"A baby, very small, she carries it on her back like a papoose." Rat's face dropped. The native misread it.

"Babies grow fast. You're at home in the woods and you have food, you'd make a good father. If it's a boy, you can teach him and have more of your own."

"I don't want a woman!" Rat exclaimed. He'd thought, just for a moment, that somehow Emmie was alive, that "they" might have saved her like they had him. The young man moved back, confused. Rat grabbed control of the raw pain, the re-opened wound. Annie needed help.

"Look, I'm sorry. I thought maybe it was my woman ... she died."

"You still want a woman for the baby? Just the baby!" His companion asked anxiously, thinking the food trade might be in jeopardy.

"Yes, let's get going. I'm afraid the baby might come when I'm gone."

"And you'll give us food?"

"Yes, we'll give you food."

They arrived none too soon. Annie's waters had broken that morning. Now she was in heavy labour. There was chaos, Bart predictively running around like a chicken with its head cut off. The woman took charge instantly, shooing the men folk out. Annie grabbed Rat's hand as he departed.

"Thank you, Rat." Eyes, huge with pain, expressed her relief.

Rat went outside. Bart tried to accost him, but he waved him away. "Not now Bart!"

He hadn't expected it to affect him like this. I should be glad for them, he reasoned, should help Bart through his ordeal, but he couldn't. The tiny light of hope, so instantly dashed, had left a pain burning. Circling the barn, he punched into wood and plaster board, skinning his knuckles. It didn't hurt. If he'd had the rifle, he'd have used it. He wanted the pain to end. He'd thought seeing Bart's child born would be balm to his soul, but it wasn't. He hated his jealousy. Knew it wasn't right, but he couldn't help it. Crawling into a stall he collapsed in anguish.

"Rat? Rat? Are you OK?" A face peered from behind the storm lamp. All around was dark. Rat blinked.

"Must have fallen asleep," he muttered. "Annie ... how is she?"

"She's fine. Had a rough time, but she's OK now."

"The child?"

"A healthy boy."

"Bet Bart's full of himself."

"Like an over fed rooster!" Rat cracked a smile. Shadows receded somewhat. "You'd best come eat, 'fore it's all gone."

Rat heaved himself up. "I'll be in in a while."

"I'll save a plate ..."

"OK, do that." He wasn't ready to face the crowd. He wished Chad was there, or even Vince, someone to tell him to pull himself together, to jerk him out of his misery.

"You not going in?" a voice sounded behind him as he lent, brooding, on the fence.

"Just getting some air. I fell asleep in the barn ... had a rough couple of days." Bill was unconvinced.

"Look, I know what you must be feeling, but you need to get in there. Your presence has been missed. Pretty soon Bart is going to come looking."

"I know. I just can't."

"You can. I know you can. If you just see their faces, it will help heal the pain."

"Nothing can heal the pain!" Rat hissed.

"Not entirely, no, but it'll help."

Yielding to pressure Rat headed inside.

The child was a wrinkled mass of peeling skin and tiny sleeping eyelids, offset by a fuzz of Bart's dark hair.

"Annie said they all look like that after they're born," Bart said defensively. "It's cos they've been in the water all that time ... give him a few days ..."

Rat peered down at the tiny form, like a shoot appearing from the earth, still half concealed in its casing. New life! He poked his finger at the scrunched hand, and, in an age-old gesture, it grasped it. The connection was made.

"He's beautiful, Bart," Rat said tapping him on the shoulder. "You take real good care of him."

"I will Rat, I will."

Rat moved towards the table and the waiting bowl of food, struggling to quell feelings striving within ... so small and help-less, so tiny and frail ... yet alive! ... if only ...

No use thinking that, he told himself. He wasn't a father, but he'd be an "uncle". The kid would need a few good uncles given the circumstances. Perhaps Vince was right, maybe he should have gone with them, made a fresh start in a new land, poured his life into someone else ... but how could he step into the future if he couldn't let go of the past? He needed answers.

He knew it was a stupid thing to do, but he was desperate. As he'd thought, no one was there, just the redwoods with their enfolding shadows. He cast himself down against a trunk. Sofia came here to talk, Bill had said, but did "Tom" still come here. Did she call him or something? Did he even want to see him?

157

That was a good question. It had been fine before he knew, but now ...

"Where are you! I need to talk to you!" the words burst forth, spiraling skyward.

Nothing happened. The only answer, a lonely bird cry and the hum of insects. He sat, head in hands. What had he expected? He was supposed to be like the redwoods, strong and protective, but he felt more like a trembling leaf on the breeze.

He didn't hear him come, no rustle of foliage, no footfall. He was just there, gazing down at him. Rat looked up, startled. Pete cracked a smile.

"Is, is it really you?!" Rat stammered. "We thought ... we didn't know what to think ... we looked everywhere! Lisa and the kids are they ..."

"We're all fine Rat, Sofia too, but seems you've been having a hard time here. I can't stay long, but maybe you want to talk about it?" Rat nodded.

"I don't know what to do ..."

"I think you know. You just don't want to do it any more ..."

"Taking care of folks? They don't need me now. Things have changed. There's so much you don't know."

"I know more than you think, and they need you more than you think ... Others too." Rat looked up.

"The native Americans?"

"That's just sharing resources."

Rat looked quizzically. How come Pete knew this stuff? "Someone else?"

"Isn't this other child, the one they told you about, just as vulnerable as Annie's?" Conviction dawned. Bathed in self-absorption, he'd forgotten the woman and her child. They should take her in. Maybe one of the guys might ...

"I'd forgotten, I was so wrapped up in myself ... We can help her, of course we can."

"That's more like the old Rat."

"The old Rat had Chad to keep him in line."

"That's true, but Chad's got other stuff to take care of now."

"Chad ... do you know ... is he ..." he hardly dared ask. How would Pete know anyway?

"Of course he's with Sal. Chad's very special, Ma too."

"Will I ever see him again? Vince said ..."

"Highly unlikely, at least for the present ... him being dead and all." The eyes twinkled.

"And you? Are you dead too? Is that how come you know all this stuff?" Rat looked apprehensive.

"No, I'm not dead Rat, as you can very well see."

"I don't get it. How could Vince see him? He said Chad pleaded for him."

"He did."

"But how?"

"The answer's right in front of you Rat."

"But ..."

"I need to go now, but don't worry. Everything is being set to rights. Some things take longer, but you must believe that. You have autonomy. Your choices make it faster or slower."

"Saving the child will make it faster?"

"What do you think? Try and see ... I need to get going. We've both got stuff to do." With a last squeeze of Rat's shoulder, he rose to his feet. "Be seeing you." His hand rose in farewell as he strolled off among the trees.

Rat stood dumbfounded. "The answer's right in front of you," he'd said. What answer? There was only one he could think of, but that couldn't be true, could it? What did it matter? He had a purpose now, to get the mother and child, a child to play with Brad and Annie's. He wondered if it was a girl or another boy ...

"So, you changed your mind." Rat gazed at their guide. They'd nicknamed him Hawk, for his hooked nose and agility. The eyes twinkled, annoying Rat.

"Can't leave her on her own with a baby, what will she do come winter?!" Hawk seemed unconvinced. Never mind, let him think what he liked.

"You'll take me there?"

"Of course. Wait a few days though and go together." The old woman seemed concerned she oversaw Annie's recovery, or perhaps she just wanted a full belly a while longer.

Rat found his steps wandering back to the redwoods over the next few days. Was he hoping to see Pete again? Had Pete been right all along? Was there a "God"?

"Perhaps you'd find the phrase 'supreme being' easier to swallow." Rat looked up. There was old Tom smiling. "People have the wrong concept you know – same with angels." He chuckled. The sound reverberated through the trees. "How's your experience been so far? Bit of a stretch from Sunday school pictures in white gowns eh?"

"Then you are an ..." Rat choked on the word.

"Messenger rolls off the tongue easier, doesn't have the same connotations."

"Then God ...?"

"You can't conceive him, he's far beyond your understanding ... but he's not an old man with a white beard, nor is he the monster you conceive him to be."

"Then why didn't he stop this, stop Chad dying, and Ma and Emmie and all the others?"

"I might ask you the same. He gave dominion to man. Man, in his pride and ignorance, gave it into the hands of evil."

"But God could have intervened!"

"He did." The voice remained calm and soothing despite Rat's increasing vehemence.

"When?"

"When he came and took your place ..." Understanding dawned.

"You mean?"

"Yes."

"But he didn't stop it! Why wait till now? Why not before?"

"It could only be at the time appointed Rat. Mankind had to run its course, to learn its own inadequacies. Only now can healing come, for mankind and for the earth itself."

"But ..."

It became a daily thing. Rat would sit beneath the trees and they would come, explaining, teaching, envisioning. Slowly Rat began to understand, to accept the impossible. Sometimes it was Tom, sometimes Pete. They never shirked a question, never became annoyed at Rat's frequent outbursts. It all made sense in a new and peculiar way, the past, the future and the role he had yet to play. Slowly, as truth replaced lie, as light replaced darkness, a glimmer of hope returned to his heart. Emmie and his child were safe he was assured. They too had their place in the plan. Even the earth itself would be healed.

The evening before their departure it happened. Drawn toward the redwoods, he heard rippling laughter. He looked for Pete. What he saw was more startling. A young child, chestnut curls glistening in the evening glow as she played, scooping up sticks and earth. She turned towards him beaming, Emmie's smile on her face. "Dadda," she lisped, reaching cubby arms towards him. He ran forward, but she was gone, only her laughter remained, transported a moment on the breeze, then it too dissipated.

Had he really seen her? It was too real to resist. Falling to his knees, head bent to the earth, he cried. Tears of joy and of sorrow, cleansing tears letting go of the past, moving on to the future.

21

The vegetable patch was growing well. Tiny seedlings, sprouted in an old tray, took the place of their cropped ancestors, steadily rotating throughout the summer months. Conversely the weeds seemed to be dying out. She supposed it was the change in weather. Grass and wildflowers had returned in abundance. Trees and bushes sported a green canopy over rubble and decay, fallen trunks and branches curving toward the sky, nourished by roots delving deep in mounds of debris.

Life was good. Yet she was lonely and feared the approach of winter. Perhaps the time had come to move on, to try to find her own kind? Later, when autumn came, she'd go. Daniel would be older, and they'd be strong from summer's bounty. Yes, in the autumn ... She looked toward what was left of the road and the old town, as she had a hundred times before. No one ever came ...

Then one day ... One day, Jack began to bark, darting off toward the old mound.

"Jack! Come back!" What had gotten into that dog? The birds also seemed disturbed, swooping up twittering loudly. Something was going on. Grabbing the rifle, she ran after Jack, slowing as she approached.

Someone was wrestling with the wheel of an old cart, stuck in the debris. The shaggy mop of hair reminded her of Greg, the same colour, but short and more curly, the shoulders too broad. It wasn't Greg, but it was a fellow human being. He didn't look like government ... could he still be dangerous? She remembered her attackers. He turned. Their eyes met. Suddenly, he was rushing towards her. She raised the rifle.

"Emmie! Emmie! It's me you fool!" The rifle dropped, as she stood, frozen. Then he was there, arms around her, drowning her in kisses. "I ... thought you were dead! ... We searched everywhere. I ..."

"Greg, is it you? Is it really you?" She pulled back his head, staring at his face, fuller than she remembered, thin lines now etching mouth and eye corners. "You cut your hair." She laughed inanely, rumpling the untidy locks.

"It was too damn hot!" They kissed again, deep and searching. Words were not enough.

Jack barked, alerting them to muffled cries from the house. She'd forgotten about Daniel ... Dropping arms, she was suddenly distant.

"Daniel ..." Joy turned to ashes. Would he understand? How could he?

"I ... have to get Daniel," she said, voice breaking. He held her still, at arm's length, eyes full of joy, forgetting his redwood visitor.

"Then it was a boy!"

"No Greg, it's not ... I mean ..." How could she break his heart? "It is a boy but ... but he's not yours. Our baby died the day they came, I miscarried." Smile gone, Greg dropped his arms, light fading from his eyes.

"There's someone else ... I'm sorry Emmie. I didn't know. They said you were alone ..."

"I am alone. Alone, except for Jack and Daniel." She nodded towards the dog. The cries were getting louder. "I have to get him," she added determinedly.

Unable to cope with overwhelming emotions, she ran off, leaving Rat standing dismally beside the cart. Was he too late? What had happened to the child's father? How could she have taken up with someone so quickly, while he ... Pain coursed through him. He felt betrayed. Anger surged, followed by jealousy. He'd wanted the child so much, wanted Emmie so much. His heart broke. His child was dead. His "true love" had deserted him for some stranger. He wanted to go, to hide away alone, but he couldn't just abandon them. He strove with his emotions.

The dog bounded back towards him sniffing at the horse and circling his ankles. He reached down to rub its ears. "Best get the cart down to the house," he muttered. "She can't stay here on her own." Jack offered no reply other than a wildly wagging tail.

She was inside nursing the child. He glanced over.

"Healthy looking little guy," he volunteered. He was trying, but it was hard, so hard!

She'd been crying, he could see the tears on her cheeks. He put a gentle hand on her shoulder.

"We have a farm ..." he began awkwardly. "The natives told us you'd need help for the winter. We have food and a place to stay ..."

"I won't give him up Greg!" she hissed.

163

"Of course not! We'll all help take care of him. Bart and Annie have a baby too. We need more children."

"Even if he's not yours?"

"He's a child Emmie. He needs food and a place to live, someone to take care of him." She looked up eyes brimming.

"Thank you, Greg." He remained withdrawn, unsure of himself. Daniel having finished she set him down among his cushions to play. "It's late, you must have come a long way. You'd better bed down here for the night ... There are plenty of beds ..." she added lamely, then bit her tongue. She remembered the kisses, the feel of his arms around her. She'd just closed the door on that, not wanting to be rejected now he knew about Daniel.

"I'll make us some food," she said hustling to the kitchen.

"I brought food. Didn't know how you were off ..." He went to the cart bringing in the bundle of supplies before unhitching the horse. Seeking oblivion in long, thoughtful strokes he rubbed it down. Jack accompanied him, tail wagging constantly.

"Don't worry lad, we'll be taking you too," Greg whispered, as he tickled Jack's upturned belly. What should he do he wondered? His world was upside down. Not in his wildest dreams had he hoped to find Emmie alive. The baby didn't matter, but he couldn't understand how she'd forgotten him so soon. She'd pretended not to know him, taken off and left him to his own devises and the comment about the beds had been pretty clear. Yet, at first, she'd seemed as passionate as he. Perhaps she was angry because he hadn't come for her. He'd told her he'd come. He'd promised. If only he'd not gone back with Chad, perhaps he would have found her. Then again, this place was far from where he'd left her ...

Hesitant he returned inside. She was busy in the kitchen.

"Do you have any water? I need to wash up a bit."

"There's a pump in the yard."

She watched through the kitchen window as he dragged off his shirt. He'd put on muscle and a little more weight since she'd seen him last. It suited him. She noted the scar marring his shoulder as he splashed water over his chest and arms. That hadn't been there before. Perhaps that was why?

He came in dripping, dabbing at the water with his shirt.

"You can use one of Dan's shirts if you want. They're in the draws through there. She pointed.

"It's OK. I'll change when we get back." So, that was the way of it, he thought. Not hard to see, she'd called the child Daniel. This must have been his place, that's why she came here. Pulling on his shirt he began to set the table.

The meal had been almost silent, air thick with unspoken questions.

"What happened to Dan?" Greg ventured, unable to stand the tension any longer.

"He died. He was a wonderful man. I wish you could have met him. I'd never have made it through without his help."

Greg bristled at the warmth in her voice. *Stop it!* He told himself. Why should she not take up with someone? She'd probably thought him dead.

"And Jack here?" he continued. "Was he Dan's dog? Seems to like guys." Jack seemed somehow less endearing than before.

"Jack likes everyone. It was him that first brought me here."

"You didn't come with Dan then?"

"No." There was a finality in the way she said it, like she didn't want to go there. "I'll get the dishes." She rose rapidly. Abruptly she turned, eyes flaring. This was a farce!

"Greg. Please, I can't do this! I can't come if you don't want me anymore!" She turned to run upstairs but he caught her, grabbing her wrist.

"What do you mean I don't want you? Of course I want you! Look, it doesn't matter you took up with Dan, or you had his baby. I need you Emmie, even if you don't care for me right now. The feelings will come back, I know they will ... I thought you were dead. I shouldn't have given up. It's not your fault, it must have been terrible on your own." Emmie stared at him blankly.

"Greg," she muttered, "Daniel's not Dan's child. Dan was an old man. He took me in, I took care of him ... the cancer was already far gone. He was like a father to me, that's why I named Daniel after him … I did think to call him Greg, but I couldn't handle it, it hurt too much."

"Then who was Daniel's father?"

"I don't know!" she turned, burying her face in her hands.

"You don't know!" There was a dangerous edge to Greg's voice.

"I was raped Greg! There were three of them. They took turns … they …"

"Oh Emmie, Emmie!" he folded her to his chest kissing her hair. "It's all my fault! I should have been there for you!"

"You tried Greg. You led them away. It was alright for a while, but then these guys came … they …"

"I should have been there!"

"I found bodies. I thought it was you, but it wasn't, just your clothes."

"A group of vigilantes found me. They didn't know about you. I came as soon as I could, but everything was destroyed."

"You were wounded right? I saw the scar on your shoulder."

"Yes. Then I was too late."

"It's not your fault Greg."

"It is. I should have kept searching."

"You'd probably not have found me anyway. They were taking me in for the reward. It was the quake that saved me. Then later I found I was pregnant. I didn't want the baby. Dan kept trying to convince me to keep it, but I just wanted it to die. He told me it was part of me too, that it would be a comfort when he was gone."

"It's not the child's fault. A child is precious, especially now."

"Yes, he was right. I could never give him up … not even for you." She glared defiantly at him.

"No one's asking you to. We'll take care of him together." Emmie heaved a sigh of infinite relief. "Though I'd kind of like to have some of my own too sometime …" His eyes twinkled, life leaped within, that precious spark she remembered. Humour defused the atmosphere.

"I think that could be arranged … You've put on a bit of muscle since I saw you last ..." She teased, sliding a provocative hand over his shoulder. "I didn't know your hair was this curly though," she quipped, ruffling the spirals at the back of his neck.

"That's why I kept it long." He laughed, sweeping her up in his arms, heading up the stairs.

"Greg, the baby!" He looked around, spotting Dan's old bed in the adjoining room.

"We can keep an eye on him from here."

Clothes were tossed aside in their frantic haste for intimacy, seeking the touch they'd so long been deprived, skin to skin. Passion soared, thrashing, gasping, climaxing in an explosion of pent emotion. Lying breathless she began to laugh.

"What's so funny?"

"We are. There's no one to disturb us, no danger, yet we go at it like rabbits." He brushed a strand of hair from her eyes.

"We have all night Emmie. Hope Daniel is a good sleeper 'cos I'd like to make up for lost time."

"He is, but nice and slow next time, OK?"

"OK. Maybe we should get him to bed first though."

"Good idea."

Daniel seemed intent to spoil the evening's designs. Perhaps it was the tense impatience with which she nursed and rocked him, feeling Greg's caresses, teasing, enticing, tantalizingly real. Perhaps it was perversity at having competition for his attention. The sun had long set, the moon out when he finally succumbed to sleep.

"At last," Greg breathed, "I see there are drawbacks with being a father."

"Do you mind?"

"Mind, how could I mind Emmie? I have you in my arms. It's been so long ... I never hoped ..."

"Yes ... we're together again, despite everything." She stopped his mouth with kisses sliding the open shirt off his shoulders, revelling in the feel of him. He took his time, exploring every remembered crevice in the flickering candlelight.

"You are so beautiful Emmie," he whispered. "I could never

understand what you saw in me."

"Oh Greg, there's so much to you, so much life it just flows out. How could I not love you?" She ran her fingers teasingly down his back, squeezing him hard against her.

"Stop that Emmie," he chuckled. "I want to take this slow, remember everything, every part of you, to reclaim every inch."

Sun beamed down, dispelling early morning mist. The whole world seemed to be celebrating or was it just her heart? She feasted hungry eyes upon him, could hardly believe he was here, lying beside her. She stroked a rebellious curl from his eyes. They opened sleepily.

"I didn't mean to wake you."

"Thought I was dreaming." He reached up, lazily pulling her towards him, lips meeting in reunion, seeking deeper. A noise startled them.

"What was that?" Greg was instantly alert. There it was again.

"It sounds like someone ... knocking?" Greg leaned out to see, retreating with a grin.

"There's someone at the door!" He laughed at the absurdity of the notion. "It's Hawk, the one who told me about you."

"What does he want?"

"Damned if I know." Rummaging for his discarded jeans he headed for the door, followed by Emmie wrapped in a sheet. Rat was greeted with a smirk, as his companion spied Emmie's dishevelled form. It had been so long since she'd seen anyone ...

"You changed your mind, huh?"

"She's my woman ... the one I told you about."

"So, she wasn't dead."

"No."

"Good thing you came." The grin enlarged.

"Yes. Now what did you want?" Rat was getting irritated.

"She's going with you?"

"Yes."

"So, we can use the farm? She won't need it now."

"I guess so. Is that OK, Emmie? ... It's pretty much your farm now, huh?"

168

Emmie nodded. "Dan would like it to be used, but how will you live? You're welcome to my garden patch but …"

"A messenger came. He said no more hunting, not many animals left. He said you have tools here, ploughs. We have men. There's still time for winter crops."

Emmie pulled the sheet tighter, becoming aware of her provocative appearance.

"There's no tools I know of, other than the ones I'm using, certainly not a plough."

"It's in the barn." He waved his hand in its direction. "Just have to get rid of the things on top."

"That's dangerous," Greg intervened. "The whole lot could come down on you. It must be done with care. Look, maybe I can stay a couple of days and help you."

"We have men," he replied proudly.

"Yes, but you might need my skills to shore it up properly. I trained as an engineer before all this."

Hawk looked duly impressed. "OK, thanks." He held out his hand.

Emmie intervened. "It's not stable. You don't even know if the stuff is in there."

"The messenger told us."

"What is all this messenger stuff?" She queried. Greg looked uncomfortable.

"Messengers from the great spirit … like big balls of light! Have you seen them?" Hawk asked.

"I don't understand? Do …"

"Look, it doesn't matter," Greg cut in. "If there's any possibility of there being ploughs in there we should try. I can help them do it safely."

"But Greg, you don't understand …" Emmie looked upset.

"What's the matter Emmie? Why don't you want us to clear the barn?"

"There's … there's a body under there! I … I couldn't bury it."

"Dan?" Greg questioned gently.

"No, not Dan … He was like a monster … I didn't mean to kill

169

him. I was so scared the rifle just went off." She tried to turn, tears welling, but Greg hugged her to him.

"Did he hurt you?"

"No ... he was outside, peering in at me. I was so scared ... His face was covered in these huge sores, like a monster ... I ..."

Greg and Hawk exchanged glances.

"It's alright Emmie. You did the right thing," Greg whispered. "He was probably crazy and almost certainly would have hurt you and the child."

"It was Jack who warned me. He started barking. That's why I had the rifle."

"Seems we owe a lot to Jack one way and another ... Now listen, if there's a body under there it's better we bury it. It may have been an infectious disease that caused the sores. Personally, I think it was probably an after effect of the venom, but better to be on the safe side."

"Venom? What venom?"

"Let's talk about it later, OK? Right now, I'd like to have a look at that debris. Perhaps you could rustle us up some breakfast?" He wasn't sure how much he should tell her, sometimes it was better not to know.

"OK, I'll get the others." Hawk took off towards the trees.

Greg surveyed the earth and lumber encompassing the barn. It would take days, possibly weeks to shift safely, but the collapsed timber could be used to shore up a short tunnel. The far side of the barn might be intact under the deluge? He surveyed the edge, testing the air. He could tell where the body lay concealed ...

A band of five men appeared skirting the kitchen window. Emmie's eyes, long deprived of human contact, took them in greedily. Greg said there were others at the farm including a new baby. How strange to be part of a community again, how precious each one. She took in the long black hair, angular faces, and lean muscular arms, hunters turned farmers. She knew little of their culture, but she'd learn. These might be their closest neighbours. The oppressive regimes were gone forever, but of what was taking their place Greg had been less forthcoming. Probably he didn't know either. New beginnings! Like the old pioneers they'd be farming and settling, hopefully on better terms with the Native Americans than before. They had, it seemed from their numbers, been more adept at survival.

Even with the food Greg brought there was little enough to set before the men. They ate shyly, embarrassed by their hunger. What would Dan have thought if he'd seen this she wondered, looking around the overcrowded table? He'd have taken them in, just as he had her ...

Dan and Bessy, she remembered!

"There's a condition to you living here," she rounded on Hawk. "Dan is buried under the tree out front, him and his wife. No farming there."

"We know these things. We honour the graves of our ancestors." Sadness came to his eyes. "They're gone now. When the mountains fell the old burial grounds sank with them. We'll honour your graves now. This was Dan's place?"

"Yes, he and Bessy lived here. They were good people, the best!" A lump came to her throat.

"Then we'll honour them, keep their graves safe. Maybe their spirits will come help us?"

"Maybe ... I think they'd like it you're here." Hawk smiled.

Emmie spent the day sorting what to bring. Space was limited, and some things she should leave for Hawk and the others. There was so much she needed to ask Greg about the farm, surely more bedding would be a help? What about the herbs and spices, they didn't take up much space?

Work proceeded rapidly. A hole was dug, and the decomposing body dragged into it, Emmie was relieved she didn't have to be party to that. Greg's team contrived to rescue two ploughs (one considerably older that the other) a bunch of other implements, and a large amount of firewood. The ploughs were designed to be dragged behind the smashed, half buried tractor. Still they were small enough to be converted.

At sunset the natives headed off, realizing there was not

enough food for another "feast". Emmie set the table while Greg headed for the pump, this time accepting the use of Dan's shirts, his own being filthy from his labours. It felt strange to relax, to know all was safe.

22

Morning mist enveloped them as they set off, Jack bounding behind, barking excitedly.

"Happy?" Greg asked as he slapped the reins.

"More than happy! Though it'll be strange being with other folks after all this time. The important thing is we'll be together." She smiled and huddled into his arm.

"I noticed a guitar in the back?"

"It was Dan's."

"A memento, or can you play it?"

"Both I guess. I can't play like Dan. He taught me a few songs, but I'm not very good. He used to play in the winter evenings. It helped, like peeking into a forgotten world. Then later, when he was too weak, I played for him."

"It sure would be good to hear some music again ..." his mind drifted back to the group of young men. "Could you play me something?"

"I have Daniel."

"Excuses! I can hold him."

"No, it's OK. He's almost asleep." She felt embarrassed about her newfound skill, also reluctant to pass on her charge. She let it drop. Though wonderful as ever, Greg was different somehow.

She was different.

"Almost there, Greg announced. "See that patch of redwoods up ahead, the tall, dark ones? They border the farm."

"Will they be expecting us?"

"They'll be expecting me, with a woman and child, but they won't know it's you. That'll be a surprise, a good one!"

"You think so?"

"They'll be so happy for me, especially Annie. She'll be glad of another woman about the place too."

"Tell me about Annie. You said her kids were killed in one of the purges, but she's together with someone now and has a new baby?"

"Right. That's why I went to find help for the birth, and found out about you, but Annie ... Well Annie is Annie. She has a tongue like a razor, bosses Bart around something wicked, and Bart's no wimp." He laughed. "Don't mind her though, she has a good heart under it all. It's just, when she saw her kids mown down, something broke inside that can't be fixed." Emmie remembered her own lost child, the tiny body, wrapped in an oily T-shirt and consigned to the oak. A cloud shadowed her features.

"What is it, Emmie?" He paused, pulling in the reins slightly.

"It's just ... just ..." tears welled, choking her voice. Understanding dawned.

"You lost a child too. I wasn't there to see it. I ..."

She nodded, gaining control. "I wasn't strong enough to bury it. I put it in a hollow in this old tree wrapped in your T-shirt. It was the best I could do for her."

"Her? It was a girl then?" Memory flashed of the laughing, chestnut curled toddler. Should he tell her? Would she believe him?

"I thought you were dead, that the T-shirt would somehow lead her to you – stupid I know ... but I felt so despairing ..."

"I don't think it was stupid at all ... it kind of did ..." His voice trailed off. She looked at him expectantly.

"Tell me Greg. You have to tell me!"

He looked away, furtive. "You wouldn't believe me ..."

"I promise, Greg. What happened?"

"So much has happened, Emmie. It's hard to know where to start, what to tell you and what not."

"Just tell me Greg. Tell me all of it, especially anything to do with our child."

"If you haven't lived through it all, how could you believe me?"

"I'd believe because you tell me. Because I trust you."

"OK, I saw her. Not a baby, but a year or so old. She was playing by the redwoods. I only caught a glimpse then she was gone, but she was happy, laughing."

"Greg, she's dead! I put her body in the hole with my own hands. You must have imagined it."

"I said you wouldn't believe me ..." He clicked the reins, picking up the pace again.

Emmie was silent for a while, unwilling to enter that fenced off void in her heart. She remembered Dan and his belief Bessy was watching over them when the pine fell, that she was waiting for him when he was dying. In a way she'd believed it too. It had been comforting to think that way for a while. She cringed as she remembered how she used to sit by the mound where he lay and talk to him about her day. She hadn't really believed, but it had been a source of comfort. Perhaps it was the same with Greg. He thought he'd seen something, perhaps even a real child, a waif in the wilderness, and it had brought him closure. Should she deny him that?

"What made you think it was our child?" she ventured.

"She had chestnut curls and your smile ... I could never forget your smile."

"What happened to her? Did you try to talk to her?"

"She just kind of faded, like I'd been glimpsing another dimension or something. Look, I know you don't believe me. I shouldn't have told you. I thought it might help, but it's just made things worse."

"I'm sorry. I pushed you. If you feel it's true, then it is for you. It's just ... just ..." She snuggled against his shoulder. "You're not mad at me Greg?" She looked up, eyes brimming.

"Of course I'm not mad, Emmie. It's miracle enough we found each other. There's so much we've each been through, but perhaps we should go slow, take one bite at a time. Speaking of which, do we have any food left, my stomach's doing cartwheels?"

She knew he was changing the subject but was happy to let

things drop, at least for the present. But try as she might, the picture of a child with chestnut locks echoed in her mind every time she glimpsed Greg's halo of unruly curls.

It was late afternoon, insects hummed lazily, as they entered the path through a field standing high with corn. A man was bent over, hard at work. He stopped, hearing the creak of the wagon.

"Rat! Welcome back!" He flung down the hoe and strode to meet them.

"Rat?" Emmie queried.

"My nickname, I'll explain later."

"You must be the woman Hawk told us about." He reached out a hand to Emmie, "The guys will sure be happy to welcome you here!" Greg laughed.

"Nothing doing, she's mine. It's Emmie you ass! Surely you remember Emmie?" Bill squinted against the sun.

"Emmie? You ... you look so different. Your hair ... Sorry, my eyes ain't what they used to be."

"Bill? Is it you Bill? ... I thought ..."

"Thought I was dead? Didn't you tell her Rat?"

"Guess I didn't get around to it. There was so much to say ..."

"Bill!" Leaning from the cart she greeted him with a hearty embrace. "And Alice? Is Alice here?" He looked down, shaking his head.

"Just me and Lenny ..."

"I'm sorry."

"It's OK. It's a miracle we survived. If it hadn't been for Vince and the guys digging us out ... But that's a story best forgotten. You're alive! And this little fellow must be ..." His voice trailed off in realisation – the child was too small.

"He's our son!" Greg chipped in quickly. Emmie looked up, overcome by this declaration. "His name is Daniel, and don't you wake him up, he's got a good pair of lungs on him." He added, laughing, defusing the moment. Bill thought it best not to ask further, catching Greg's eye over her shoulder.

"Well Bart and Annie's boy will have a playmate. It'll be good to have another woman around."

"I'm looking forward to it," Emmie replied. "It's been a very long time since I had a woman to talk with."

"Well, Annie's not your usual type of woman, if you know what I mean."

"Don't worry, Greg already warned me."

"Want a lift to the house? It's about time to head back now?"

"Sure, sure. Can I stuff these tools in the back?"

"Yes, just watch out for ..." Too late. Jack rose startled and snarling from the midst of the bundles.

"Jack, down boy! It's OK Jack, it's only Bill. He's an old friend." Bill deposited the rest of the tools more carefully before holding out a hand for Jack to inspect. Emmie was laughing.

"He's usually a friendly guy, you must have startled him."

"Well, being awoken by a bunch of tools crashing down on you will do that." He moved to scratch Jack's ear. "So, looks like we have another newcomer, eh."

"There are a couple of Pete's dogs at the farm, and some other livestock too, but I'm sure Jack will make friends," Greg explained to Emmie, as Bill swung up to join them.

That first meeting was a chaotic rejoicing that left Emmie feeling overwhelmed, so many people, so many faces. She was secretly relieved when Annie, self-appointed administrator, ushered her into a tiny room, leaving Greg to sort and unload the cart.

"It's a bit small, we thought it'd just be you and the baby. No way were we expecting Rat's lost love. Most of the guys bed down in the barn, but I guess he'll be sleeping here from now on?"

Emmie nodded. "I'll get settled in then ..." she whispered.

"Suit yourself, but everyone's expecting you for dinner ... want to hear your story and stuff."

Hear my story! She'd barely managed to parry all the gibes and greetings, let alone share what had happened with this brash bunch of strangers ...

Greg came in a few minutes later carrying the sack of baby things.

"Something wrong?"

"It's all so strange, so many people. Annie said ..."

"Never mind what Annie says," he bit in. "Annie says a lot of things. Pay her no mind."

"But it's not just Annie, it's everyone ... I'm just not used to all this ruckus. It was fine with Hawk and the others, but these ..."

"They're a rowdy bunch, I know. Look, you don't need to go out there if you don't want. I'll tell them you're tired and need to rest." She looked up.

"But Annie said they'd want to hear my story and ..."

"I told you, never mind what Annie says. They can wait. None of their business anyhow. Any explanations about Daniel and stuff I can give, OK?" She nodded.

"Thanks Greg. And yes, if I could just stay here for tonight ... I ..."

"No problem. Just tell me what you need off the cart and I'll bring it in, and I'll tell Annie to get off your back."

"No, please don't do that. I'm sure she meant well. It's just all a bit much right now."

"Don't worry I'll explain ... tell her ... tell them all, you've been through a lot and need some space. They'll understand, they've all been through it too in their different ways, they know how it is."

"Thank you Greg, thanks for understanding."

Greg went to finish unloading the cart. Annie could be too much, he knew that, but the others? ... It'll take time he thought. Emmie's sojourn had been so different to his own. They'd changed, grown in different directions. She'd become more reclusive, self-sufficient, would she also withdraw from him?

They ate quietly in the room – once Sophia's, he remembered. It was not a happy thought. Sophia had never fully recovered from her ordeal ... Still, they were together, hope blossomed, anything was possible.

Daniel, having slept a good part of the way, was eager to

explore his new domain, but with all their things scattered around and hazards at every turn it was no place for a baby. Emmie tried to nurse him to sleep, but he clearly wasn't interested. She was tired, Greg could see.

"Why don't you let me take him for a wander round while you finish your food and get settled," he offered.

"It's OK, he doesn't know you. He's not used to lots of people either." She was being protective.

"At least let me try, you need to eat."

"I'll manage, but if you could clear a space it would help."

Greg looked around. "That's going to be a bit of a job in here. Why don't I take him out to the barn, there's a couple of milk cows and some chickens. I'm sure that would divert him ..." Finally, after another round of Daniel's tears and fretting, she yielded. Much to her surprise he was co-operative.

Emerging from the room, Greg was once more inundated by well-wishers, anxious to see the new member of their community. Daniel seemed to enjoy the attention. Faces were pulled, objects dangled, and no one was stupid enough to ask the baby's parentage, they could all do the math, no one but Annie, that was. Sensing a "professional", Daniel reached out to be held, squirming in Greg's arms till he passed him along.

"So, what gives Rat, who's the father?" Annie asked in her usual obtuse way. May as well get it over with he thought.

"She was raped. Doesn't want to talk about it, so please. Drop the subject, OK?"

Annie's face softened. "Sorry Rat, I didn't know."

"It's OK, he's a great kid and as far as I'm concerned, he's mine, OK?" She nodded.

"Good for you Rat. I won't say anything, I promise. She must be having a hard time of it."

"She loves the baby, but I think she might find it hard to adjust here. She was on her own so long, she's not used to having a bunch of folks around."

"I see ..." Annie was pensive. "I think I got off on the wrong foot with her." Greg smiled. "Thought so. She just needs time ..."

his voice cracked a little.

"You're worried, Rat ..." she stroked his cheek, one of those rare motherly gestures that sneaked through now and then since the baby. "Wanna talk about it?"

"No. Maybe."

"Come on, let's take this little fellow for a walk."

"What about ..."

"Having dad time. Those two get on great. Bart's a natural, never grew up himself!" She laughed.

"Maybe I should ask him for some tips."

"Maybe ... So, out with it Rat. It's the baby, isn't it?"

"No, the baby doesn't matter. Well, not that much ... it's more ..."

"That she's changed." He nodded.

"It was so wonderful seeing her again, to know she's alive, that she still loves me. I ... I thought it would be just like before, but ..."

"But it's not, right? You've changed, she's changed. Life moves on. You can never, never go back. That's something I've had to learn. It won't be like before, but it can still be good. You guys love each other, you'll work it out. You just need to give it time, Rome wasn't built in a day and you'll need to rebuild your relationship from the ground up."

"But that's just it ... I ... I'm not sure she still loves me ... at least not the same way."

"What makes you think that?"

"She's changed. Even from the first she was strange, didn't think I'd want her ... that I'd reject her because of the child."

"Some men would." Greg pushed open the barn door.

"But I'm not that way, she should know that." He lit the oil lamp, sending shadows racing. Daniel squealed in delight as the old collie wondered over to great them.

"Perhaps she feels as uncertain of your love as you are of hers. It's been a long time."

"I'd never stop loving Emmie ..."

"But does she know that? After a woman's been raped, particularly if she's had a child, she can feel devalued. She needs to be reassured you love her now, just as she is, child and all."

"I've told her that."

"Then keep on telling her till she believes you."

"But what if she doesn't love me back?"

"She'd be an idiot not to. Men like you don't grow on trees – especially not now. Unless? ... How is she in the sack? It can happen after ..."

"Annie!" He glared. "You're about as sensitive as a brick wall!"

"Just trying to help! No need to bite my head off. I'm just saying ..."

"Sometimes you need to think before you say Annie."

"So, is it that?"

"No!"

"Then there's nothing to worry about, just give it time."

Further conversation was curtailed as a lowing sound drew Daniel's attention.

Greg found Emmie curled up asleep. Returned to "captivity" Daniel began to fuss again. Greg went in search of Bart for some father to father tips.

23

Morning dawned. Emmie woke to find both Greg and Daniel sleeping. Seizing the opportunity, she ventured out, finding the farm semi-deserted.

"They're in the fields." Annie confided. "I saved some breakfast for you guys. Seems Greg was up pretty late." She winked, nodding at her own little bundle, cosseted in a hay filled tin bath set on a kitchen chair.

"He got off schedule on the trip," Emmie explained. "Greg should have woke me."

"Probably wanted to let you rest." Annie set a mound of french toast before her. Emmie's mouth watered.

"I haven't had eggs in years!"

"Plenty here, the chickens lay well. Well, they did before that dog of yours came. He's gonna have to learn farm ways." Annie chuckled. "Thought it was chicken for breakfast. Sure woke up those critters!"

"Oh no! I'm so sorry. He used to hunt and bring back the odd squirrel. I never thought about the animals here."

"No harm done. Bill's set him on a long leash for the present. Ain't right to keep him locked up. Maybe you or Rat can teach him some manners."

"We will. Jack's saved my life, more than once. Where is he?"

"He's round the back of the barn. No critters round there and plenty of space to run free."

"I'll go see him. He hates being tied up. Maybe I can take him for a walk, start teaching him."

"I'd eat first if I was you, no telling how long the little guy will sleep, and it looks like you're enjoying that French toast." Emmie felt bad for Jack, upset that they'd felt free to tie up her dog. Her first reaction was to go right then and free him, but annoying as it was, Annie had a point. Daniel was sure to wake soon, and Jack would be more upset if she had to leave him tied to go get him. She watched as Annie headed back to the ball of dough she was kneading.

"Looks like you could use some help. It can't be long since you had the baby. You should be taking it easy." Emmie ventured trying to ease things between them.

"Sure could. It's like feeding an army with these guys. Normally they'd help out, but they're all needed in the fields just now. Still, I still got Lenny here." She nodded toward a gangly youth, balanced on an improvised crunch, precariously dragging a potato sack through the door.

"Let me help you." Emmie scrambled up. Annie shook her head.

"Leave him be. He likes to do it himself." Lenny smiled triumphantly.

"It's OK. I do it all the time." *Lenny* ...? Realisation dawned.

"You're Lenny, Ben's son Lenny!" He beamed.

"And you're Emmie. I remember you." Hobbling to the sink he filled a bowl with water, waiting as Annie moved it onto the table for him.

"Lenny's my best helper," Annie proclaimed. "Knows a lot about herbs and stuff too. Closest thing we have to a doctor. Couldn't do nothing about the leg though ..."

"Liz taught me," he announced proudly.

Who was Liz ...? "I was a nurse before. Maybe I could have a look at your leg. Perhaps there's something ..."

"Don't think so. Liz said the bone wouldn't set right. You could look though ..." Emmie saw a faint glimmer in his eye.

Quickly finishing up the food, she was alerted to a substantial wail proceeding from the direction of their room.

"Sorry, got to go. Sounds like Daniel woke up."

"Got a good set of lungs on him that one! Tell Greg about the food, OK?" Emmie nodded as she sped out.

Jack was glad the see them, tail wagging prodigiously. Daniel gurgled, reaching down from his sling toward his old companion. It hurt to see him so confined after all he'd done. Was the rope really necessary?

"Sorry Jack, we can't let you free just now ... Least ways not around here," Emmie added a little rebelliously, as she wrapped the cord around her hand before untying it. Rounding the barn, Jack immediately made a dash for the chicken run, only to be pulled short by the leash. He looked round reproachfully.

"No Jack, no! Looks like you're gonna have to learn. Those chickens are not for eating!" She could see she'd have her work cut out. Poor Jack, she'd always applauded his hunting skills. Seemed she was not the only one with some adjustments to make ...

ჯჯჯ

Annie was nursing a now fractious child. Lenny was up to his elbows in dish suds.

"I'm sorry, I meant to come back and help, but Jack was so

upset about the leash, I wanted to take him someplace he could run free a bit," Emmie explained guiltily. "Daniel's asleep now, if I can find a place to put him, I can help."

"Mostly done for now. Lenny's just finishing up. Maybe tomorrow you and Jack could take the food and stuff out to the guys in the fields, save them coming in. They've started on the harvesting and it's hard work. Kill two birds with one stone that way. For now, grab a plate and set him down in your room." She motioned to the pantry shelves and a covered metal bowl.

"Sounds like a plan."

Annoyingly, Daniel woke up while being set down. Her first morning had been a little daunting. It was strange having to fit in with other people's ideas, after being the sole one in charge. Annie for sure didn't make it easy. Still she could see many needs she could fill, not least with her nursing experience. Life was tough here, but she liked a challenge, starting afresh with a new kind of society, a little as she'd known before, but different.

It was not to be. That night Daniel was fussy. Greg had collapsed to sleep soon after dinner, precluding their nightly lovemaking. Even when she edged out of bed to try to settle the bawling infant, he didn't stir – Annie was right about harvesting being exhausting. Again, and again she set him down, again and again he awoke giving vent to his frustration. He finally settled as predawn light was invading the sky. Nerves frazzled, she sank into oblivion.

She awoke, exhausted, to more angry cries of frustration. Greg was already gone. Daniel's cheeks were flushed, had he developed a temperature? He'd always been such a healthy child. There were no antibiotics, nothing to reduce a fever out here. She'd never wanted the child but now he held a tight grasp on her heart strings. She felt guilt for her night's anger and frustration. He was sick, even his natural appetite disturbed. He fussed at the nipple, alternately sucking and screaming with frustration. She felt his forehead, his back and tummy. He didn't feel hot, for sure not a high fever. If only she had a thermometer …

A head appeared around the door. "Is everything OK? I heard

him going off during the night, woke up mine, then again just now. Getting his teeth in, is he?"

"I think he might be sick. His cheeks are flushed, and he doesn't want to nurse ..." Annie came over to look down on the complaining babe.

"Sure looks flushed. You could ask Lenny if he has anything that'd help ... Gotta go. Do you want me to bring you some food?"

"No, I'll come get some." She was irritated by the idea an untrained teenager might have something to help. Some of the women at the camp had sworn by herbs and such, but she remained unconvinced. They were far from the old town and anyway the drugs counter was long buried. There'd been a few old packets of aspirin etc. in the bathroom cupboard at Dan's, why hadn't she thought to bring them. She'd just have to let it run its course and hope to God it was nothing serious. Annie was far from helpful. *"Don't look too bad to me. Probably just the teeth. I heard they can get feverish with 'em sometimes,"* was not what she wanted to hear.

ꙮꙮꙮ

It was like treading on thin ice, Greg reflected. Daniel's first happy encounters were not repeated. He'd become fractious, fussy and no amount of coaxing would tear him from Emmie's arms, and he was too tired after a day in the fields to fight her about it. Annie suspected he had his first tooth coming in. Emmie, worried to death and mortified by her son's fretting and nightly wails that woke the whole house, spent most of the day on long, solitary walks with Jack, baby tied Indian style on her back – the only thing that seemed to pacify him. Not wanting to shirk his share of the harvesting, Greg left her to it. Things were not going well. She was withdrawing more and more.

Trudging back, he felt drawn to the redwoods. He'd not visited there since finding Emmie. There was so much she didn't understand, so much he'd learned, was still learning, that she knew nothing of. Annie's comfort and advice had helped, but it wasn't enough. He needed more, and instinctively sought the

184

place where his questions had been answered.

Tom was waiting, old straw hat, dirty boots and all. Greg reflected that a being of such infinite power would take on such a humble disguise. It was for his sake, he knew.

"Hi Rat! Or is it Greg again?"

"Tell the truth, I don't think I can ever be Greg again, Tom."

"Things not going as you expected?"

"Yeah, you could say that. I'm so thankful to have found Emmie though. I've you to thank for that. You knew, didn't you?"

"Yes, I knew, but I didn't want that to influence your decision. You needed to be ready to take the child, to have already made that choice, and, don't thank me, it was part of 'the plan'." Greg grinned. Tom had this way of putting everything in perspective.

"And now? Is there a plan for this?"

"There's always a plan." Greg didn't have to explain, Tom always knew.

"So, tell me, what is it, Tom?"

"Ah!" Tom smiled that slow smile of his. "You want a quick fix. It's not that simple, unless you want to just cut loose."

"Not that, never that."

"Then you must have patience. Imagine a tangle of string or a big snarl of hair. You can't just yank it, that makes it worse. You have to ease it gently, loosen the strands, keep brushing the edges and figure out how to untangle them." Greg recalled the times he'd helped comb out the snarls the pack straps were prone to make in Emmie's hair, smoothing the strands between his fingers, it was always a prelude to other things ...

"Had some experience?" Tom winked. "Well it's the same now. Pulling won't work, you have a lot of sorting and smoothing over to do, not to mention a lot of explaining. What do you suppose she'd think if you told her you were chatting with a 'celestial messenger'?" Tom grinned.

"She'd say I was crazy. She didn't believe me about our child, why would she believe me about you? I had a hard-enough time of it! Maybe you could just ..."

"And scare the life out of her? She's not you and that would

185

constitute pulling. Perhaps though, you might mention me – in my Tom persona of course – I could introduce myself that way, as I did with you? It's a good place this, quiet ..." Tom was fading as he sometimes did.

"Tom, wait, I've things to ask you."

"Sorry, I got to go." Greg stood gazing up at the redwoods, remembering his calling. How he wished he might have their peace.

Leaves were beginning to turn, autumn on its way, yet today the sun beat down, her back a wall of sweat from her hot little bundle. He was quiet, but not sleeping, as evidenced by frequent turns of his head. The flushed checks had subsided, but he remained restless. He liked it out here, the rustle of the leaves, an occasional flutter of tiny wings, the animals slowly returning.

She didn't want to go back yet, relishing the quiet stillness. She glimpsed the redwoods, knowing Greg had frequented there of late. It looked cool and inviting under their shadow. Perhaps she might even put Daniel down to play a while.

Sadly, she was not alone, a stranger sat dozing against the trunk, a farmer by looks of it. A few weeks ago, she'd have rejoiced at company, but not now ... The eyes flickered open as she turned to go.

"No need to head off, come sit down. It's just me, Tom. You look like you could use a rest." *Tom? of course ...*

"You must be Emmie, Greg told me about you. In fact, he talks of little else." Emmie flushed. What had Greg been saying?

"That guy has got it bad. Heart broke he was when he thought you were dead," Tom continued, patting a place beside him. "Come on, sit yourself down and take a rest. Nothing to fear of an old cogger like me. Why not let that youngster have some fun with the fir cones. He'll like that." She was about to resist when Tom threw a cone in the air and caught it, instantly capturing Daniel's attention. Why not, she reasoned, heaven knows she could use a rest. Untying the shawl that held him in place, she propped him against her legs, setting Tom's proffered cones in easy reach. Fascinated with these new playthings, he settled happily.

"Now, how about a drink? It's just water." He held out a flask.

"Actually, that would be great, it's pretty hot today."

"Yes, getting milder already." It seemed an odd thing to say with autumn approaching, but she said nothing. He reminded her of Dan. There was something comforting about him, perhaps it was the age? The water was deliciously refreshing. He waited patiently while she drank, smiling as she passed it back.

"So, how are you finding it here?"

"OK, I guess ..." He raised an eyebrow. "Well ... Daniel's been fussy and ..."

"Finding it hard to cope?" Tom cut in. She looked down. How did this stranger know so much about her? Should she go? He was so much like Dan, his insight, hitting straight to the point. Memories flooded back. Could she trust this guy? Greg did it seemed, and ... there was something about him, something peaceful, reassuring ...

"You miss him, don't you?"

"Miss who?"

"Dan."

"How do you know about him?" she said startled.

"Greg told me. You can't help but miss someone when you go through so much together."

"Yes, I do miss him. If only I could talk to him now. I ..." She stopped herself. It was so easy to confide to this stranger, as if she already knew him, but was it wise?

"Things are different from what you expected?"

"Yes ... It's not like before, Greg's not like before ... and I have Daniel and ..." He caught the catch in her voice as the words tumbled out.

"It'll be OK. I promise it will. You've both been through a lot. It'll take time. You can't go back to the past. You must start again, build a new future. He tilted her chin to get her to look at him just as Dan used to do. For a fleeting moment she thought he was Dan – just an illusion – but enough to trigger a deluge of tears.

"I ... I have to go ..." Grabbing Daniel she seized the cloth to bind him on. Interrupted from his play he let out a howl.

"Pour little guy, he'd just got those cones piled up right. Here let me help you." Magically, Daniel went willingly to Tom's arms, calming instantly. "Here," he continued, drawing a hankie from his pocket. "Let's wrap these up so you can take them home." How he managed to wrap the cones one handed she wasn't quite sure, but he did, presenting the bundle with a flourish to the tiny fist. "Now let's get you strapped back on, little fellow."

"You really have a way with babies, Tom."

He smiled. "Well anytime he gets too much for you just come see me. I'm often down here under the redwoods. He's a lovely little fellow, gonna do great things one day ..."

That night the first tooth came through, a tiny slit of white against swollen red gums. She wished she hadn't dashed off like that. She'd enjoyed talking with the old man. It brought back memories, but that too was overwhelming. She felt embarrassed by her outburst, the way she'd dashed off. He'd said nothing, letting her keep her dignity. Still, it was some time before she ventured back ...

There was no sign of Tom, hadn't been the day before either. Why had she run off like that? She sat a while against the trunk, Daniel seemed to like this place, giggling and laughing as he crawled around inspecting rocks and cones. Greg said he'd seen another child playing here ... *Stupid!*

The rustle of leaves disturbed her reverie, a woman was approaching. Chubby and white haired, dressed in a floral print dress, her wrinkled old face radiated smiles.

"Tom said I might find you here. I wanted to see the baby," she called out. *Tom said? Could she be his wife, she looked the right age ... Greg had said nothing about a wife ...?*

Daniel ceased his play as the old lady approached, greeting her with an enthusiastic grin.

188

"Little Daniel!" she beamed. "Oh, he is the cutest little thing! Such a good boy too!"

"Well I don't know about that. He's been getting a tooth in. I was hoping after it came through, we'd get a good night's sleep again but no ..."

"Tom said he was teething. Let's have a look, shall we? Can I look at your new tooth young man?" Daniel obligingly opened his mouth for examination, something he never did. "Ah! See that. Right there, next to the new one, where the gum is swollen. He's another one coming. Poor little guy, two at once, first go, no wonder he's fussy! He's sure getting them in early, my guys were much later."

"You have children?"

"We had two, no grandkids though. They ..." Her smile dimmed a moment as if in remembrance of some past sorrow. Emmie asked no more – everyone had lost someone ...

"There are so few children now. I do love children, such pure souls."

"I could sure use some advice sometimes. Annie's had kids but ..."

"Annie's not too easy to get on with from all I've heard." She laughed. Emmie smiled back. They chatted on a while; Daniel happily diverted by the older woman's ploys.

"Well I'd better get back," she said at last.

"Yes, Tom will be wondering where you are."

"Tom?"

"Yes, you're his wife, aren't you?"

She grinned. "Me, no. I don't think Tom has a wife." She seemed to find the idea funny. "I'm Bessy. Still, I do need to get back, perhaps I'll see you another time." With a kiss and cuddle for Daniel she was off.

Emmie stood thunder struck. Bessy, she'd said. Bessy! Two children ... No, it must be a coincidence – had to be a coincidence. Bundling Daniel into his perch she set off back to the farmhouse, thoughts tumbling.

24

"Anything wrong?" Greg looked up. Emmie seemed distracted, been that way since he got back from the fields.

"No, not really. I was just thinking about something. Does Tom have any relatives around here?"

"Not that I know of. Why?"

"I met a woman down by the redwoods. She seemed to know Tom." Greg was startled but tried not to show it. There were no women for miles around and definitely Tom had no relatives. Unless ... "Could she be one of Hawk's group?"

"No, she was white and old, definitely Caucasian ..."

"I don't know, but I'm pretty sure Tom's on his own," but was he? Were there female messengers? Best not make too big a deal out of it. "Maybe he has someone staying."

"What now? It's not like before, people don't come visit."

"No, but people have turned up before, like the guys Vince and the others went off with. She might have been looking for someone to team up with?"

"Maybe ..." she didn't sound convinced, but it was the best he could come up with.

"I'll ask her if I see her again. You should have seen her with Daniel, she was incredible. He never fussed the whole time." *No, he wouldn't.* Greg thought.

ɤɤɤ

There was no one there the next day, nor the next, though the second tooth came through and Daniel returned to his sunny disposition, much to the relief of all concerned. Free to help in the kitchen, Emmie kept busy, but the thought kept returning. No matter how often she told herself she was being silly, crazy even, she couldn't shake the feeling, wanted to confirm it was just a coincidence. Was she becoming delusional? She'd known it happen, people who'd been through intense trauma ... schizo-

190

phrenia could set in. Had it happened to Greg with his whole baby thing? Greg, though different, seemed "normal", but she had all the signs – social withdrawal, emotional swings, depression even, when she should be over the moon with happiness! She had to know, was Bessy real, or a figment of her imagination? She withdrew even more into herself. Greg noticed – she knew he noticed.

Perhaps Annie ... Surely if there were any other woman around, she'd know, but dare she mention it to anyone else? Finally, she summoned the courage, but Annie didn't know either, only looked at her a little oddly, compounding her fears. Day after day, she found herself returning to the redwoods, only to find them deserted. Jack was slow to learn and still had to be tethered much of the time. Emmie took him for walks as often as she could.

Evening was coming on, the nights drawing in. Someone was there. She picked up the pace. No, not Bessy. It was a man, Tom maybe. Tom would know. Jack suddenly lunged forward, tugging the cord from her grip. Barking ecstatically, he raced for the figure.

"Jack! Jack! Come back!" she yelled. Jack began jumping and circling as the figure bent to pet him, slowly turning to face her. No!! No, it couldn't be. She ran. Forgetting Jack, forgetting everything!

Greg returned from the fields to find Emmie sobbing wildly, Daniel fussing. He bent to pick him up – they were becoming used to each other. Perching him on his knees he eased down beside her. "Emmie, Emmie honey, what's wrong? Tell me ... Did I say something? Did I ..."

"Nothing! Nothing's wrong! I'm alright, I tell you! I don't want to talk about it!" she snapped.

"Look, anyone can see you're not OK. Let me help you."

"You can't help me. No one can! I'm going crazy!" She looked at him wild eyed.

"Oh Emmie, it's not true. Why would you think that? You've

been through a lot. We all have, but you're not crazy!"

"You don't know!"

"Look, is this about that woman you saw? I could explain ..."

"No, not that, even worse."

"What? Tell me Emmie. How can I help if you don't tell me?" He shook her gently by the shoulders forcing her to look into his eyes.

"I ... I saw Dan. I'm delusional Greg, I ... I think ... maybe I'm becoming schizophrenic!" She looked questioningly into his eyes, seeking reassurance.

"No, no you're not, Emmie." He pulled her into his arms cradling her against his chest. "Others have seen things too. Vince saw Chad and I saw our child, remember?"

"Don't you see, Greg? We've all been affected. PTSS at the very least. We're seeing things, things we want to see."

"No Emmie, you're mistaken. It's real. I had a hard time with it at first too. There are these messengers here to help us ..."

"Messengers?"

"Yes, they have these amazing powers and ..."

She pulled away, sobbing. "No Greg, can't you see, can't you see ..."

He should have kept his mouth shut, but she was in such pain. What could he do or say to convince her? He searched his mind finding nothing, but to hold her close and whisper. "Emmie, Emmie, you have to believe me. You're not crazy, you'll understand later. It's just a lot to process ..." Again, she pulled away.

"No Greg, I don't want to process it, I don't want it to happen again, ever!"

"Emmie OK?" Annie asked. "She's been acting a bit strange the last few days."

Greg ladled food into the two bowls, pausing to consider his answer. "She saw something she's having a hard time coming to terms with."

"Like when Chad and Bart came back talking about aliens and stuff?"

192

"Something like that."

"I had a hard time with that. Thought they'd gone nuts."

"Yeah, well she's scared she's going nuts. It's the medical training. She can't believe what's happening is real."

"I have a hard time believing it myself. How come I've never seen anything? What did she see anyhow?" Greg hesitated. Annie meant well, but could she keep her mouth shut?

"Look Greg. It's obviously bothering you too. Out with it."

"She said she saw Dan, the guy who died back on the farm she came from. They were close ..." Annie looked pensive.

"You know, I'd give anything if I could see my kids again ... just to know they were OK ..." Greg shrugged uncomfortably. Every time he opened his mouth about these things, he made it worse. "What?" Annie knew him too well – saw he was hiding something. "Tell me Greg. You know something about my kids?"

"No Annie." He moved to go, but she gripped his arm like a vice.

"What Greg?"

"It's not about your kids." She held firm, waiting.

"I ... I saw my child. Not Daniel, the one Emmie lost."

"Where?" She shook his arm.

"Down by the redwoods." She loosened her grip, mesmerised. Greg took advantage to scuttle away.

Emmie felt along the bone in Lenny's leg. The underlying protuberances told their story. Whoever this Liz was, had not been able to set the multiple breaks and fractures caused by the impact. She'd done well to stabilize it as well as she had.

"I'm sorry Lenny, there's nothing I can do. Perhaps if you'd been able to go to a major hospital ... even then ..."

"It's OK," Lenny said stoutly. "I'm used to it now. It was worth a try." Tears welled as he swung it down off the bed. Had she made it worse she wondered, given false hope?

Jack returned that evening seeming none the worse for his time away, though from that time on, he ceased to worry the livestock. Instead he ran along beside her as she took out the midday food. The paths were deeply rutted and she'd yet to fully master the reins. Still, the old stock horse knew the way and scarce needed her guidance. Waiting while the men removed the food and fresh water, and loaded the morning's produce, she glanced around. Greg was busy as usual. Was he avoiding her? She'd missed their nightly couplings. Every night he came back dog tired, exhausted by the harvesting ... She wandered off a little, gazing out over the fields. With extra hands and an end of government surveillance they'd extended the farm, Greg had told her. They'd not realised the work involved bringing in the crops by hand ...

Jack became excited, jumping up and down, barking. He raced off, then stopped, turning as if to call her to follow. What or who did he see? Hair rose at the back of her neck. She stood frozen, as, giving up, he raced off toward the trees edging the field.

"What's with Jack? Spotted a jackrabbit or something?" She felt Greg's hands on her shoulder, his breath warm on her neck.

"I don't know. I don't think so ... He generally doesn't stop like that, just high tails it straight for them." There was only one reason she could think of why Jack would do that. She couldn't voice what she was thinking.

"Why don't you stay and eat with me?" His tongue was teasing her ear, hands slipped to her waist. Good as it felt, she couldn't stay ... she just couldn't.

"I need to head back, Annie needs my help," she lied, rushing to the cart, now fully loaded.

"Aren't you going to wait for Jack?" She could sense the hurt, see it in his eyes, but she was scared – scared what she might see ... needed to be alone, away from other's eyes ... Scrambling up she flicked the reins. The cart jerked into motion.

"What's got into her?" Bart queried. "Way she took off ... Now if it was Annie, I'd get it, but Emmie ..."

"Nothing that I know of. She's been acting a bit strange since she came back."

"You can say that again! Women! Ha! More trouble than

they're worth!"

"You don't mean that," Greg cuffed Bart playfully on the head, but inside he was disturbed. They'd always been good in bed ... He recalled Annie's words, "as long as that's OK, I wouldn't worry," but was it still OK? Why had she rejected his advances?

He returned to find Emmie absent from the meal. "Went out for a walk," Annie chimed in, Daniel nestled on her lap. "Said she needed some time alone." Greg pushed the bowl away.

"I'll eat later," he told her. "Save my food for me?"

"Sure Rat." Looks were exchanged as he headed out the door, nearly bumping into Lenny.

"Looking for Emmie?" the boy queried. "She looked upset, Rat," the eyes widened in concern.

"Yes, which way was she headed?"

"Toward the redwoods by looks of it. Is everything OK?"

"I hope so Lenny. Thanks for that." He set off at a run, legs aching.

"Emmie! Emmie!" She turned. It was Greg. How did he know she was here? Why did he have to come? She couldn't face him or anyone right now ... She pretended not to hear, but he broke into a trot, speedily gaining on her. Breathless, he turned her to face him, noting the tear stained face, the look of utter despair.

"Emmie." He crushed her to his chest, cradling her head against his shoulder. "What's wrong Emmie, is it me? Don't you want to be with me anymore?" She didn't answer, how could she explain ... Worried at her silence, he pulled back to look in her eyes. She stood mute, unspeaking. He held her close again, his own tears brimming forth.

"Emmie ...?"

"It's not you Greg." She muttered. "It's not your fault. I just need some time alone ... I can't be with you right now. I ..." Tears sprang up again, choking the words.

"If that's really what you want." The eyes were hurt, the tone icy.

"I ..."

"OK, have it your way Emmie. I don't know what else to do or say. Everything I say just seems to make it worse." Heart breaking, he pulled away, striding back toward the house.

There was silence as Greg re-entered the kitchen. Snatching up his bowl he retreated to the room, face like thunder.

"What ..." Bart was silenced by a hard dig in the ribs from Annie.

"You shouldn't have sent him away," a soft voice whispered. Ellie looked up startled.

"Tom! I've been looking for you."

"I've been around, but seemed there were others wanting to talk ..." He nodded toward Greg's retreating figure. "He's a good man Emmie, one of the best. You shouldn't have pushed him away like that. He's just trying to help you."

"I know. It's just ... "

"You're scared he might be affected too?" Like Dan, Tom seemed to see right to the heart of the matter. Maybe it came with age ...

"Did he tell you?"

"In part, not everything, but I can read between the lines. Why don't we sit down, and you can tell me all about it? Don't have to go no further than me. Who am I gonna tell anyways?"

"Greg?"

"Think you'll find Greg knows all about it anyhow." They nestled down, backs to the redwood. He kept silent, waiting.

"Well ... I ... I think maybe I'm going crazy – delusional!" she blurted. "Greg has some of the signs too ... I don't want to push him over the edge ... I ... I don't know who to talk to. I should be the one helping others."

"Because you were a nurse?"

"Yes, but even when I try to help it backfires. Like with Lenny."

"You thought maybe you could do something about his leg?" She nodded.

"But I just made it worse ..."

"You can't say that Emmie. It was good to try. Weren't nothing

196

you could do, Lenny knew that ... Now, you said you saw things. What did you see?"

"A woman came to see Daniel."

"She scared you?"

"No, she was lovely. Daniel adored her, but she said her name was Bessy and she had had two kids ... just like Dan's Bessy. Do you know who she is? Please, tell me she's real, that I didn't imagine the whole thing." She looked up, eyes pleading.

"If Daniel sat and played with her, it's my bet she's real. You wouldn't both be hallucinating!" Tom had a point.

"But what if I imagined the whole thing – Daniel too? Do you know of a woman living around here called Bessy? Greg said maybe she was staying with you or something?"

"Sure ain't staying with me," Tom chuckled, "but that don't mean she's not real."

"That's not all. I saw Dan too, and Dan's ..."

"Dead?"

"Yes, I buried him with my own hands." Tears began to stream as bittersweet memories surged. Tom put an arm around her shoulders, hugging her to him.

"Now, you just have a good old cry. Let it out. Nothing wrong in a few tears for those we care about."

"But it's not a few tears, Tom. I'm always crying. That's another reason I think I'm unstable."

"Nothing unstable in crying for those we love Emmie. God put those tear glands there for more than to keep our eyes clean."

"So ..." she sniffled, "you're a believer."

"Sure am. Reckon Dan probably was too, in his own way."

"Maybe. He didn't talk religion, but he sure thought Bessy was watching over him."

"Ever thought he might be right?" She looked up startled. "Well it'd make a heap more sense than that you're delusional." Tom chuckled, lightening the mood.

"Don't tease me."

"I ain't teasing. Though it would do you a heap of good to laugh. Don't take yourself so serious. Stop worrying about your mental state and think about how much you're hurting Greg just now. What does he think about all this stuff anyway?"

"He says he saw our baby and ... and that there are these messengers and ..."

"So, he doesn't think you're crazy?"

"No, he says lots of people have seen weird things."

"Well Emmie, seems you have a choice to make, to believe these things are happening, like Greg says, or believe you're going crazy. One will make you happy, the other destroy you. I know which I'd go for in your situation."

"But it's not true. It can't be true!"

"Well, that's a matter of opinion. Dan believed it, so does Greg and some of the others."

"Annie doesn't."

"No, but she'd like to."

"You think?"

"Yes, I do. Just imagine if she could see her kids, the ones she lost, and know they were OK, if you could see Dan and sit and talk with him again. He was a good man. Greg said he could tell you still mourned for him."

"He was like a father to me. I miss him so much."

"Well if you see him again, maybe you should stay and talk rather than run away then," again he chuckled. "If being happy makes you think you're insane then I'd go with it. You're not going crazy though Emmie." He took her hands, looking deep in her eyes like Dan used to. There was so much in Tom's eyes, such peace and assurance, like looking up at the stars or the moon. It calmed her ravaging emotions, soothed her fears.

"Don't try to fight it Emmie. It's like when you're drowning, you can struggle so much you hurt those who are trying to rescue you." A picture flashed to mind when she'd slipped crossing the river and got caught in the rapids. Greg had come to rescue her. She'd been so frantic he'd had to slap her to gain control.

"You know what I think?" Tom continued.

"What?"

"I think you have to face your fears, decide what's real and what isn't, an' I don't mean who's real. Stop worrying about that. As I recall it, schizophrenics generally imagine bad stuff, people trying to hurt them, not old ladies who play with babies." He smiled. She nodded, that was true.

She returned to find Daniel tucked up in bed, Annie listening for him from the kitchen.

"Everyone's turned in. Didn't expect you to be so long," she muttered crossly.

"Sorry, I ..." Her heart pounded. "But didn't Greg take him?"

"No idea where Greg is. Haven't seen him since he came, grabbed a bowl, and took off. Never seen him so upset. You two had a fight or something?" Annie looked accusing. No doubt whose side she was on.

"No, it was ... all my fault. I didn't mean to hurt his feelings. I'm such a mess!" She broke into tears once more. Annie relented.

"If I was you, I'd tell him that, then bed him good and proper. Never fails with Bart and believe me, we have some tussles. Best wait till morning though, he'll be sound asleep by now."

The bed was empty. More alarming, Greg's stuff had gone from the room. What had she done? Had she lost him forever? This couldn't wait till morning, by morning he'd be gone to the fields. The barn, maybe he was sleeping there? She lit the oil lamp, glancing back at Daniel, did she dare leave him? No, she'd done enough leaving. Gently she lifted him onto her shoulder, heaving a sigh of relief when he didn't rouse.

He was there! Dousing the lamp, she settled Daniel down in the empty feed trough. It would have to do. Nestling down beside Greg, she pressed against him, lips teasing the curls at the nape of his neck and ears, hands reaching to explore the tight muscles of his belly. He was deep asleep, but as her fingers probed on down, he awoke with a jolt.

"Emmie?"

"Who else were you expecting?"

"You said ..."

"I said I needed some time alone. I've had it. Now it's you I want, Greg." He turned to face her, grasping her wrists to dislodge the tantalising grip.

"Look, you can't play me like this Emmie. Either you want me or you don't."

"I'm sorry Greg, I was so confused. I didn't want to make you crazy too. I thought ..."

"Look, it's not like it's catching or something. Anyhow there's nothing wrong with you Emmie. It's all in your head."

"Exactly, and I didn't want to put it in yours."

"So now what?"

"Now I'm gonna show you how much I love you, and to hell with everything else!" Again she slid her hand down encasing him.

Greg gasped. It had been a while. Exhausted as he was, he rose to the occasion.

"You drive a strong argument Emmie," he muttered. No more was said as words were drowned in kisses.

Suddenly he stopped. "Daniel? Where's Daniel?"

"In the feed trough. Where else?" He laughed, turning to pin her beneath him.

"You know what you're asking for, don't you?"

"Oh yes, I know ..."

25

A scrawled note, in Bart's handwriting, met Emmie's glance as she wondered why her ever-early bird was still sleeping.

"Daniel's with Annie. They thought we might need a lie in," she told a sleepy-eyed Greg.

"Then come back to bed. Let's take advantage of this."

"But Annie ..."

"Annie can handle it, believe me. Probably her doing if I know anything about it." He reached up, grabbing her hand and pulled her back to "bed". She smiled, remembering Annie's advice.

"You sure you're up for this?"

"I'm up alright!" Greg pulled back the blanket to prove his point. She laughed.

"Don't you think I should go rescue Annie now?" she asked as passion subsided.

"I guess so, and I ought to go help in the fields. The first stuff is almost in but there's more to come."

"Couldn't you use the old tractor somehow?" She nodded to the rusty old machine in the back of the barn.

"Sure, if we had gas. That attachment would cut a darn site faster than us, but the gas ran out long before we came. Don't know where the hell we could get it now ..." He paused. A picture came to mind. The old army camp – there'd be gas in abundance there, tools too, bedding, pots and pans ... Maybe later they'd check it out, but it was at least two days' journey from here ...

His mind was changed a few days later.

Horses were coming, the sound of hooves rousing Greg from his evening meal. Dashing out to the yard he saw two horses, looking suspiciously like the ones they'd lost during the great quake. The former housed Hawk. Was that someone behind him? The second carried a small child held in place by the enfolding arms of what appeared to be his father. Both were rake thin. Hawk jumped down to reveal a woman, dirty and dishevelled. It was left to Greg to help her down, Hawk was full of his mission.

"We found them in the forest. I thought I'd bring them here. You said you had food, we're still a little ..."

"Of course, of course, Hawk. It's harvest time, we have more than we can eat." The woman stumbled as Greg set her on her feet.

"Aren't those ...?" Greg silenced Bart with a look.

"Help her, can you, Bart? Don't just stand there like a pudding!" Bart stiffened, remembering his former nickname ... and those <u>were</u> their horses. Annie stuck her head out.

"Come on Bart, bring her in, she looks close to fainting – and you two," she glared at two emerging forms, "help that guy down. The kid's asleep in the saddle!" They sprang to help, the kitchen erupting into chaos. Greg was left with Hawk.

"Don't worry, we'll take care of them. You were right to bring them here." Greg reassured him. "You have horses now?" he continued. Hawk grinned.

"Yes, a messenger led us to them soon after you left the farm. They'd been running wild. Seemed as glad to see us as we were to see them, especially the mare. The saddle had been rubbing her raw."

Should he say anything Greg wondered? They had horses at the farm. Hawk's people's need was greater and for sure they'd looked after them well.

"It's late, why don't you come eat with us? The meal's probably gone by now, but Annie can rustle you up something." He could see Hawk was tempted. He remembered the hungry faces. "Maybe you could load up a sack of something for your folks on the spare horse to take back, tide you guys over till your crops come in. Seriously, we have more than we need. It was a bumper crop this year."

"Can't stay. I need to get back, but if you have some food to spare ... We could pay you back when the harvest comes ..."

"No need Hawk. I owe you more than I could ever repay for finding Emmie, not to mention helping Annie give birth. It's a gift. You help us. We help you. It's how it should be." Hawk smiled, extending a hand. The firm shake was more than any pact or treaty could ever be.

Hawk was soon underway with a sack of grain. Tearing off bites of a fresh baked loaf thrust upon him by Annie, he sped off.

"I don't get it Greg. Those was our horses he was riding!"

"I know."

"Then why the hell didn't you say something?" Greg looked frustratedly at Bart.

"They need them, Bart. We have a couple from Pete. They'll do us for now. Besides, he said a messenger led them to them. They're meant to have them."

"And that sack of grain?"

"They're starving. All they have is what they can forage and the stuff from Emmie's little plot till the harvest comes in."

"Sorry Greg, I should have thought ..."

"Not to worry Bart, you weren't to know."

The newcomers were half starved and exhausted. Annie took charge, bedding them down in the barn for the present, after dishing them up the remains of the stew and several large hunks of bread.

"Don't have bedding for them all, nor a proper place to put them. Guess Bill and Lenny could be coaxed to lend them their room. That little'un don't look more than five or six. It's a wonder they survived out there."

"I'm betting they didn't, or not for long at any rate. We'll need to think about bedding. Emmie brought some, but it won't be enough come winter. We left all ours at the cabin and God knows if that's still standing – probably not, that whole area collapsed in the quake."

"What we gonna do then?"

"I have an idea. Let me talk it over with Bart."

"With Bart!" Annie bristled.

"Well, I'd need him to come with me and him being a new dad and all ..."

"You're thinking to go back to the camp, aren't you, Rat?"

"Smart girl, Annie."

"Well, it's true there'll be plenty in the way of bedding, pots and pans too. I could sure use some bigger ones with you lot to feed."

"Not to mention gasoline for the tractor! That would make a heap of difference."

"Do you reckon it's safe though?"

"Only one way to find out. For sure there won't be any troops there now – least ways not live ones. I'd feel better taking Bart though. We've been through some rough stuff together."

"What are you expecting, Rat?"

"I'm not expecting anything Annie, I just like to be on the safe side. The government guys may be gone, but that doesn't mean there's no bad guys left. Vince brought that up. It was part of the reason he left with those guys, a kind of self-appointed body-guard. Other folks might be scavenging too ..."

Bart agreed to the venture, though they had to delay a few days in order to get the last of the early crops in. It turned out, as Greg had suspected. The family had been hidden away in an uncle's basement for much of the time. Though not approving, he'd baulked at handing them over to the authorities, figuring that, given time, they'd "come to their senses". His wife had brought them food from time to time, *"for the little one."* Some-times they'd even taken Alex above ground, pretending he was a visiting grandchild. For a few weeks he'd eat well, till ques-tions were asked, and he was returned below. As for Thad and Jules, their food supply depended on the mood of cousin Jeff. While not condoning turning them over, he wasn't above leav-ing them to starve a while to *"help them see sense,"* particularly at those times Alex was "above ground."

Then, one day, hunger had drawn them out. There'd been no food for weeks, not even one of Jeff's "visits" to talk them into "being responsible". They'd emerged to find the house empty.

They'd spotted Tina through the kitchen window, while raid-ing the shelves for items that wouldn't be missed. She lay still, bedraggled, beside the laundry basket, clothes half hung. The car was not in the drive. Jeff must be out! Throwing caution to the winds Thad had run out to see if he could revive her. Horri-fied, he discovered she'd been dead a while.

They'd stayed hidden, slowly eating their way through the kitchen supplies, but Jeff never returned. No one came. They saw no one. The township was deserted. They'd helped them-selves to the usable food from the small shop down the road, even venturing into other homes. Again, and again they found bodies, frozen in action, gnawed on by rats and vermin.

Then a group of men had come, armed with pistols and pock-etknives, claiming the territory. They'd barely escaped. Since then they'd wandered the mountain slopes in search of berries, or anything edible. One of Hawk's friends had found them and taken pity on them, but since they had barely food for themselves, he'd had brought them here. It was a sad story from beginning to end and tended to confirm Greg's fears. They were lucky to be out here in the wilderness away from everything and everyone. He wondered about the bodies though. Jeff and his wife had not been military, nor, probably, were the other folks. He asked Thad if there had been any sign of why they all died like that. Thad had no answers. As for the family, they fitted in well, only too glad to help out. Though not yet fit for the heavy work of harvesting, they were extra hands around.

The primary harvest safely stored away; Greg prepared for the trip. They'd take the cart, which would make it slower going but enable them to carry more. If the jeeps were still there, maybe they could split up and share the load. He'd feel safer with a rifle at hand, but the guns were long gone. For sure Pete had never owned a gun of any sort.

The camp appeared unchanged save for the wreckage of two helicopters near the perimeter. They approached with caution. Greg took the lead, Bart following out of sight, should backup be needed. It appeared to be deserted, gates open, the only sign of human occupation a smattering of disintegrating bodies. Greg nodded. Signalling Bart to stay put, he entered in.

"Rat get down!" a voice yelled. He hit the deck as a shot rang out above him. *No guns! They'd said no guns! Seems someone hadn't got the message or chose not to follow it.* He scrambled behind an old army truck, the only available cover. The warning voice sounded familiar – knew his name. His memory reeled trying to place it.

Whoever it was behind that rifle knew their stuff. No way could Bart get through the gate or over the fence to help him without being picked off. His only hope lay in the voice. It had been female, definitely female ... He had little time to ponder. A woman stepped from one of the cabins, no gun, no form of defence.

"Sophia! No!" Greg yelled, leaping from his shelter. A shot rang out, shattering the silence, but she didn't crumple. They must have missed. The gun turned to him as he rushed forward.

"Lana! It's me! Don't hurt him. He saved me!" the voice yelled.

"Sophia? Sophie is that you ... is it really you?" the rifle clattered to the ground as a woman emerged, wild eyed and haggard. Greg stood mesmerised as the two embraced, emotional, muttering inaudible words in a foreign language.

Bart used the opportunity to gain access, slipping through the gate. He looked at Greg in confusion.

"What ...?"

"Don't ask me," Greg replied, edging to pick up the rifle – just in case. His assailant ignored them completely. "Maybe she was scared. Good thing she missed Sofia."

"But that's just it, Greg. She <u>didn't</u> miss. Hit her square in the chest, bullet went right through! I saw it."

"Couldn't be, she didn't even falter."

"I tell you that's what I saw. Didn't believe me about them aliens either but it was true! Maybe she's been taken over by them, maybe she's ..."

"Bart, they weren't aliens, OK."

"Then what was they? huh?"

"Messengers, celestial messengers ..."

"You're as crazy as I am Greg, crazier in fact. But that's beside the point, I tell you the bullet went right through!" Their talk was interrupted as the women broke off, Sophia turning to make introductions.

"This is Rat. He's the one who rescued me. This guy too. I don't know his name."

"Bart, I'm Bart." Bart thrust out his hand. Weird, Greg thought, shaking hands with someone who was just taking shots at you. He stood uncertain, but there was no hesitation with

Lana. Seizing and embracing him hard, she kissed his cheeks again and again. "You saved my sister, thank you! Thank you!" Even stranger Greg thought. Still it made sense now ...

"I've been searching for months," she continued, freeing Greg from his ordeal. "Some lowlife I caught pillaging told me she'd been taken here, along with a bunch of others, but then the trail died out. The place was deserted. I've been here a while, hoping for a lead."

"Then there's no one around? We need some supplies. Look, we have the farm where Sophia used to live. You're welcome to join us if you want."

"Thanks, but I'm going to stick with Sophia. Nothing's going to part us again, ever ... I was so scared for you, Sophie. I thought I'd never see you again ..." Sophia looked down, teary eyed.

"I can't take you with me Lana, but if you go with Rat, maybe I can visit you there."

"But why? I don't care where it is, I'll go." Understanding dawned in Greg – the bullet! It all made sense ...

"Sophia, you're with Pete, aren't you?" he whispered.

"Yes."

"Lana," he turned to face her. "She's not alive anymore. Well no, she's alive, but not like you and me. That's why the bullet went right through her ..."

"I shot her? I shot Sophie? No, I couldn't have done. I missed!"

Sophie smiled. "You didn't miss, Lana. When did you ever miss a target at that distance? But it's OK. Like Greg said, you can't hurt me. No one can ever hurt me again."

"You mean you're a ghost?"

Sophie laughed. "No, not a ghost. My angel came to get me, he was there all the time."

"Sophie don't be childish. That was just mama's stories. You know that!"

"Oh! but they're real Lana, just not at all as I imagined them ..."

"Tom? It was Tom, wasn't it?" Greg interrupted.

"Now Rat ..." Bart tried to get a word in and failed.

"Yes, it was Tom. Do you know him?" Greg nodded. "He came for me and Liz, the children too," she continued. "We all went together."

"Went where?" Lana said sarcastically.

"To God of course. That's why you can't come with me yet, but you can go with Rat. He's a good man. You can trust him."

"Trust a crazy guy who believes in angels and stuff! Don't be an idiot!" Lana hissed her contempt.

"Look," Bart interrupted. "I don't know about this angel stuff, but Rat's a good guy. You can trust him, and we have food."

"I have food here." She nodded toward the camp.

"But it won't last forever, and you'll be a might lonely out here on your own. 'Sides, Annie could use the company. You two should get on great." He eyed the rifle.

"Who's this Annie?"

"She's Bart's partner. Good with a gun. Bosses him about something rotten." Greg attempted to lighten the mood. "Like I said we have Pete's old farm, stock, fields, everything. It's a good place to start. We took in a new family in a few days back, that's why we need extra bedding and stuff. I wouldn't mind betting there's more folks out there with no place to go and nothing to eat too. We have a chance to start from scratch, build something new, something better, a whole new society without the greed and corruption."

"It's what you always wanted Lana. You remember when we were young, how you'd go on about it. That's why you joined the rebels in the first place," Sophia muttered.

"You were a rebel fighter?" Greg asked.

"In Venezuela. She was always the crazy one. I was the good girl." Sophie smiled and hugged her sister. "Now please, go with Rat, Lana, so I can come see you now and then. You'll like it there."

"OK. OK, but let's get this straight, there's no such thing as angels!"

"Whatever you say," Greg smiled. Could they really handle another Annie?

"I need to go Lana. I can't stay long just now. I just wanted to see you, make sure things went according to plan."

"Plan, what plan! You're coming too Sophie. You hear me?" Sophie was fading as she spoke. Lana made a grab at her, but her hands met only air.

"No! no! Sophie, come back!" She collapsed on the ground, weeping and beating her fists in the sand. Greg attempted to comfort her, but she shrugged him off snarling with anger and frustration. Bart stood open mouthed.

"So Rat, you think this guy Tom is an angel?" Bart pulled a face.

"Celestial messenger ..." Greg corrected, but the words didn't make it sound any more coherent.

"Look, I'm gonna go see if I can find some gasoline. Stay here till Lana decides what she wants to do, OK?" Bart opened his mouth to object, then, silenced by Greg's look, closed it again. Maybe Greg thought him more fitted to deal with this crazy woman. Lord knows he'd had plenty of practice.

Sure enough, after a while she quieted.

"She ... she just vanished, just like that. You saw, didn't you?" She looked heatedly at Bart. He nodded, following his usual tactic of "least said soonest mended". "No one just vanishes. Right? It's impossible. There has to be an explanation!" Bart was not about to field his thoughts on the matter.

"Beats me," he responded as a safe option.

"Think I should stay here in case she comes back?"

"Said she'd see you at the farm. If I were you, I'd come back with us. Either way, if she comes great. If not, at least you'll have some food and company."

"What if she comes here?"

"She won't. She was clear about the farm." Slowly Lana nodded, her practical bent kicking in.

"What is it you guys needed anyhow? May as well make a start." Bart heaved a sigh of relief, that went better than he'd expected.

They loaded up in silence. Greg had said next to nothing and

Lana appeared steadfastly engaged in her tasks. They'd refuelled two of the jeeps, figuring to take all three vehicles, Greg rendering the task of escorting Lana and the jeeps to Bart, saying he was more used to driving the cart and would follow at a slower pace. Bart knew it was an excuse but went along with it. He sensed a tension in Greg. Probably wants to avoid all the questions arising with Lana's coming, he thought. He himself was not looking forward to it, but he at least could duck them, Rat could not.

The jeeps took off at a much faster pace. Greg was happy to fall rapidly behind. He took in the tranquillity of the surrounding trees. Though the highway no longer existed as such, parts were more negotiable for the jeep than the scrub and woodland. He'd instead chosen the route they'd come, shorter but more challenging. He'd always loved the trees, the foliage, and most of all the sky. There was an infinity to them, a continuance, serene, eternal, beyond the transience of man. Sometimes the farm with all its occupants got him down and he longed to be alone, away from all the drama and emotions. He breathed deeply, taking in the quiet stillness of nature ...

That night he camped out under the stars, unhitching the mare to amble around, munching on the freshly replenished sward. Leaning back, he closed his eyes, pondering the day's events. Some things were clear. Sophia had disappeared with Pete and Liz. She was now ... some kind of something? Definitely no longer human, but probably not an angel (he'd reconciled himself to the term, but with a whole other frame of reference). Lana on the other hand was unquestionably human, very much so, and a force to be reckoned with. Had he been wrong to invite her? What else could he have done? And what of Bart and his whole alien thing? Now Bart would go telling everyone that Rat thought Tom was an angel. He remembered Bill's reaction ...

"It's not your job to convince them Greg," the voice sounded behind, startling him.

"Tom ..." Greg relaxed.

"Need some answers Greg?"

"You can say that again!"

"You don't need to worry. You were right to invite Lana. She needs help. Don't know it yet, but she does."

"But she's so ..."

"Strong headed?" Tom chuckled. "You can say that again! She'll need help to come to terms with everything. You'll find a lot of the survivors like that; else they wouldn't have survived." Greg half smiled.

"So, what do I do Tom? Couldn't you just appear at the farm or something?"

"So you can be vindicated?" Tom laughed.

"No ... well yes, I guess so." Greg smirked. Tom saw right through him.

"What about them? You saw how Lana reacted when Sophia had to go." He had a point. "I know it's tough, but it's better this way. A bit at a time, just like me and Pete did with you."

"But what should I do, Tom?"

"Just keep on like you have been Greg. Have patience, be there, but don't push things. Let them all find out in their own time. Follow the plan."

Greg smirked. "It might help if I knew what the plan was."

"You'll know when you need to – like inviting Lana. It's put in you to know. The plan is not some set thing, though it has a set goal. It grows and evolves according to choices. Time for you may not be the same as someone else. You need to understand that."

"But suppose people make the wrong choices?"

"Then the plan adjusts for that. Look, you chose the more direct path back while the others took a longer route, but you'll all get there in the end." Greg nodded. "Well God's great at materialising other routes and He'll bend those paths around again and again till they finally make destination. 'Course some folks take a mighty long time ..."

"Like Emmie?"

"I wouldn't worry too much about Emmie. I got that in hand."

211

"Thanks Tom. I always feel better after I talk with you."

"Emmie does too, but she doesn't know about me yet. You mustn't tell her. Let her find out in her own time."

"I wanted to ask about Sophia – and Pete and Liz. What are they now? Are they angels, or turning into angels?" Tom laughed prodigiously.

"No, Greg, no! Where did you get that idea! Mankind is mankind and angels are angels. No, they are something completely new, the next step for mankind you might say. They're the ones who'll take over down here eventually. Right now, you might say they're learning the ropes."

"You mean they'll form some kind of government?"

"Not like you're thinking. They'll be here to serve, to help. Like I'm helping you just now and how Sophie helped keep you from getting shot."

"Will ... will it be Pete? Here I mean?"

"Well, he sure knows a lot about the area and the folks in it."

"I'd like that – Pete I mean."

"Thought you would, others too. We'll see ... Well gotta go. You're not the only ones I visit, you know." The smile turned to a glow as lights erupted, a spinning vortex that rocketed into the heavens at incredible speed. Greg smiled. Tom had generally strolled away after that first startling demonstration, but perhaps he felt Greg needed the encouragement of re-experiencing it.

26

Lana was well received. Even in faded fatigues and baggy shirt her curvaceous figure and large, dark fringed eyes, were drink in the desert to men long starved of female company. Annie and Emmie, for their part, were simply glad of another woman. The rifle (which she'd refused to relinquish) put her up several notches in Annie's estimation, though she was glad to see Bart showed no great interest, other than to get her settled.

How different to Emmie's entry. Lana was only too keen to tell her story and boast of her anti-government exploits, though, Bart noted, she stopped short of speaking about her sister's appearance. He knew better than to bring it up, perhaps it was wise, how were they to explain all that? The challenging look she'd cast his way was more than enough to convince him.

Annie, mindful of devouring eyes, suggested Lana sleep on the couch, but she declined, choosing instead to bed down in the hayloft.

"I sleep with my partner," she nodded at the rifle, winking at Annie. "The guys won't be bothering me."

"A woman after my own heart." Annie responded.

Greg returned the following evening, much to Emmie's relief. After Thad's story, she'd feared for him travelling alone with the loaded cart. With the three vehicles, there were spoils aplenty, pots and pans, tinned food, several sacks of grain, bedding, clothes (though primarily army fatigues) and plenty of gasoline.

"We left most of the food," Greg explained. "I figured other folks might come who needed it." There was a mumble of disapproval from one of the men.

"If folks keep turning up out of the wilderness, we'll need food for them all. We've plenty now, but when winter comes ..." Greg felt bad for the father of the family standing by.

"We have enough and to spare, for winter too. I never saw such a harvest!" Ben chimed in. "I'm with Greg. When Pete took me and Lenny in, he could have said they might not have enough. We were laid up a mighty long time, 'fore we could be much help."

"I don't think we need to worry," Greg continued. "From what Thad said most folks are dead. I think it behoves us to try to help all we can who survived."

"What about those guys who drove Thad out. Guy's like that don't deserve to survive."

"Who are we to judge?" Greg reasoned. "Lana would have had a hard time without the food stores." A lively discussion erupted ending only when Annie summoned them to eat and food closed hungry mouths.

"I hear there was quite a fervour this evening," Emmie quipped as she lay Daniel down to sleep.

"You can say that again," Greg responded. "I thought they'd all see it but seems not everyone agrees."

"Most do. It's only one or two really. They look to you Greg, they really do."

"Well Chad kind of appointed me and Vince and now he's gone ... It's never been like I want to be in charge or anything."

"I know you don't, that's why you are so good for it. You were right. It's what I'd do too. Everything I have came from Dan, and from you guys of course." She nibbled his ear affectionately.

"That reminds me. I have something for you. Now where did I put it?" Rummaging he pulled out a small kit bag. "For you!" he announced with a grin.

"Clothes? ... Bath stuff, cosmetics?" she added hopefully, feeling the lumps through the canvas.

"I'm afraid the army guys weren't much into that stuff. No, this is something even better." Unzipping she squealed in joy.

"Medicine and first aid stuff! Oh Greg, Greg you are the most wonderful ..." The rest of the sentence was cut off as she flung herself into his arms.

Unlike the new family, who were just thankful for food and a place to sleep, Lana made her presence known with an opinion about everything, frequently in opposition to the codes of behaviour they'd long established. Thus, Greg's gentle remonstrations, that they'd been told no more rifles or hunting, also fell on deaf ears. "Who says!" was her only response, followed by mocking laughter when Greg tried to explain.

"I told you! None of this angel/messenger stuff!"

"And I'm telling you, no more killing or hunting if you want to stay here."

"And who put you in charge!"

"No one really. In fact, I'd sooner not have the job."

"Then for God's sake get out of the way and give the job to someone with some balls!" Greg bit his lip resisting the desire to throttle her.

"Look, it's not just me. I'm just the spokesman ..."

"So you tell us! ... Well I'm off to get some fresh meat and I don't care what you say. Bet you everyone will be only too happy to eat it." She stormed off, rifle in hand. Greg sighed in exasperation.

"Well, that went well," Annie chimed in, emerging from the kitchen. "You got your hands full with that one!"

"You can say that again!"

"What you gonna do? You can't force her. I hate to say this but she's the only one armed around here and she sleeps with that thing."

"I don't know Annie. Maybe I'll get everyone together while she's gone and discuss it. I wanted to get the tractor hitched up and try it out, damn it!"

Lana was angry. Perhaps she should just take off. She didn't need them. Still they were right, it was a well set up place. Greg was the problem. She was pretty sure she could persuade the other guys to her way of thinking. She'd seen the way they looked at her, like dogs drooling at the mouth. She'd used it before and could again. First she'd bring back meat, nothing like the smell of roast meat to win them over ...

She became aware of a rustling among the leaves. She swung round, gun at the ready.

"You planning on shooting me with that thing?" A voice rang out, as an old man emerged from the foliage. "Ain't much meat on me, girl!" He chuckled. "Not much game in these parts either. It'd be a shame to go hunting the few that's left."

"What's it to you?"

"To me? I like the critters. What they done to you anyways?"

"Nothing personal. Just want some fresh meat for a change."

"And that makes it OK?" She shrugged.

"Look old man, it's none of your business what I do. Get the hell out of here!"

"Boy, what's got you so riled up?"

"No one tells me what to do. I make my own rules." She glared angrily.

"Don't think it's such a good idea, going off all riled up with a gun in hand. Someone could get hurt."

"Sure, and who's gonna stop me – you?" She smirked her derision.

"Might just be, if you push this too far."

"Get out of here before I shoot you!" She levelled the rifle threateningly. Tom merely smiled.

"OK, Lana, guess you won't listen any other way ..." Lights erupted, encircling, spinning. Taken back, she pulled the trigger again and again. He stood there grinning as the rifle melted away in her grasp. Then, more terrifying, he began to change ...

"What? Who the hell are you?"

"Someone who doesn't like to see any more creatures, or humans for that matter, get hurt." Though the voice was the same, the figure, encased in lights, before her was anything but old and feeble. It resounded with power and magnificence. "You were told no more rifles, no more killing." The voice too changed becoming deep like the rumble of thunder or the pounding of waves.

Lana stood cowed, petrified. Was this what Rat had seen? Was this why they'd abandoned their guns? For years she'd relied on her rifle, her skills, but now it lay, ashes on the forest floor, her skills useless ...

"If you want to be a part of this, you have to listen. The killing is over. No more. You understand! Not man, not beast, ever! It's your choice Lana, you can stay or go, you can listen or go your own way. Think about it!"

Then, whatever it was, was gone, hurtling into the heavens leaving nothing behind but the pile of ashes that had once been her sole ally.

She stood riveted, terrified. Even had her rifle survived it proved useless, anyway it was gone. She felt naked without it.

She could take one of the jeeps, return to the camp, get another rifle or something bigger? Perhaps these beings, whatever they were didn't operate there, but maybe they did, and she somehow knew no earthly weapon would be of any use.

Battle raged. In her heart she wanted to stay, wanted to be here in case Sophie came, but surrender was unthinkable. She'd never been subject to anyone, least of all some trumped-up woodsman like Rat. Her pride revolted at the idea. Why should he tell her what to do! Yet he'd been right about the "messenger". Was he perhaps right about other things too? He'd said he didn't want to lead, that it had been thrust upon him. He hadn't seemed domineering – except about the gun. It was one of the reasons she'd rejected his leadership, thought him soft, ineffective. Perhaps she had him all wrong, but what if she went back now, without meat, without the gun she'd so proudly vaunted? No, she couldn't face that, could never do that ... Defiantly she strode off toward the farm. She'd need to wait till dark. They set no lookouts. It would be easy.

Belly empty she crouched watching as the last of the lights went out. Maybe she could sneak in, grab some food? No, too much chance of disturbing someone. That baby of Annie's was a light sleeper, who was to say Annie wasn't awake with it already. No, she'd been hungry before, there'd be food enough at the camp and with her own vehicle ...

Sliding the extra can of gas into the back she moved toward the driver's seat. She turned the keys. Nothing. Not even a splutter.

"Damn!" she hissed. What was wrong with the engine? It had been fine on the trip. Finally, with a roar, it kicked in. She needed to get going before the others woke. Pounding the accelerator, she headed off at high speed. Trees flashed past, the jeep bouncing erratically along the rutted forest path. Forced to slow she gripped the wheel in frustration. It took a while to reach the gravel road she remembered from her trip. Anger and impatience pulsing through her she floored the pedal as she mounted the incline and swung out into the road. Suddenly a figure stood before her, face white in the headlights. Screaming she rammed on the breaks – too late!

"Sophie! Sophie!" She yelled, scrambling out of the seatbelt. She'd somehow missed killing her sister before, but this time, this time ... Why did she do these things! Why hadn't she just gone back to Rat and the others? Expecting a torn and battered body, she stumbled from the car. No body lay on the gravel, no blood on the bonnet, not even a dent or scratch on the fender. Nothing! "Sophie! Sophie!" she called, but there was no answer. Collapsing on her knees, she surrendered. She couldn't fight anymore.

It was two days before Lana returned, cowed, bedraggled, daring any to ask what had happened or where she'd been. She spoke only to Rat.

ɤɤɤ

Annie approached the redwoods. She knew it was stupid, nothing was going to happen, but if she didn't try, she'd never know. Lana had said nothing of her hunting trip, or of what had happened to the ever-present rifle. No one ventured to ask, perhaps afraid of what the answer might be. Even Annie had held her tongue, afraid to unleash a torrent. Rat must know, he'd spent hours with her on her return, though he'd been uncommunicative, saying if Lana wanted to talk about it, she would in her own time. So here she was, furtively slipping away in search of answers.

"It took you long enough Annie!" a voice chimed from under the firs.

"What are you talking about?"

"About how long you've been fighting this."

"Don't know what you're on about. I just came to get some peace. Rat said this was a good place to chill." She glared belligerently at the old cogger. He just chuckled. This had to be him. This had to be "Tom" ...

"You came looking for peace alright, that much is true Annie, but are you ready to handle it yet? That's my question."

"I can handle anything you got to give!" she retorted angrily, taking in Tom's shabby, rustic clothes and country clod demeaner. He was not what she'd been expecting, how could she be so dumb … Emmie was right, Rat was delusional. "You've been manipulating folks, playing on their feelings."

"Have I Annie? Perhaps you're not ready yet. Do you want to know about Jess and Debbie? Do you want to know they're safe and happy? That they want you to drop this façade and be happy too."

"How dare you say that, you …" Annie leapt at him fists raised in fury. He caught them easily, with surprising strength.

"Annie." Glaring up in fury she encountered his eyes. "It's alright Annie, let it go. Just let it go …" Her arms went limp, she had no more power to fight, just to feed and feed on the peace she saw mirrored there. A damn broke. Tears erupted in heartrending sobs. Tom nestled her head on his shoulder as he slowly drew her down to sit against the redwood. How long they sat there she didn't know, saying nothing, just inhaling comfort as endless tears broke forth. Night came on, shadowing them in velvet wings …

A voice broke the stillness. Bart was calling her.

"Annie! Annie! For God's sake Annie, where are you?"

"You'd better go." Tom gently raised her head. "Come again though." She nodded, clambering up to head toward the voice.

"Annie, I was so scared. I thought I'd lost you. I've been looking for hours!"

"I just wanted some time alone. I was down by the redwoods."

"I looked there. Looked there twice. Rat thought that might be where you'd gone. We've been searching for you, all night …" She glanced at the red shimmer gilding the sky, how long had it been?

"What about Adam. Who's taking care of him?"

"Emmie has him. He's fine. You scared us Annie. Don't you ever, ever do that again, you hear! Or I'll, I'll …" Tears glistened

219

as he grabbed her in a rough bear hug. "You know I love you, Annie."

"Yes, I know, Bart." She ruffled his hair affectionately. She'd known of course, but he'd never said it before. "Come on, let's get back and let the others know. Don't know what the fuss is all about. I can take care of myself."

"I know, but you'd never leave Adam that long. When you didn't come back for his feed ... I took him to Emmie and went to look for you, but no one knew where you'd gone ..."

"Well, we'd better get back. She must have had a pretty hectic night of it."

"But where did you go?"

"I told you I was under the redwoods. Maybe you should get some glasses Bart."

"No place to get glasses out here. Anyhow ain't nothing wrong with my eyes ..." His words fell on deaf ears. No way was Annie going to talk about what happened. She understood why Lana was so reticent.

"I'm telling you, Emmie. I said it all along. It's aliens. I've seen them too, big circles of light, an' they got weapons! Wow, you should have seen what they did to that insect thing!" Emmie was regretting asking Bart's opinion.

"You mean, you think Annie was abducted by aliens?"

"Well, she sure as hell wasn't under the redwoods, an' I checked there twice over. Annie has her faults but she ain't no liar. Why should she lie about it anyhow?" He had a point. Something had happened to Annie, not only her disappearance, but she was different in herself. The hardness was ebbing away. But could an alien take on another form, was it possible? Re-runs of the classic *Taken* series ran through her mind. Could an alien have taken on the form of Daniel ... Bessy even? Surely not. Yet it was definitely a better explanation, far more comforting than they were all going crazy. She ventured the question.

"Do you think they could take on other forms?"

"D'know, I only ever saw the spinning lights, but Ben said

Sophia seemed to think Tom was some kind of angel, Rat too! I thought Sophia was taken by aliens, but now you mention it, maybe Sophia wasn't Sophia at all." Emmie was stunned.

"Greg thought Tom was a ... a ..."

"Yep. Floored me that one too."

"You think Tom ... is an alien?" She recalled the timeless eyes, the comfort she'd received. Could it be true?

"I never met the guy, but if he is, he's good. Why, without those guys we'd all be dead several times over. Ain't never heard anything bad about Tom. Of course, maybe it ain't Tom at all. Maybe they can impersonate folks." She'd never seen Bart as the intelligent type, but he'd sure given her plenty to think about.

Annie slunk off, baby in tow. Bart and the others were off in the fields trying out the tractor and Lenny was watching over the kitchen. There were questions she needed answers to. Not least of which, why the sharp-eyed Bart hadn't seen them under the redwoods?

He was there, leaning against the trunk as if waiting for her.

"Hello Annie." He held out an arm. It was a few minutes before she could speak. Somehow comfort flowed from Tom, like the father she'd never known. She felt safe, secure, with him. Perhaps that's what Emmie had spoken of with Daniel ...

"Tom, I need to ask you something." She pulled away catching his gaze. He waited. "Bart said he came looking for me here – twice. Bart's not always the smartest cookie in the jar, but he's not blind. Matter of fact he probably has the sharpest eyes of all of us. How could he not have seen us?"

"I think you already know ..."

"He thinks you're an alien. I heard him talking with Emmie."

Tom chuckled then grew serious. "What do you think?"

"I don't know what to think. He also said Rat thinks you're ... you're ..."

"An angelic being? Or 'celestial messenger' as he prefers to term it."

"Yes," Annie breathed.

"And you? What do you <u>want</u> me to be?"

"I ... I want you to be someone who can bring my kids back!" she blurted out.

"Only God could do that Emmie, and I sure ain't God, but ..." She looked up, eyes full of longing.

"If only I could see them, know that somewhere, they're OK ..."

"They are OK, Annie."

"If only I could believe you."

"You can." Looking again into those timeless eyes, she caught a glimmer, more than a glimmer ...

"Tom! Oh Tom! Thank you! I don't care who or what you are, or how you did that."

"I'm just old Tom, think of me that way. You need Tom right now more than you need angels or aliens."

"But ... but which are you? Who's right?"

"Does it matter?"

"No ... you're right it doesn't matter, not now at least."

"Later you'll see and so will Bart."

"So ..."

"Hush now, Annie." He placed a cautionary finger on her lips. "All you need to know right now is that it's all gonna be OK."

"But my kids. Will I ever see them again?"

"Yes, but not here, not now. You need to build a new life with those who are left. I just wanted to let you know they're OK. You have a new baby to love ..." She'd forgotten Adam, slung across her back, scarce noticed his presence till now. "He's going to be important – they all are. You're needed Annie. He'll need your love and support in the brave new world he's entering. That's why you survived, why you didn't die along with them."

"Then why did they die!" she retorted angrily. "If I was kept alive, why not them? Why didn't you save them?"

"To go through all you've been through, the horror and the pain, just so you could have them with you? You saw where they are. If you had the choice which path would you choose for them. Would you want them to get hard like you did?" Slowly

Annie shook her head.

"You're a good mother, Annie. In fact, you're a wonderful mother, use that gift. There will be children coming, many children. You can teach, help. Rat might be great at building and handling men, but he sure doesn't know much about kids. None of them do. Your heart is big enough to encompass so many if you'll only let it mend."

Annie nodded. She understood – kind of. She had to let go of the past and move forward. She was needed.

Annie was ... well she was not Annie. That was all there was to it, Greg thought. She'd changed – radically – since the night she went missing. She'd been talking with Tom she'd told him, but had said nothing of what they'd spoken, or why they'd been unable to find her. Everyone had their secrets he guessed. Only Annie and Emmie knew of his experience with his daughter and no one knew of his talks with Tom and Pete. They'll all come to know in their time Tom had said. Perhaps this was Annie's time? It had certainly been Lana's! He remembered her shy, stuttered admission, so different to her former attitude, apologising for her rebelliousness. She'd lost far more than the rifle that day. She'd seen "Tom" in all his glory, felt the immensity of his power, again interacted with her sister and returned cowed by the experience. Instead of upbraiding her, he'd found himself coaxing her back into the circle, if indeed she'd ever been part of it. For her part, she wanted no further confrontations, understood entirely why the no rifle stipulation was to be obeyed.

Annie watched as Lenny dragged the sack across the floor. He was fourteen by their reckoning, an age which should be imbued with youthful exuberance, slowly gathering strength for manhood. He was strong, she had to give him that, but his exploits were curtailed by the ever-present crutch, the limp and determined expression, that defined him to those who knew him well. The grin and cheerful countenance were a choice, masking an inner resolve to play his part. He deserved more.

She'd hoped, against hope, that Emmie might have been able

to help him. If anything, it had made it worse, made him question ... She'd heard rumours about Vince, that he'd almost lost a leg to gangrene, that he'd somehow been healed. No one had been keen to talk about it, Vince least of all. She'd prised most of the story together, piece by piece, but holes remained. In their first exuberance at surviving the quake, she remembered, they'd told of globes of light amid the vortex of annihilation that surrounded them ... Then there'd been the whole rifle issue. Those guys' rifles had been their only resource for food and protection, yet they willingly forsook them. Even Lana now embraced the "no more rifles" doctrine. What had changed her? What had changed them? More to the point, could Bart's "aliens" have some kind of healing power? Had one of them healed Vince? If so, was Tom one of them, or different?

She watched as Lenny grinned at her, noticing her gaze. She smiled and looked elsewhere but the thoughts lingered.

"You want to what?!" Emmie gasped.

"Look, I know it sounds mad, but if there's even a chance ..."

"I'd give anything to see Lenny walk freely again, but this ... this is crazy. I never thought ..."

"You never thought I'd say something like that. I know, I know, believe me, but I saw my kids, Emmie I saw them, I tell you!" Emmie stopped, taken back by the statement.

"Then you think ... you think Tom is some kind of alien?"

"Angel or alien, what does it matter if there's a chance he could heal Lenny. Look, I'm not asking you to come with me. I just need you to cover for me with the lunch and stuff. Will you do that? ... for Lenny." Thoughts tumbled through Emmie's head. Annie had seen her children? ... Could it be that what Greg said was true, that he'd really seen their child? Could it all be true, and, if so, who or what did that make Tom? Here was a way to test it. If he really could heal Lenny, she'd know for sure. If not, they'd lost nothing.

"I'll do it! Please though, don't tell Lenny what you want to do. It would break his heart to have his hopes dashed again."

Annie smiled. "Don't worry, I won't. I don't even know for sure Tom will be there. I planned to say we'd go for a picnic as a reward for all his help. That will encourage him if nothing else and if Tom is there ..."

"You really believe it, don't you, Annie?"

"I do. Yes, I do, Emmie."

They set off the following morning as soon as the clear up was done and the bread in the ovens. Lenny rode the horse not needed for the cart, revelling in the freedom this gave him. He'd ridden before but Annie held the lead rope, just in case.

"Where are we heading, Annie?"

"There's a place under the redwoods folks hang out a lot. It's smooth and shady. Plenty of space to sit and spread our blanket."

Drat, Tom wasn't there. She'd felt so sure ... Well she'd come again and again till he was. She wouldn't give up ...

They'd almost finished their feast when a voice broke the stillness.

"Hello Annie, nice to see you again. And who is this you have with you?" Tom thrust out his hand and Lenny strove to rise and greet him.

"I'm Lenny." He mustered a hand, scrambling somewhat with the stick.

"Lenny, this is Tom. He was a friend of Pete's. Perhaps you've heard about him?" Lenny's eyes lit up.

"Yes, Pete used to talk a lot about you, Tom."

"Well then, why don't I join you a while. If that's OK with you guys. Then we can all sit down. Looks like it's a bit tough for you standing Lenny."

"I do OK," Lenny answered with a grin, but a shadow passed beneath which Tom was quick to catch.

"Lenny's very strong. He helps me a lot in the kitchen. Don't know what I'd do without him." Annie leapt to his defence.

"I can see that. But you want me to heal him, right? That's why you came?" Annie squirmed.

"Can you Tom? Vince's leg was healed, why not Lenny's? He

225

deserves it more." Tom's eyes twinkled.

"What about you Lenny? What do you think?" Lenny was confused.

"Are you some kind of doctor? Emmie looked at it but said there's nothing that can be done."

"Ah! But I'm not Emmie." Tom chuckled. "There's more to me than you see. Let me look at it." Tom grasped Lenny's leg, sliding hands down either side, pausing at the protrusions. A warm tingling sensation began. Annie watched intensely.

"Now, how's that feel? Tom asked.

"It feels kind of weird," Lenny replied. "What did you do to it?"

"How's about you try it out and see?" Tom extended a hand, pulling Lenny to his feet.

The stick fell away as Lenny staggered forward, hesitant at first. Then, growing in confidence, he began to run and jump.

"Annie! Annie! Look! It's gone. The limp has gone!" Tears streamed as he span and leapt for joy. "How did he ...?" They turned to Tom, faces radiant, but Tom was no longer there.

"He must be an angel, like Sophia used to say! He's got to be an angel!" Annie smiled, inclined against her better judgement to agree. Lenny picked up the crutch that had been his constant companion. "I don't need this anymore!" he yelled, flinging it off into the bushes.

"Come, let's go tell the others!" Annie exclaimed.

Emmie was washing dishes when she spotted Annie's head rising above the bushes. Throwing aside the dishcloth she bounded to the door. If Annie was riding ... if Annie was riding ...

Lenny appeared, bounding towards her. Grabbing her in a tearful embrace, he swung her round.

"I can walk! No more stick, see?" She saw indeed but could hardly conceive it. Annie had been right, and this could be no delusion.

"Let me see! Let me see your leg Lenny!" she exclaimed. Annie swung down from the mare.

"Tom?" Emmie asked, breathless. Annie nodded, beaming.

Lenny meanwhile rolled up the baggy combats he was wearing. The leg was thin as ever. With trembling fingers Emmie felt along the bones. The lumps were gone, the bones straight and true.

"Oh Lenny, Lenny, I'm so happy for you!" She grasped him to her as again tears erupted. She was happy, not only for Lenny, but so much more. Fears were vanquished. She was not going crazy. Greg was not delusional ... Her child, her precious, precious child, forsaken so long ago in the old oak ... could it be she was somewhere safe and happy, and Daniel, had she really seen him? The world was filled with new and amazing possibilities.

Lenny rode with her, eager to share the news with all. They laughed gaily as the old cart hobbled along the track. She could see them now, bent over, hard at work. Lenny stood up on the duckboard, waving wildly. Heads rose, mouths opened in surprise as he leapt down, racing toward them.

"Lenny ... Lenny!" Bill clasped him in his arms. "What ... what happened?"

"My leg's better, Dad! I can run, jump, everything!" Bill was too choked to reply, words wouldn't come. "It was Tom, Dad. You know, Tom, Pete talked about. Sophie was right! He must be an angel! He just put his hands over it, and it felt all tingly and ..." Men gathered round adding to the hubbub, as Lenny gabbled on, catching only half of what was said. Greg looked up at Emmie for an explanation.

"Annie took him for a picnic by the redwoods and Tom came ..." Tom! *Ah that explained it,* Greg thought, as Emmie was inundated with questions. Had Annie taken Lenny there deliberately, he wondered?

There was great rejoicing that evening. Annie made a cake and a keg of Pete's cider, long secreted in the cellar, was breached. There was laughing and dancing, accommodated by Bill's old harmonica. Yet beneath the surface jubilation, many questions rose. Who was this Tom? What was this Tom? Could anyone go talk to him?

Emmie at least was convinced. Tomorrow she would seek him out.

27

Resolute, Emmie strode toward the redwoods, Jack, their ever-present outdoor companion, bounded alongside making Daniel giggle and squirm against her back.

"Jack, Jack, settle down. You'll have Daniel out of his sling," Emmie admonished. Jack, however, took no notice, bounding and jumping as if affected by her own anticipation. Nearing the trees, he took off, barking excitedly. Emmie froze. Could it be? If it was, could she face it? Doubts hurtled, breaking her resolve. Jack was returning, a familiar figure at his side.

"Emmie! For God's sake don't run off again. I just want to see the baby." She couldn't move, couldn't run. Her mind rebelled, heart ached for it to be true. "Bessy said he's a strong little fellow …" he continued striding ever closer.

"Then … then you are together?" Emmie stuttered.

"'Course we're together! You made sure of that when you took that damn chip out. I'll be forever thankful for that, Emmie." He was close now. She searched his face, relaxed, pain free, looking younger than she remembered. Emotion overwhelmed her.

"Dan. Dan, is it really you?" Relinquishing reason, she ran into his embrace.

"Of course it's me. Who the hell else do you think it would be?" He wound his arms around her as she wept on his shoulder. "Bessy? Is Bessy here too?"

"No, Bessy got her chance to see him. We can't stay here. We're just able to visit sometimes. I wanted to see the tyke." Daniel seemed eager to pursue this new acquaintance, wriggling in protest at his confinement. Emmie released him to Dan's arms as they strolled down to the redwoods to sit and talk. There was so much to say, so much to share. Words tumbled out – of the fearful time alone, of Jack's bravery, of the birth, the quakes, of Greg's coming and the ensuing confusion.

"So, Greg thought this little rascal was mine," Dan chuckled at the child playing in his lap. "I must tell Bessy that one!" Emmie smiled, then grew serious.

"Dan?" He looked up, catching her tone. "Did you hear me, when I used to sit and talk to you and Bessy?"

"I heard, but weren't nothing I could do back then. We was watching you, me and Bessy both, couldn't see clearly though, not like now. I was wrong about the tree, the one that fell right on the chopping block. It weren't Bessy."

"Was it Tom?" Emmie whispered. "Was it all Tom, all the stuff that happened with Greg and his guys too?"

"Damned if I know, Emmie. You'll have to ask him, but this I know, there's a bunch of them around, not just Tom. This guy Pete, he's something to do with it too. Nice guy, seen him around a few times, but don't know how he fits in."

"Pete's the one who had the farm here. Greg met him a few times. But tell me Dan, this Tom ... You do know Tom?"

"Sure, but not like you do."

"Is he some kind of alien like Bart says?" Dan erupted in laugher.

"An alien! Ha! That's a good one. He's an angel, Emmie. Surely you guessed that? But not like any angel you ever saw in Sunday school books, that's for sure!"

"I've only ever seen him as an old man," Emmie confessed.

"Well I can tell you, you're sure missing something!"

On and on they talked, neither wanting it to end. Finally, Daniel, who until then had been content to indulge himself in playing with his new "grandpa" and exploring every nook and cranny of their surroundings, grew restless.

"He's getting hungry," Emmie said. "Eats like a horse!"

"Got to get big and strong my boy," Dan teased his namesake. "Can't go chatting on through mealtime."

"Will ... will I see you again Dan?"

"We'll all be together sometime, you and me and Bessy and all, but that's a long, long, way off. You've stuff to do here, a whole new world to help build. How I envy you that, Emmie. You do it right this time, you hear? Build a world fit for Daniel to grow up in. You made a good start with those guys at my farm."

"You know about them?"

"Sure do! Me and Bessy were right happy about that, glad the old place will be used. There's this little girl comes and puts flowers on our graves, can't be more than two or three. She sits and talks to us like you used to do ..."

Emmie smiled. "I'm glad Dan. I'll always remember you even if I can't sit and talk anymore. Do you think she's lonely like I was?"

"Probably, ain't seen any other little guys around, but one of the women is pregnant so maybe later she'll have some play-mates."

"Oh Dan, you can't believe how much I miss you. You always seemed to be able to calm me down, help me see things right, even about Daniel."

"Life moves on Emmie and we must move along with it, but we'll always be special to each other."

"I thought I was going crazy for a while ..."

"You got Greg now. He's a good man Emmie. You just listen to him when you gets all tied in knots."

"I know he is, Dan. I wish you'd been able to meet him."

"Oh, I did. A few days back out in the corn field. Didn't let on who I was of course. He seemed to think it odd, me out here passing through. I let him think I was one of the Mormon guys." He chuckled.

"That's strange he never mentioned it. It's still a bit of an event seeing folks around here."

"Guess he thought it wiser. You haven't been exactly receptive when he's shared stuff he's seen, my girl." He raised an eyebrow.

"No, I guess not. But that's going to change from now on."

"I'm glad to hear it. There's some wonderful things going on right now, Emmie, don't let that head of yours get in the way. God wants you to be happy, He always has."

"God ... so there's a God behind all this. Really Dan? I mean ..."

"Yes, Emmie. I always knowed it, somewhere deep down. Bessy, well Bessy, she always believed. She kind of brought me along with her somehow. Now, ha! Now everyone knows it, or will soon, but he don't like to force himself on folks, goes gentle at it like with a wild critter. He just holds out his hand kind of and hopes you'll come."

"I have so many questions ... I ..."

"Greg did too, or so I've heard. He might answer some, else come down here, Tom or Pete are often around an' they can answer better than me."

"Tom, is he really ... I mean ..."

"Of course he is, Emmie. You just wait and see. It's all going to work out fine now. God's took the reins and all kinds of wonderful things are happening. You wouldn't believe the half of them, but you will ... later. Well I'd better be going. Greg will be back soon, and that little chap wants his supper. Take care of him for me."

Dan gave one last hug, a strong manly hug, such as he'd never had strength for before, then, as he stepped back, he began to fade. Emmie was dazed. It had seemed so "normal" sitting and talking like old times. It was odd to remember things were not as they'd been. Even so her heart was suffused with joy. She'd faced her fears – found them groundless. If this was insanity, she'd embrace it ardently!

"Greg," Emmie asked between mouthfuls. "Did you meet someone recently, a stranger, passing though." Greg looked up guardedly. He'd become very careful what he shared with her of late. Still, this surely couldn't upset her.

"I met a guy up in the fields while we were harvesting, me and Bart. Nice young guy, didn't stay long. Part of the group the other guys were from I think."

"You didn't tell me."

"Didn't think you'd be interested."

"Just a minute ... did you say he was young?"

"Yeh, couldn't have been much more than late twenties." Emmie looked puzzled.

"What did he look like?"

"Nothing out of the ordinary, blond hair, average height, skinny, big grin. He had a guitar though, that I remember. He played me a song. Pretty good, though I say it myself."

"What did he play?"

"Oh, some old song from way back. *Annie's song* he called it. We had a laugh about that, Bart in particular." Emmie put down her spoon stupefied.

"Emmie ... Emmie what's wrong?" Greg floundered. What had he said now? She looked up teary eyed.

"It was Dan, Greg. At least I think it was Dan. He said he met you out in the cornfield ..."

"Yes, it was the cornfield, but this guy was young, like I said. Couldn't be more than thirty. Young, strong and definitely not dead."

"No, not dead. At least not anymore." A smile spread across Emmie's face.

"Then you believe me?" Greg asked.

"Of course I believe you. I should have believed you all this time ..."

"You met him? You met Dan!" Emmie nodded. "Oh, I'm so glad Emmie, so very glad."

"Yes, we met under the redwoods. He wanted to see Daniel ... But he ... he was old. Well, not as old as I remember him, but still old. Bessy too, that's why I thought she was Tom's wife."

"Well I guess they're not old anymore. Maybe he just looked that way to you because that's how you remembered him."

"Oh, I should have loved to see the young Dan though."

"He was so full of energy, all smiles and glistening eyes and the way he played that guitar ..."

"It was his song Greg. His and Bessy's, all about love and nature. It just seemed to fit him so well."

"I can believe that."

"They really loved each other you know. They still do, even now."

"Like us?" There was question in Greg's eyes.

"Yes, like us. I mean it Greg. I never loved anyone like I love you. I ... I know it's been hard. We've each been through so much. It tore us apart in some ways ... I'm sorry I didn't believe you ... about the baby and stuff. I mean to do better, really I do. Dan said ..." She paused.

"What did Dan say?" He brushed a strand from her face.

"He said you were a good man. That you'd help me, like he used to do."

"We'll help each other Emmie. I could face anything with you by my side. It's a strange new world we're entering into. There's so much potential, so much good, but it's all so overwhelming, easy to lose our bearings. There's so much to learn, to build, to understand, we have to take it a bit at a time."

"I guess so," Emmie whispered against his shoulder.

"Come on Dad. You have to come. I really want you to meet him ... Shouldn't we at least go thank him?" Reluctantly Bill caved. What could he say after all? Lenny had been healed, no doubt of that. Still, he couldn't reconcile the healing with the old guy who had cautioned him to mulch the crops, if indeed it was the same guy?

Autumn sunlight lit the trees, but beneath the redwoods was a pool of shadow. A figure was waiting. He couldn't make it out.

"Is that Tom?" Bill asked. "My eyes aren't what they used to be."

"No, I don't think so Dad ..." He hesitated. "I think it's ... It is! It's Pete!" Lenny yelled, bounding off.

Pete embraced him, spinning him round. "Why just look at you Lenny! I heard about your leg, but you seem to have taken on a whole new lease of life ... and look at the size of you! Been eating jumping beans?"

Lenny laughed. "Just the usual stuff and lots of it. But where have you been, Pete? We thought you were dead. Rat was sure you and Liz were OK, but ..."

"We're fine, just fine, Lenny."

233

"And the kids? I tried to find them, but I was so slow. I'm sorry Pete ... I ..."

"Nothing to be sorry about Lenny, the kids are fine too. Anyways, no way you could have stopped them, no matter how fast you were."

"But what happened? I thought maybe ... Bart thought you'd been taken by aliens."

"Of course not Lenny. Unless you think Jesus is an alien." Pete chuckled. "We were gone, just like that. Didn't even get time to put the hoe down. You heard the story about how he'd come get us, Liz used to tell the kids."

"Yes, but I didn't believe it. I thought they were just children's stories. Dad said ..."

"And what did Dad say now?" Bill asked stumbling up. "And where the hell have you been all this time Pete. You scared the hell out of me and Lenny."

"Not hell, that's for sure!" Pete pointed upwards, grinning.

"You expect me to believe that?"

"No more than you believe Lenny is standing and running and jumping around." Bill was silent a moment. What was there to say? "Probably aliens like Bart said?" he mumbled. Pete laughed.

"You'll grasp at any straw just to prove me wrong, Bill." Bill's communist leanings had always precluded any sort of spiritual or religious notions.

"Tom's an angel," Lenny ventured. "Least ways Sophia thought he was. He healed my leg."

"Doesn't mean he's an angel. Could have been some sort of advanced science thing ..."

"Could have been, but it wasn't Bill. Why do you find it so hard to accept God is real?"

"Rubbish Pete. Look you're welcome to believe whatever you want, but that means I am too, an' I say this angel stuff is nonsense."

"And Lenny's leg?"

"That's real alright, but it don't mean it was an angel."

"What about the fact that all this stuff that's happened is

written down in the Bible, like the story Lenny heard?"

"Maybe aliens made the Bible."

"When there are historic records about the men who wrote the stuff. The whole book of Revelations was written by John on the Isle of Patmos. I suppose you think he was visited by aliens?"

"Could have been ..." Bill muttered defensively.

"OK, OK, Bill, call them what you will. It doesn't matter, the principal is the same. They are a different species, it's true. The real reason you don't want to use the word angel, or 'celestial messenger' as Greg prefers to call them, is because you don't want the God connotation in the picture. Don't you understand, he exists whether you believe it or not. He doesn't need your ratification to be."

"Look, I've had enough of this stuff, Pete. I don't have to stay here and listen to this nonsense. We came to thank Tom for healing Lenny's leg, that's all." Bill turned and stormed off, turning to add. "You coming Lenny?"

"No Dad, I'm sorry. I want to hear what Pete has to say. I'll catch you up later." Bill's face turned to thunder.

"'Spose you're happy now. Filling his head with all your non-sense!" Bill glared at Pete, then strode off towards the house.

"None so blind as those who will not see," Pete said sadly. "But I'm glad you stayed Lenny. That must have been tough for you." Lenny grinned.

"It was, but you know how Dad is about some things."

"You think I was too hard with him?"

"Sometimes things have to be said. There's no easy way with Dad ... Look I'd better not stay too long but please, tell me about what happened – with you and Liz I mean. Did you actually see Jesus? What was it like?" Pete smiled, face glowing.

"It was like being in the presence of love, total love. I can't really describe the experience except to say it was nothing like the pictures you see. It was like a presence that was everywhere and yet so close and personal, full of light and colour – all these beautiful colours I never saw before and I felt ... I felt like I'd come home after a very long, long journey, so long I'd forgotten what home was like. Like coming to a place I belonged, that I'd always belonged, but been far from. Like waking from a dream to find reality far more wonderful."

"I wish I could have seen it."

"You'll see it all one day. Meanwhile, you have things to do here. You may not have made the rapture, but you were chosen to live on. You all were, even your dad. We'll be around to help, me and Tom and stuff, but really it's up to you folks and the choices you make."

"But what about Dad? He's never going to come around to all this." Pete chuckled.

"You know when I was young, I went deep sea fishing once. I knew nothing, but my friend's dad, he was an old hand. He'd get one of these strong old fish on the line. He didn't want it to break, so he'd let it out, let it swim, think it got away. Then, slowly, slowly, he'd start to reel it in. Those smart old fish would realise what was going on, that the line was still there, so they'd dash off again trying to break it, to get away, but he'd just let it out, let it out, then start reeling it in till those fish just wore themselves out with the effort and they couldn't fight anymore."

"I think I see where your going with this!" Lenny laughed.

Bill stormed through the kitchen.

"What the hell's got into you?" Annie quipped, looking up from the stove.

"Pete! That's what! Coming back here with his damn stupid ideas!"

"Pete?" Annie dropped the spoon. "You mean Pete who used to live here?"

"What other Pete is there?"

"But Pete's been gone ..."

"Well he's back now!" Bill interrupted. "Got no right coming in here ..."

"But it's his place. Does he want it back? The farm I mean."

"How the hell would I know?!" Bill slammed the door. Already Adam was wailing at the noise.

Annie bent to pick him up. "Hush now, hush," she whispered. "Everything's fine, go back to sleep," but inside thoughts were tumbling. She'd never seen Bill upset like this, never. If what he said was true, suppose Pete wanted them to move out? They had no right to the farm really ...

"Rat," Annie asked. "You knew Pete, the one who used to live here?" Greg nodded. "Well Bill said he's back. Seemed real steamed up about something, Bill that is ... Do you suppose Pete wants this place back?"

"Pete's been around a while Annie, and no, he doesn't want the place back. As a matter of fact, he's happy we're all living here."

"What's Bill so charged up about then?" Greg smiled. He could guess.

"Don't worry, he'll calm down, just give him some space."

"But where will Pete live and what about his family? Are they around too?"

"Haven't seen them, they must be living somewhere else now, Pete too."

"Around here, do you think? It would be lovely to visit." Greg grinned.

"That might be a bit hard, Annie." Grabbing his bowl, he headed out the door evading further questions. Annie was changing by the day, but he was never sure how much to tell her.

28

"What happened with Bill today?" Emmie asked, snuggling down beside Greg under the old quilt.

"Annie said he'd met Pete. You know the one I told you about." She nodded. "I suspect Bill got more than he bargained for," he continued.

"He seems a bit of a sceptic."

"That's putting it mildly. He still espouses the old communist philosophy of religion being a tool to keep the people in submission. How he could have lived side by side with Pete all those months I'll never know, but Pete, well Pete was special. He met everyone where they were at."

"What were they like, Pete and Liz?"

"Oh, they were like something out of a fairy tale to me back then. Their place was like a little oasis in the middle of hell. They had so much love, not just for each other but for everyone. You should have seen how Sophie took to Liz, just like that."

"I'd like to meet them someday. Do you think that's possible?"

"Pete for sure. I've met him around a few times. Not sure about Liz and the kids ..."

"Speaking of kids." She threw him a cheeky grin. "I've something to tell you Greg." He looked up, startled.

"You're not? Really?" He lifted the covers to stare at her belly.

"There's nothing to see yet, you imbecile!" She laughed.

"But you think you are?"

"Well my monthlies never started after Daniel, but I know the signs. My mouth tastes like gunmetal and I have to eat first thing if I don't want to throw up. No way I'd mistake that." Greg recalled those days of early pregnancy, crumbs in bed and dashes to the sick bowl.

"You seem to be doing much better this time."

"Yes, well it's my third, remember. I feel healthier too, all this good food and stuff. So, you happy Greg?"

"Happy, I'm ecstatic! I'm the happiest guy in the world right now and that could be literal you know." Emmie laughed and kissed him.

It was easier to get away now Lenny was able to get about. He'd always expressed an interest in the kitchen, herbs etc but now he could virtually take over, putting to use all he'd learnt.

Sadly, beneath the trees was empty. She settled down to nurse Adam, enjoying the still calm and birdsong. Patterned sunlight danced windblown shapes in the shadow. She sighed deeply; eyes heavy.

She was awoken by a light girlish voice. A woman stood before her, tiny, slightly on the chubby side, with dancing eyes and beaming smile.

"I'm Liz," the visitor announced. "I've been waiting to see you. We need to talk about the children. You know Emmie's going to have a child?" Annie shook her head, speechless. "Well she is. You'll have more too, you and Bart. There'll be lots and lots of children. You need to think about how you'll bring them up, what you'll instil in them. They are the future – they'll live longer and do wonderful things. Oh, I've so much to tell you Annie ..."

Emmie tucked Daniel into his little draw bed, pausing to add her combats to the pile of clothes residing on the chair back, before snuggling in with Greg.

"I was wondering, when the rest of the harvest's stored do you think you could work on a bigger room or something? It's gonna be awful cramped when the baby comes."

"Of course, Emmie. I've been thinking, the new family need something bigger too. It was good of Bill and Lenny to give them their room, but they need more space. I thought for now to just build some extra rooms on the back. That would be easiest. Then maybe we can plan to eventually build a place of our own or something."

"I know at first I said it was too much living with all these folks, but well, I'm used to it now and it sure is easier working together. Imagine if we were on our own and I had to cook and clean and take care of two kids."

"The pioneer women did it."

"Well I'm not sure I'm quite that calibre, Greg."

"Sure you are, but don't worry, I'm only teasing. I didn't mean way off, just maybe a few separate buildings, like a little village or something. We could all work together on the farming and stuff, even share the cooking etc. if we want, but we wouldn't be so squashed up. After all there's plenty of space now, why not use it?"

That sounds great Greg. Do you think the others would agree?"

"We can ask them. If some want to go off and start their own places there's nothing to stop them, but I don't think they will."

"Why's that?"

"Well for one thing I'm the only one around here who knows anything about building and without Bill's farming knowledge we'd all be stumped." She laughed.

"There's something else I want to ask you Emmie. I've been thinking, we've been so busy just surviving, trying to work things out, understand what is going on ... but now. Now there's time and things are more settled ... I ..."

"What are you trying to say Greg."

"Suppose we get married, Emmie? It doesn't have to be a big thing, couldn't be a big thing. You know I love you. I want to make it a commitment ... Well you know, I've always been committed to you, right from the beginning, but there was never time to ..." He floundered. "Unless you ..."

"Greg, you imbecile! Of course. Yes! I could think of nothing I'd like more."

"If you have doubts tell me now, 'cos I want it to be forever ..."

"I want to be bound forever, like Dan and Bessy, to love together and grow old together. I want it so very much. However, this is not what I'd rate as a romantic proposal," she laughed.

"You mean you want me to go down on one knee and all that stuff?"

"Don't look so worried Greg, I was just teasing."

"Well then, let's tell the others."

"But who on earth could marry us. Tom? For sure there's no registry office, not even a pastor."

Greg laughed. "Tom? That really would be something! I don't think it matters really, it's our commitment that's important, but I was thinking maybe Pete. It might be a good way to introduce him to more folks." His eyes twinkled.

"Greg, is there something you haven't told me?"

"Maybe, but now is not the time. Now, I want to show you just how much I love you ..."

"But Greg ..." his lips stifled her questions.

"So Pete isn't really human anymore?"

"Well he is. He looks the same, but he has powers he for sure didn't have before. I've seen him fade like Tom does."

"Tom fades ...?"

"Haven't you seen him do that?"

"No ... but Dan did. It was like he was crossing into another dimension or something."

"The spirit realm."

"So is that like ..."

"Look, I don't really know, Emmie. I'm guessing. What I do know is that Pete, Liz and their kids, Sophie too, all disappeared. I've seen Pete many times. I had questions and ..."

"And Pete helped answer them. Dan told me."

"He and Tom, yes. I saw Sophie too. Just the once. She stopped Lana from shooting me."

"She what!" Emmie's face registered her alarm. "She never said anything about that."

Greg smiled. "Well, she wouldn't, would she?"

"Seems there's a lot you haven't been telling me."

"You weren't ready."

"I guess not, but I am now. From now on you tell me everything, OK?"

"Deal."

"So Greg," Bart queried, "what's this I hear about you and Emmie getting hitched? Is it true? You know Annie is going to hound me when she hears."

"Not if you ask her first, Bart."

"But ..."

"You want to, don't you?"

"Sure, I'd be OK with that, but s'posing she says no?"

"She shares your bed every night and she has your baby ..."

"Yeah but you know how she is. Maybe she's just using me. Ain't many guys around just now."

"Remember how upset she got when she thought you were up

to something dangerous?" Bart's face brightened.

"That's true, but you know Annie, no knowing which way she'll jump."

"Guess you have a point there, Bart."

True to form next evening Annie, having picked up the gossip, gave Bart the cold shoulder. Wrapping the quilt around her, she turned to face the wall.

"OK Annie, what I done now?" Silence.

"Is this about Rat and Emmie?"

"Hmph!"

"Look Annie, I thought about asking you, but I was afraid you'd get mad."

"Get mad? Why would I get mad?!"

"'Cos you always get mad." Bart chuckled. Annie turned, fuming.

"So, you leave me to fend off all the comments, huh!"

"Comments?"

"Yeah folks asking if we were planning to do the same. Been at it all day. I no sooner silence one than someone else asks." In truth there had been only two comments, but in Annie's mind any comment was too much.

"Look Annie, if you want to get married it's fine with me."

"Oh thanks! Thanks very much, So you'll marry me to get off the hook will you? Well I wouldn't marry you if you were ..." She flung out her hand to slap him, but Bart was used to such manoeuvres. Grasping her wrist, he swung his weight over her, pinning her hands to the pillow.

"Look Annie, you know that ain't true. I told you I love you."

"Sure, but not enough to ask me."

"I was scared," he muttered.

"Scared, you?"

"Yeah, I was scared you'd say no. We've been together a while, but I figured if I tried to push you into a decision you might ..."

"You thought I might think again and walk out on you."

"Yeah."

242

"Oh Bart, you idiot. Why would I do that? You might not be the smartest cookie in the jar and sometimes you can be a bit of a dunderhead, but you're my dunderhead. Besides I don't think anyone else would put up with my shenanigans."

"I love your shenanigans! So, will you ...?"

"Let me think ..." she paused for a moment. "Well there are some things I'd miss if you went and found another woman ..." She slid her hands down his back pulling him toward her.

"Annie. Ain't nothing doing till you give me your answer. A guy's pride will only take so much."

She laughed. "Playing hard to get?"

"Hard alright, but not hard to get. It just takes a single word."

"N ... yes!" she teased. "But look don't let's steal Rat and Emmie's day. We could wait a few weeks. Meanwhile I'll be able to answer any more comments. So ..."

"At your service Annie ... as ever," he breathed under his breath.

Though far too short for Annie, Emmie had found a dress of Liz's that could be altered to fit her. She was thankful for her practice making baby clothes and taking in Bessy's things. Life might be primitive, but she didn't want to be married in combats. Greg would have to make do, but it didn't matter. Greg was ... well, Greg was Greg. He didn't need to dress up to fill the room with life and energy.

Pete had agreed to perform some kind of ceremony, exactly what form it should take was open to conjecture. No one recalled much of the old formal words, anyway it seemed irrelevant. This was a new world they were stepping into. They'd each written promissory vows to read to each other and Pete would doubtless have some profound words to say over them. It would suffice.

Greg stopped astounded. He'd only ever seen Emmie in pants or the shapeless dress she'd worn that dreadful day. Today, hair shining, eyes gleaming, even minus the usual bridal cosmetics and hair styling, she took his breath away.

Pete stood waiting, a grin spreading from ear to ear. Introductions had been a little awkward, no one quite sure how Pete fitted into the picture, but he'd quickly put them at ease with his gentle humour. All but Bill that is, who was on "best behaviour" not wanting to spoil Greg's day. The sun shone and a gentle autumn breeze made music through the leaves as Emmie moved to set her hand in Greg's. The "service" (if such it could be called) was simple in extreme.

It was time for Greg's vows. "I always wanted you Emmie," he began. "From the first time I saw you stagger into camp, pale and half starved. You brought joy and hope into my life. I thought there was no way I could love you more, but having lost you for a while, I do. Our time apart changed us both, made us stronger, but more vulnerable. I need you more than ever. Every morning I wake and find beside me I thank God for giving you back. I love the child you brought with you and the seed of our love that grows inside you. I'll always love you Emmie. You complete me and make me strong. No matter what comes, we'll face it together, always ... till we grow old and crotchety." He added breaking the intensity of his speech.

Emmie grasped her paper, but instead spoke from the heart.

"You say you don't understand what I see in you, Greg. I see so very much. Life and strength permeate you. When I'd given up on everything you came and rekindled the flame. You were even prepared to surrender your life so that I and our child could be saved. You're like the great trees of the forest. The storms of life do not overcome you, rather they make you strong and flexible like seasoned wood. I don't understand why you love me. I so often feel weak, but you're like a rock I can lean on. I'm so thankful you came to get me, not even knowing it was me, that you waited patiently for me to adapt, to surrender my doubts and fears. You never gave up, never lost faith in me. I want to be together now and forever. I promise to be a good wife and companion, the mother of your children, to love you forever and never ever lose you again."

"None could be happier than I to join you both together," Pete concluded. "May your love grow and flourish as the seed in the field, encompassing many. May you find strength and inspiration in each other to fulfil the many tasks that lie ahead. As this world embraces a new beginning, so let your love embrace the new and wonderful life before you. May it bring forth fruit in abundance bringing light and truth in its wake. Though your physical bodies may grow old and fall away, let your love remain forever strong."

There was a strange stillness after Pete's words rang out. All stood in accord, waiting. For what they didn't know. Twin globes of light emerged, lighting the horizon, spinning at great speed to converge above their heads. Alarm broke out, but Pete spoke strong and calm. "Don't be afraid. It's just Tom, come to add his blessing." All stood, awestruck, as one of the spheres slowly descended, dancing incandescent lights illuminating faces with rainbow colours. Slowly the whirling eased. Tom stepped forth, straw hat and dungarees oddly in contrast to the glory surrounding him.

"Thought I'd make an entry," he chuckled. "We just wanted to add our blessing on the proceedings."

"Our?" Greg's throat was dry, his tongue glued to the roof of his mouth. He was familiar with Tom, had seen him incognito and in his natural state, but who or what was in the second globe?

A pulse of light beamed from the sphere above, like a wave on the shore or a gathering explosion and he knew, oh yes, he knew, as did all those gathered below. Love reached out, bathing them in its presence, cleansing, healing love and complete acceptance. Bill cowered in fear as the waves washed over him. Lana clung to Annie, apprehensive. Was she forgiven? Greg looked up, joy enthusing his heart. He was loved. Not only by Emmie but by the very creator himself.

They stood spellbound even after the vision had faded and the lights rocketed off across the sky. A presence remained, a presence so tangible it filled them and overflowed into their surroundings. Emmie slipped her hand in his.

"Now I know," she whispered. He turned and kissed her long

and deep.

No one said much. Overawed by what they'd witnessed they sought solitude, time to assimilate all that had transpired. In those few moments hearts had been laid bare. No mask could evade that overwhelming presence, no argument remained against the presence of God. Jesus had touched them. Not to condemn, of that there was no need, their own thoughts, their own minds condemned them, their pride and virtue as filthy rags before the perfection of his all-consuming love. He had come in compassion to heal, to love, to encourage. Though filthy in their own eyes, they were loved. Loved without condition, without sense. The overwhelming, never ending, reckless love of God encompassed them, bringing hope, bringing cleansing. The past slipped away like an old ragged blanket. They were reborn, reborn to a world of endless possibility. A world cleansed of the old, corrupted governments and economics of man, springing forth in fullness.

Greg took Emmie aside, arm at her waist.

"How long have you known?" she asked. He smiled.

"Since before I found you again. Pete and Tom told me, explained it all, but I didn't really grasp it till now. Then it was head knowledge, but now I know in my heart. I feel it all around me."

"Oh Greg, I do love you so."

"And I love you Emmie. I always will … Let's go consummate our union." He grinned.

They made love well into the evening. As if enhanced by the creator, love flowed between them in every touch, every kiss, every caress. No one disturbed them, not even Daniel for Annie had taken him.

Rousing from dozy slumber on Greg's shoulder, Emmie's eyes lighted on the guitar sitting neglected among the baggage. She squirmed in his arms.

"What?" He bent over kissing her forehead.

"I never played for you Greg." He looked puzzled.

"Dan's guitar. I never played it. I thought you might laugh at me. I'm not very good."

"As if I would. Go on, get it. Let's hear a song. What about the one Dan played me and Bart? Can you play that one?" She nodded. Scurrying over she grasped the neck. It was dusty. Gently she dusted it off on the sheet and adjusted the strings. Sweet notes sped forth. It was as if Dan were there guiding her fingers, as if Bessy listened.

"You fill up my senses like a night in the forest ..."

A realm, magically glimpsed with Dan, had become her reality.

Greg sighed. She'd said he was like the trees. Was that really how she saw him? Rat dissolved into the past, leaving only his strength, his wisdom. Greg was reborn in peace, in love.